THORNE

KETLEY ALLISON

CHAPTER I
EMBER

I pull at the thin gold chain around my neck, dragging it across the pad of my thumb until it burns.

"We're almost there," he says.

I call him *he* because … I don't know what to call him yet. His thick blond hair flows back from his face, the silver highlights catching in the meager sun when it decides to show itself as we drive through the low-hanging gray clouds. Crow's feet line his striking blue eyes, and the stubble on his jaw sparkles with the same silver threads, framing his full lips.

Staring, studying, I look for similarities in his face but find none.

He notices my attention, his eyes darting to mine before going back to the road, but thankfully, he does nothing except clutch the wheel tighter.

When I first met him two months ago, I didn't have the wherewithal to search for a ring on those long, slender fingers. I do now. His left hand is bare, the only adornment an expensive matte metallic watch wrapped around his wrist. It peeks out through the cuffs of his blazer—the man picked me up in a *suit*—

along with a thin, black threaded bracelet knotted so tightly, its frayed ends puff out as if strangled.

I wrinkle my nose at the time-worn band. The rest of him is so put-together, like his handsomeness is his brand, but I can't think of him as good-looking. I don't want to think of him at all.

The view out the passenger window offers enough of an escape, and I stare out at the cliffs and the white spray of the ocean crashing against the rocks below. The winding seaside road carries us to the top, driving into bottomless clouds, only to come out of the fog and do it again. I'm protected by the car's cabin, but the salty mist seems to have crusted against my skin regardless. I drift a finger down my cheek, wondering if my flesh has turned to granules the incoming storm will lift to the sky.

"It'll be okay, Ember."

My hand drops from my face.

Are you saying that for yourself or for me? I don't voice a response. Nor do I turn from the window.

"I don't intend to steal you away forever." He clears his throat. "In fact, I was hoping during these past few weeks you would've come to understand the advantages of coming to Raven's Bluff." He pauses. "Do as I say, and you can see them again. One day."

The mention of my parents has me whipping toward him. "I plan to."

In truth, I don't know if I want to see my parents any more than I want to live with this man, but I refuse to offer any reasons to continue this conversation.

A muscle in his cheek clenches, but his attention doesn't stray from the winding asphalt. It can't, considering how narrow and close this road is to the edge of the cliffs. "I'd like to take this opportunity to get to know you as well."

My lashes flutter into my vision as I shut down and go back to the window.

He sighs heavily but doesn't push it.

What he calls advantages, I see as fractures growing and expanding through the life I thought I knew. He came to my home two months ago and ruined everything. I was happy, settled, and eager to start the summer with the knowledge I was at the top of my class after my junior year. Captain of the debate team. Co-president of the coding club.

It was perfectly laid out, all of it, and this man took it all away with a simple snap of his fingers and the question, *Wouldn't you want Winthorpe Preparatory on your college applications?*

Of course, he prefaced it with a hangdog look and the hollowed-out eyes of a man who was just as shocked to see me as I was him. Our background noise was my mother's sobs and my father's sharp growls, demanding proof yet refusing to answer *my* questions, my devastation.

Is it true, Dad? Mom? I'm adopted?

The memories echo inside my skull, not unlike the caves carved into the cliffs by the angry ocean below.

"Are you all right?"

My eyes snap open at his concerned tone, tense anger replacing the grimace tightening my features. He doesn't have the right to be worried about me. He's neglected me for almost eighteen years of my life. I'd dismissed him entirely, screamed at him to leave, to stop lying in my home, *you are not my father*, to which he responded with his own hoarse cry. *I never knew I had a daughter!*

You would think neither one of us would want a relationship after that.

Yet ... he knew how to reel me in with promises of a position at a prestigious, impossibly attainable school, an academy in his hometown where he was an alumnus. If I agreed to live with him for my senior year, he would get me in.

To a school where the entire graduating class made it into the Ivies.

A place where the academic brainpower of rare, handpicked professors made the other top high schools in the United States seem like kindergarten play.

The one spot that held the most coveted tech internship and scholarship in the country. An award I fantasized about receiving but never actually believed I'd have a chance in hell of qualifying for.

Somehow, *he* understood my weakness and pounced on it. He made it seem like such a sure thing that even my parents couldn't argue once they finally admitted the truth. At least, that was how he made it appear. I doubt he would've given them a choice, but I was too angry with them to argue to stay.

The adoption was illegal, he said. *I never gave my consent. Once I found out, I was determined to meet you.*

That only made my mother sob harder, her shoulders quaking as she confessed how desperate she and Dad were to have a baby. So fraught with emptiness, they were willing to drain their life savings for a baby and never questioned my origins after being told my mother died in childbirth.

The thought makes me sick. And while this man didn't come out and say it, his insinuations that he would file kidnapping charges against my parents if I didn't submit to his wishes were enough to make me feel putrid, wrong, and boxed in.

Then he pretended to give me eight weeks to think about it. My summer break, reeking with the hidden poison under the offer of a bright future.

I've been lied to my entire life, and now the person gaining the most advantage is taking me to his home, all because I can't resist the road to perfection.

I should ask myself again, who is the weaker of us two?

The car slows, redirecting my focus to the front. We turn a

hard left to pass through iron gates with the twisted iron cursive of "Weatherby Manor" lining the top. Instead of a long drive leading up to the house, there's a circular driveway. While consumed in my internal rage, I'd missed our turn away from the ocean to a crowded street of mansions, each hidden behind large brush, stone, and iron, sitting five or six yards from the main road.

He slows the car in front of the black double doors, each showcasing identical, elaborate door knockers. At this vantage point, glimmering black twines around the iron circle like snakes, with bumps and ridges like the features of a face resting in the middle.

A *splat* against the window has me jumping back. Then another and another. Soon, Medusa's double heads blur into distorted ink as raindrops start falling in buckets against the car.

"Shit," he mumbles while twisting to reach into the back seat.

I flinch at the close contact, a motion he doesn't miss. For a moment, his brows sag in disappointment, but he quickly smooths his expression as he hands me an umbrella. "Marta and Dash have left for the day, so you'll have to make a break for the door without assistance."

Frowning at his notion of needing help to step out of a car, I open the door. The mansion seems close enough, so I sprint to the house, leaving the unopened umbrella to bounce against my side.

By the time I make it to the entrance, my hair sticks to my temples, and my black tank sags against my torso. Rain droplets fall into my eyes as I turn under the stone awning and watch him step out of the black sedan and head to the trunk—umbrellaless.

Did he give me his only umbrella? My fingers tighten on its handle.

He lifts the trunk, the rain drenching the top of his head and his shoulders, falling so hard it blurs the landscape into white streaks as he pulls out my luggage.

I can't very well stand here and witness him struggle with my things in a storm—though it's tempting—and I don't have a key. The umbrella *thwicks* open at the press of a button, and I jog back to the car, helping him with my two carriers.

"I got it," he says, ushering me back to the house. His previously coiffed hair falls into his eyes. The blue sky seems to have taken shelter in his irises until the storm passes.

"You're soaked," I say.

"So are you," he counters, "and without a jacket. Wait for me at the doors."

Ignoring his request, I'm about to shove the umbrella into his chest and grab one of my roller bags when movement behind him catches my eye.

The rain seems to lighten as my attention focuses across the street. A figure leans against a stone column, legs crossed at the ankle and eerily still despite the cascading rain, their umbrella tipped just enough to disguise their face. Smoke drifts from underneath the nylon canopy, the pungent smell of weed soon following, even at this distance.

Their eyes are hidden, but I *feel* this person watching my movements.

"Who's that?" I ask, a crash of thunder almost stealing my words.

Lightning flashes, placing the figure in stark relief. The person hasn't moved, as if impervious to the sharp crackle of thunder and deadly spikes of lightning.

"Ignore him."

The man grips the back of my arm and ushers me away, but I can't peel my gaze from the boy across the street—because he is a guy, I can see it now that he's raised the umbrella and his broad shoulders come into view, then his face.

Keys jangle as the front door's unlocked, but my stare remains on the figure. His features are obscured, but his pale skin and dark hair come through the rain in stark relief.

So does the moment when the joint falls from his mouth, his lips part in disbelief, and his eyes lock on mine.

He jerks back, doing a double take, but then blinks out of it, turning rigid. That face—oddly mesmerizing in the blur of the storm—hardens before his mouth turns up into a sneer, and he whirls from the stone column on one side of a curving driveway, disappearing into the thick foliage beyond.

My brows pinch together. "What's his problem?"

"When I say ignore him," the man says as he pushes open the door, "I'm not kidding around, Ember." He waits for me to step in first, but as I turn my attention to him, I notice the sky has left his eyes. "He's the son of a terrible man. You'd do best to stay away from him."

I sneak a final look across the street before stepping inside, but the boy is long gone.

Terrible man, huh? You mean, he could be an enemy of the guy who upended my life simply out of curiosity and a desire for control?

I think I'd do best knowing everything about him.

CHAPTER 2
EMBER

We step into the entryway, darkened by both the storm and the lack of indoor lighting. The door shuts heavily behind me, echoing its creaking discontent, and I jump at the sound.

The thud of my suitcases soon follows, along with his heavy sigh.

I don't turn to him, and instead, I scan the interior. Ebony wood crawls up the walls and winds through the twisting staircase directly in front of me. An incredibly—almost impossibly—large all-black chandelier hangs from the center of an intricately carved white ceiling. It must be cut from something expensive. It glimmers every time I move my head, even in the shadows.

The new angle of my head leads my eyes to one of two large portraits hanging on opposite walls of the foyer. Ancestors, maybe, or the first owners. Wait ... is that *him* painted with his arm around a wide-eyed blonde?

"That's Julie."

His voice at my ear comes unexpectedly, jolting me again.

"Apologies for scaring you," he says. "She's ... she was ... my wife."

My stare narrows on her features, painted softly with high cheekbones and an angular chin.

"Not your mother," he murmurs, reading my thoughts, then sets his jaw, leaving it at that.

I let him, considering I've yet to wrap my head around him as a father. Besides, I *know* who my mother is even though she's now a liar. I'm the child of Barbara and Gene Beckett, raised by them in Boston where I lived a predictable if hardworking life. Dad has his own landscaping company, and Mom's part of a cleaning service. Because of their long hours and strict routine, my schooling continued after classes at home, including dedication, perseverance, and the strive to do better, always. To *become* better. Dad managed success after I taught him how to input his drawing talents into computer software and started his own landscaping business (nearly losing his stable job because of the risk, leading to my first real fight with Mom). Perfection is attainable if you're focused.

It still is. It must be. I refuse to think about how my picture of them, of us, crumbled into dust as soon as *he* walked in.

He lingers beside me as if expecting to hear more questions. When it's clear I'm going to remain silent, he adds, "Let me show you to your room. Unless you're hungry?"

I shake my head.

"All right then. This way."

He leads me up the winding staircase to the upper level, where we turn into a hallway adorned with pictures and artwork of all shapes, sizes, and decorative frames staggered against the red damask wallpaper. He stops at the last room on the right, twisting the brass doorknob and motioning me inside.

"I trust it's to your liking."

Peering around the doorframe, I half-expect more strange

self-portraits or odd landscapes adorning the walls, but instead, walls of robin's egg blue greet my vision with a simple, white-framed mirror sitting atop a dresser of the same color. I step farther inside, taking in the domed ceiling, the creme canopy bed, and a fireplace, crackling its hello behind an elaborate iron grate.

"Whoa," I whisper.

"Barb, your ... mother" —he has trouble saying the word— "told me your favorite color was light blue."

I twist around. "You painted this room for me?"

He nods, his stare steady on mine. "Since you'll be here for quite some time, I wanted you to feel comfortable."

The reminder of his blackmail snuffs any remaining awe.

He seems to sense it. "Your uniform for tomorrow's orientation is in the closet over there. Your attached bathroom is the door next to it. Breakfast is served downstairs at seven o'clock sharp. I expect you down there, fully dressed, before you're driven to the academy."

I nod before all the words even sink in. I'm used to a rigid schedule, so I'm almost comforted by it.

"Good." He works his jaw, scanning the room aggressively like he's looking for weapons or spoon-dug tunnels I've secretly been working on before arriving. "Not to frighten you, but this house makes strange sounds at night. It's been attributed to the wind that comes off the cliffs, but if you hear howling, like animals in pain, it's not real."

I raise my brows at that.

"And the creaking wood flooring," he continues. "It's ancient, annoying, and often sounds out at night as the house settles."

"Okay." But I drag out my acknowledgment with extreme suspicion. Did I just agree to live in a haunted house?

"If you need anything, I'll be in my study on the first floor. Behind the staircase, third door on the right."

I note the time on the analog clock ticking down on my nightstand. Ten at night.

"You don't sleep?" I'm not sure why I should care, but the question comes out anyway.

He shakes his head. "Not much. Search for me anytime."

"Thanks. Um ..." I search for a way to acknowledge him out loud.

His eyes soften for a moment, his hand still clutching the doorknob. "You can call me Malcolm."

"Malcolm." I test the name out on my tongue.

"Good night, Ember."

"Night."

He shuts the door with a soft click. The fireplace activity amplifies in sound, its spits and whooshes encasing the room. I close my eyes, thinking of the last time I went camping with Dad, covered in grit and smoke from building a small fire, then falling back into the grass and staring at the brilliant night sky as the flames flickered between us.

Holding on to that thought like a childhood stuffed animal, I crawl into bed. I keep my eyes shut and pretend I'm at home, that Malcolm never came into my life, and my parents just kissed me good night before my first day of senior year.

I SPEAR UP IN BED, the howling in my nightmares continuing with heartbreaking speed. My breaths spike as I frantically look around, forgetting where I am or who I'm with. Everything I'm surrounded by is unfamiliar and terrifying.

The wind from the cliffs ...

Animals in pain ...

Malcolm's foreboding words rise from the depths of my

mind, slowing my breathing and unclenching my fists from the sheets.

I'm at Weatherby Manor. *His* home. In a pale-blue room blanketed in shadows, the fireplace nothing but sputtering cinders.

Rubbing my chest, I listen to the continued howling outside, a cry that seems to wrap itself around the mansion and continue in circles, over and over.

Outside. Not in.

I ache for water to quench my parched throat, but I didn't bother to do anything but crawl into bed last night, foregoing pajamas.

Maybe I could drink from the faucet in my bathroom, but I can't seem to get my legs to move. A tickling feeling on my cheek continues down my neck, traveling through my body, quivering with the thought that someone else's fingers initiated the goose bumps along my skin.

But that's impossible because my bedroom door is locked. I made sure to do that much so I didn't make myself vulnerable in a strange, possessed house. Besides that, Malcolm stated no one else was in the manor except for him, and he wouldn't sneak in and touch me while I slept.

That would be *beyond* creepy.

I fumble for the bedside lamp, finding the chain and yanking until golden light floods the room. Chasing the shadows away is enough to level out my breaths, and I slide out of bed.

The hardwood floors creak under my footsteps, and I wince at each whine, but the sound is better, safer, than what's moaning outside in the storm. Branches clack and claw against the bay window, joining the bone-rattling orchestra, and I want nothing more than the noise-canceling headphones I know are somewhere in my suitcases.

Malcolm propped them up against the far wall, where it's

still dark, but I tell myself to pull up my big-girl panties and just find the headphones so I can curl up in bed and get warm again.

Now that the fire's dampened, a cold draft floats through the room, and falling asleep in wet clothes hasn't exactly helped. I undo my jeans as I head over to the luggage, stepping out of them and tossing them nearby. I do the same with my shirt, discarding it and heading the rest of the way in my bra and underwear, shivering.

I step in something wet.

Squealing, I recoil, nearly slamming against one of the bed's pillars holding up the silk canopy. A puddle sits close to my luggage but far enough away not to be originating from it. The puddle spreads, edging against the wall, as if ... as if it came *through* the wall.

That's impossible. It's not part of the house's exterior.

Folding my arms around myself for warmth, I hedge closer, tangled strands of hair falling into my face as I bend slightly and stare at the water as if it could tell me why it's there.

Why *is* it there?

I look up, scanning the plaster, the more panicky bits of me wondering if it's a false wall and there's a secret passage behind it.

While not ludicrous, it's definitely something I'd rather not be true. Who would want to sneak in here, anyway? Who would walk through the storm, then traipse through this room in darkness to bend over my bed, watch me sleep, and touch me?

Images of the guy across the street flit behind my eyes, but I blink his face away before my brain can convince me it could be him. It's all too easy to imagine him standing over me, stroking my cheek and sending shivers into my dreams. To have a guy be that enamored with me after only seeing me for a few seconds, it —well, it's a gothic fairy tale I don't have the right to star in.

The hollow ache that follows after I shut the image away

leaves me the most surprised. As if I'm disappointed I didn't get the chance to open my eyes and see him up close.

Jeez. Get a grip, Ember. He'd assessed me with such revulsion by literally stumbling back a step after we made eye contact across the road. He was eerie, beautiful from a distance, but most assuredly *not* interested.

Odds were better it was Malcolm, sneaking alongside the mansion until he found the passageway into my room ...

Ugh. No.

Retreating, I massage my temples.

The puddle is nothing. Just remaining waterlog from my luggage ... four hours later. After a steady fire warmed the room.

The wind picks up its howls, and another tree branch tries to claw its way in.

I swallow a whimper and unzip my suitcase as fast as I can, searching blindly for the cold, metallic feel of my headphones.

The tips of my fingers hit something hard, and I latch on, pulling it through the tossed clothing. The headphones appear out of the fabric, and I clamp them on my ears before I even stand, blissing out at the instant white noise of my blood pounding in my ears and nothing else.

Crawling back into bed, I let the amplified, rhythmic beats of my heart lull me into a state of relaxation as I stare at the ceiling through the sheer canopy, carved with swirls of cherubs and angels. My eyelids grow heavy, and I fall back to sleep.

With the lamplight on.

CHAPTER 3
EMBER

T hanks to my dead phone and the old analog bedside clock I couldn't figure out how to set an alarm on, I'm late waking up. Shoving my hair out of my face and pulling my headphones off, I go in search of my charger, then plan to take a shower as fast as I can.

Digging through my luggage graces me with a power cord, but further inspection of the room provides me with zero electrical outlets.

Frowning, I do another search, going so far as to try to move furniture away from the wall, but everything is so heavy, I'm unable to shift even a leg.

There's a bedside lamp whose cord I can't follow behind the bed and electrical sconces in the hallways, so there must be outlets *somewhere*. Figuring I'll find one eventually, I toss my phone on the unmade bed and head to the bathroom.

But freeze in the doorframe after I swing open the door.

To say the bathroom is opulent is an understatement.

Cream marble countertops and a claw-foot tub are the first things I notice, as well as glimmering brass fixtures. A separate shower with clear glass sparkles in one corner with the same marble sheen, next to the water closet—basically a toilet sitting in its own tiny room with a door. On the way to it, I scan the walls for outlets, still finding none.

My reflection stares back at me as I strip off my underwear from last night, still smelling like rain. The overhead light combined with the cold, sterile background paints me as washed-out and pale, my ash-blond hair nearly the same color as my skin. Usually, the strands are a dishwater platinum, dull and unremarkable in most environments. But here, the strands are so white they appear gray. If it weren't for the jarring contrast of my dark brown eyes, I'd swear Weatherby Manor turned me into a ghost.

The unforgiving bathroom light forces the fact that this summer was harder on me than I thought. I turn away from my sallow edges as soon as I can, stepping into the warm, thankfully modern spray of a wide showerhead and wash off the remnants of my travel to Raven's Bluff, Massachusetts.

I'm ready in twenty minutes, deciding on simple makeup and a low, damp ponytail for my first day at Winthorpe High. During the summer, I'd devoured internet searches on the school and tried to scope out the social media accounts of any students I could find. Strangely, all accounts were private and locked. There wasn't one public persona I could scour to try to get an idea of how to fit in. That left me with the school website and online brochures featuring students (or actors) laughing in bright-green grass or sharing hilarious secrets while clutching books to their chest and strolling the opulent halls. Everyone was perfectly groomed. No one rebelled with above-the-knee skirts or top buttons undone. Any keywords I attempted to search for to find the *real* Winthorpe High School provided precious little.

I'm left to my own devices. My stomach skips with my steps to the closet as I peel off my robe and get dressed, hoping I do this right. If the fashion game is anything like it was in public school, the way I wear this uniform will either make or break me.

During my eight weeks of "thinking about it," I never reached out to Malcolm, so I have no idea if the tailoring is correct on the uniform I find hanging in the walk-in closet. A lot of other clothes are there, too—blouses and slacks, dresses and skirts—and they are all in my size. I hum in thought as I pull the uniform off its hanger and use my other hand to brush against the expensive, wrinkle-free fabrics in mostly pastels and grays.

Did Malcolm expect me to join him at a country club?

Not to be ungrateful, but I mostly get by on T-shirts and jeans, sometimes mixing it up with sweaters and shorts. Seeing all this preppy, over-the-top attire makes me think that during this summer, Malcolm didn't bother to get to know me, either.

Except for the blue bedroom.

A frustrated sound leaves my throat. I won't let Malcolm chip away at my armor. I *won't*.

I turn to the floor-length mirror hanging on the back of the closet door, using it to slip on the Winthorpe uniform.

Shockingly, it fits. The black pleated skirt with blue and white plaid detailing falls just above my knees. The white, long-sleeved blouse caps off perfectly at my wrists, as does the black blazer with the silver-threaded shield on the right breast, surrounded by flowers encapsulating the Winthorpe crest. I knot the black cross-tie at my collar with amateur flair, pull on white knee-length stockings, then call myself ready.

Even the backpack is school-issued, and I hook it from its cubby above the closet's selection of coats, using its side pockets to shove my phone and wallet into but leaving the main compartment empty, considering I don't have books yet.

After tying my school-issued Mary Janes, I leave my bedroom at seven o'clock but get lost twice on the first floor. The mansion appears as lonely as last night, except when I pass a butler on my way to the dining room. He doesn't startle at my presence, so I must be an expected addition to the manor. With his help, I'm directed to something called an atrium, not the dining room.

After stumbling down the wrong hallway, doing a U-turn, and finding another one near the back of the house, I eventually come to the opening of a glass-domed room covered with carefully tended plants, vines, and flowers. The scent of roses and soil hits me first, and as I wander inside, I find Malcolm sitting at a wrought-iron garden table with a newspaper open and one covered plate.

I follow the small cobblestone path to him, marveling at the shades of green with rainbow sparks of color that wrap entirely to the ceiling. Dad would be *astounded* by this room, gabbing nonstop and pointing out the rare horticulture, explaining which were native and what was imported, his body practically throbbing with the desire to record each and every flower.

But to my amateur eye, I'm only seeing roses. Different types, sure, and many rare ones, but they're all the same species and kept in perfect full bloom condition.

The newspaper snaps, capturing my attention. Malcolm doesn't look up from his reading when he says, "You're late."

"It's a big house. I got lost."

I immediately bite my tongue, annoyed at being even slightly sassy with him. I'd promised myself to be numb, uncaring, and devoid of emotion while I was here. I can't let the exhilarating sight of so many roses—a reminder of my *father*—dissuade me.

"Understandable. Try not to have it happen again. Please. Sit."

I take the seat across from him. As if Malcolm snapped his fingers, the same butler I asked directions from appears between us and lifts the silver dome from the single plate.

"Thank you, Dash," Malcolm says before staring at me expectantly.

20

Steam wafts into my nostrils, sweet and savory. A stack of pancakes, bacon, scrambled eggs, and mini-sized ketchup and hot sauce bottles greet my vision.

"Holy crap," I say without thinking.

"I wasn't sure what you preferred for breakfast, so I had the cook prepare a spread."

I glance up from my plate. "I'm expected to eat this every morning?"

Malcolm answers with a slight nod. "If you'd like."

"I'm okay with some yogurt, or cereal, or a smoothie or something. Your cook doesn't need to go all out."

Though I try not to, my attention drifts to his steaming mug and the French press beside it.

Malcolm notices and makes a noise in his throat. "You're a little young for coffee, aren't you?"

I try to give Malcolm credit where it's due, and considering the vast emptiness of this house, he probably hasn't been around teenagers very often. Especially the caffeinated ones.

"I do, with about a billion packets of sugar."

One side of Malcolm's lips quirk, his pale blue eyes gleaming with what I think is amusement. He motions behind me to Dash, who I assume was hiding behind a rose bush in wait because he startles me with his sudden reappearance.

"Another mug," Malcolm says to him, "and a saucer of sugar cubes."

"And caramel sauce," I can't help blurting out.

Malcolm's answering shudder is noticeable, but he nods his consent to the lean old man dressed in butler attire. Dash's face, while heavily lined with age, doesn't twitch in response. He merely departs from the atrium on silent loafered feet.

"He doesn't ... I mean, nobody has to wait on me," I say to Malcolm. "If you show me where the kitchen is, I'll be happy to grab my own coffee next time."

21

"Nonsense. They're paid handsomely. Not to mention, it's been a long time since they've had a young ward to fuss over."

Considering Dash's weathered, unresponsive face, I doubt he's kicking his feet up in glee at the thought of cleaning up after a young girl.

Malcolm clears his throat, the conversation suddenly over. I turn to my food, ravenous despite my pledge to be unmoved and unamused at all things Weatherby, especially if someone spent their morning cooking this just for me. Malcolm's side of the table is empty and crumb-free, leading me to believe he doesn't eat breakfast and most definitely does *not* ask for pancakes in the morning.

"Are you ready for your first day?" he asks without lifting his eyes from the paper.

I chew the remainder of my pancake bite and swallow. "Sure."

"Nervous?"

"No," I lie.

This conversation sounds remarkably like a father-daughter bonding session, and I want no part of it.

The smell of roses remains pungent yet soothing as memories of Dad slicing a spade through the soil as I ran circles around him as a child and tried to pick all the flowers he'd painstakingly planted flood my mind. It brings a heavy, lonely feeling, and I bunch my fingers in the napkin on my lap. That memory's tainted now. Stolen.

Dad knowingly took me away from the person sitting across from me, yet I still feel closer to Dad. I want Dad.

So immersed in my confusion, I don't notice the way Malcolm's watching me until it's too late.

"This was my wife's favorite room," he says softly. "She took it upon herself to tend the garden and keep the place bright and fresh. I'm afraid, with her absence, I've let it grow wild, but I can't seem to let it die."

A beat of silence passes, and I'm sure he believes I'll fill it with questions and curiosity.

I don't.

"Do you like gardening?" he asks.

"Not really." I toss the napkin on my half-finished plate and stand. "But my father does."

Malcolm winces, and I push down the resulting nugget of guilt that lodges in my throat. I've spent eighteen years with my parents and less than twenty-four hours with Malcolm. He can't possibly expect me to switch loyalties that quickly, even knowing my parents' heartbreaking duplicity.

"What Mom and Dad did was illegal," I admit, though it hurts. I clasp my hands in front of me, holding on tight. "But my emotions can't follow the law so easily."

Malcolm's lips crimp. He nods tightly and pushes to his feet. "I'll have Marta make your coffee to go. Otherwise, you'll be late. Dash will drive you. I apologize for not doing it myself, but there's a meeting I can't avoid."

During my late-night plunges into the online depths of my new life, I'd also did a few searches on Malcolm. He's old money. The Weatherbys founded an import and export business, and Malcolm is the current CEO.

"It's not a problem," I say, forcing my hands apart so my fingers can relax.

"Well. Good luck to you, then." Malcolm's arm jerks as if to shake my hand before he sets it back to his side, pretty much summing up our awkwardness.

"I'm sure I'll be fine," I say.

Malcolm's crystalline eyes grow small as he studies me. "Try to have some fun, too."

At that, I snort. "Academics aren't fun. They're the hardworking key to a comfortable future."

He cocks a brow as if to acknowledge that we're cut from the same cloth. Wisely, he stays silent.

"I'll see you at dinner," he says instead. "Eight o'clock sharp."

The mention of this evening raises my head. "Before I go, I wanted to ask ... are there secret passageways in this house?"

Both his brows rise. "There are servants' tunnels, yes, from some time ago. I suppose you could call them secret passageways."

"Into my room?"

He frowns. "Most of the tunnels are inoperable and have remained closed off for years. The structural integrity alone causes concern. If one leads into your room, I wouldn't know, but you can rest assured no one else does, either. I suggest you don't go exploring in them if you find one."

"I wouldn't know where to start. I was just wondering ... There was a puddle, and ..." I drift off, realizing how ridiculous I sound.

Malcolm answers, "An old house like this has some leaks, I'm afraid. I do what I can with upkeep, but with just me living here, I've neglected certain wings, including yours. I contracted some work to be completed over the summer, but there's still more to be done. Will you be all right until then?"

No. I want to go home. But the fear of my parents being dragged out of their house in handcuffs has me answering, "Yes. It'll take some getting used to."

"I'll see you tonight, Ember."

"Maybe some outlets. Eventually. In my room." I can't muster the graciousness to say goodbye, so instead, I turn out of the atrium and leave him standing there, strangely exposed and vulnerable despite his impeccable three-piece suit and hundred-dollar haircut, surrounded by the immaculate flowers of his dead wife.

CHAPTER 4
EMBER

The cold ocean mist pricks my exposed skin as I stand in front of Winthorpe Academy, perched on the highest cliff in Raven's Bluff and bordered by twisted and gnarled oak, pine, and beech trees.

The school claims a refurbished castle as its home base, named after some noble lord in eighteen-century England. It was constructed as a two-story rectangle with turrets on each side, but upgrades and refurbishments give it strange, modern limbs stretching out in cast iron and glass-paned relief. The center remains traditional, keeping its original bone-white, crumbling stone with climbing vines along the walls.

Underneath such an imposing structure, the center court-yard bustles with the modern uniforms of the students. Rather than stand out like a sore thumb as I wander in without anyone to talk to, I pay attention to the perfectly landscaped, squared-off garden bordering the stone pathway to the entrance. Wild roses, daisies, hydrangeas, and rhododendrons burst with life within their stone confines, their scent drifting into the fog and wrapping around my shoulders like a soothing blanket. If anything, I can escape this day by coming here and finding a vacant stone bench, closing my eyes, and pretending I'm home.

I must've made that fantasy a reality because I'm roughly shoved aside and open my eyes before I nearly topple into the very dreamscape I'd crafted.

"Watch it, you fucking moron," a voice snaps.

Righting myself, I lift my head and meet feline eyes of cold steel. They narrow when they latch onto mine, and she clasps her friend's hand as she sneers, "If it isn't the carpetbagger."

I'm too shocked to be insulted. I know these kids are smarter than the average student, but... "I'm sorry?"

"Somebody who takes advantage of other people's tragedies for personal gain." The girl's long auburn hair glistens in the waning sun as she gives me an unimpressed once-over. "I guess bottom-feeders have to figure out some way to swim to the top. Fair warning, you'll be drowned during your trip up."

The brunette friend standing next to her titters in amusement.

"How is tripping me into a rose garden making me a bottom-feeder? Or ... carpetbagger?" I'm honestly curious.

The redhead blinks as if not expecting the retort. "Because you're a slow mover in the middle of a crowded walkway, and you look like you just crawled out of the ocean and over the rocks."

I self-consciously find a damp strand of my ponytail and twirl it around my finger. "Unless the ocean smells like strawberry shampoo, I doubt that's where I came from."

The girl's eyes narrow as though I'm the weirdest person she's ever met. I probably am.

"Leave the Weatherby bastard alone, Aurora," a low, dark voice says behind me.

My shoulders stiffen at the sound, goose bumps skittering like spooked insects as if he'd whispered it near my nape.

"Is that who she is?" The girl, Aurora, tilts her head, inspecting me now as a circus freak. "I wondered how somebody managed to take Savannah's reserved spot."

"Excuse me?" I look back and forth between the redhead and her friend. "Who's Savannah?"

The male voice answers softly behind me, "I'm also curious how she got here."

Call it kismet, an unknowing *knowing,* or simply instinct, but I'm aware of who the voice belongs to before I even turn around.

Him.

The boy across the street.

Instead of spinning all the way, I show him my profile but keep my eyes on Aurora. "I'm not a bastard. And I think you have me confused with somebody else."

"What are you then, little pretty?" He comes up beside me, bringing with him the scent of soap, pine needles, and something foreign. A scent that's sharp and predatory. "A kidnap victim? Motherless orphan? Escapee of the child sex trade? There are all kinds of rumors swirling about you." His shadow covers my entire form with ease, and I'm almost afraid to look up into his eyes as he continues. "I was hoping you'd be more interesting to look at up close. But you're just as waterlogged and pathetic as you were from a distance."

Aurora laughs, a light tinkle of chimes against a subtle wind.

I don't know what it is that makes me shrink under his towering form. Maybe it's the menacing rasp of his voice or the hurtful words. Perhaps, it's the comparison of the boy I hoped was standing over my bed versus the reality of this asshole.

Any one of those makes me want to counteract the urge with a simple statement. "I must be somewhat fascinating since when you first saw me, you looked like you'd seen a ghost."

"Mmm," he acknowledges. "A ghost you'll never live up to."

I don't cower. His insult only brings more questions. "Why does Malcolm Weatherby think your father is a terrible man?"

The guy jolts, his torso stretching the buttons on his shirt before snapping back into rigid stone, replacing his nonchalant stroll around my body. "And who the fuck are you to ask that?"

I tip my chin, at last meeting his eyes. I halt my sudden inhale at the sight of his irises, so pale blue they're almost white, with a dark indigo outer ring.

I'm supposed to want to know everything about him, this enemy of my enemy. His father and Malcolm don't get along, and it's only natural I question why. How. I'd like to use it against Malcolm in some way. It could be the key to gaining the freedom to return to my parents without punishment.

I angle my head as I take him in, studying and assessing. Yet also secretly admiring, mesmerized by every aspect of his angular, carved-in-brimstone face.

His nostrils flare, one of his brows moving with the tiniest twitch of surprise at my blatant study.

"Jesus," Aurora says from nearby. "What the hell's wrong with her?"

I ignore her, saying to the boy instead, "According to you, I'm the Weatherby heir, so I should have a right to know why Malcolm and his neighbor don't like each other."

His thick black lashes lower to half-mast, the marble carve to his features edging out sharply against the hazy background of the sky. "Being Malcolm Weatherby's *mistake* doesn't gain you any ground with me. And some free advice? If you want to survive this semester, you'll make yourself scarce around me and anyone associated with me."

"It's impossible for her to be invisible, Thorne," Aurora whines. "Look what she's done. If Savannah ever comes back ..."

Thorne. His name is Thorne, a fitting name for a boy whose gaze shoots up and pins Aurora like a shredded butterfly. "What

28

have I said about your inane predictions? Don't make me warn you again."

Aurora's lips clamp shut, her jaw trembling with the effort. She glares at him.

One murderous second passes, my lungs tightening with shortened breaths as they stare each other down. Then he returns to me and grins, showing off impossibly white teeth with pointed canines. "I'd rather call you prey instead of a bottom-feeder. See how long you last at my school. That's right, little pretty. *Mine.*"

A shiver runs up my spine, both pleasure and dread at hearing such foreboding words come out of such a devastating face. I can't break eye contact even if I wanted to. He holds me captive, and the quirk to his full lips tells me he knows it. "Sadly for you," he murmurs to me, "I'm very patient with my victims."

A different female voice cuts through the electric buzz in my ears. "Don't you vultures have anything better to do?"

She's loud enough to sever Thorne's and my connection, and I jerk in the direction of the voice. A Japanese girl uses her elbows to come between Thorne and Aurora, breaking them apart and forcing the two to step back. "Get away from the new girl, Thorne. Go pick at somebody else's bones."

"I'd go for yours," Thorne muses, "but there's not much to occupy me for long."

"I'm devastated." Nonplussed, the girl swoops her arm around my elbow and pulls me toward the entrance.

"Watch yourself, Aiko," he warns at our backs.

"Always do," she chirps.

A crick forms in my neck as I twist to get one last look. His eyes have the same impact from a distance, and a shudder of caution rattles my bones, yet curiosity keeps me from breaking our stare first.

Thorne turns to Aurora, whose icy features thaw into a brilliant smile once she regains his attention. He says something, and she laughs, bright and loud.

I've known Thorne for maybe five seconds, but the last vibe I get from him is *funny*.

"You're okay, now." Aiko squeezes my arm. "They're a terrible welcoming committee, but I promise we're not all like that." A tiny line forms between her brows as she stares ahead. "Well, some of us aren't."

I huff out a laugh. "I'm not worried. They aren't my first bullies."

Life at my public high school wasn't the greatest, but I made it as ideal as I could by keeping my head down, focusing on my grades, and padding any free time on campus with extracurriculars or study hall. Basically, I ensured I was never left alone in a deserted hallway and picked off like the weakest animal straying from their herd.

Sadly for you, I'm very patient with my victims …

I have the awful impression bullies are different here.

"Yeah, but these people are a separate breed of hellions," Aiko says as if reading my thoughts. "You think your old high school had problems? Wait until you see the shit they get up to at Winthorpe."

I try to match Aiko's easy stroll through the rest of the courtyard, but I'm distracted by the constant stares in my direction, the mutterings behind hands, and the suspicious arching of brows. "Lawson High had the typical jackasses who vandalized, shoved, and threatened their way to the top. You're saying it's not like that here?" I ask.

"Well, no, but yes. You're with the heavy hitters, now. The politicians' kids, the heirs of billion-dollar companies, royals of countries you've never heard of but who are rich as hell, and I think there are even mafia don children and drug cartel members scattered around. Those kinds of titles come with a different sort of aggression. Vicious but quiet. The kind of undercutting you don't notice until it's too late."

"Great," I whisper, her words hitting me harder than I'd like. Dealing with Malcolm Weatherby is enough. "And where do you fall?"

Yikes, where do I get off being so nosy? Thorne's sudden proximity flustered me more than I thought. I'm about to apologize, but Aiko answers easily. "I'm the only child of a high-ranking military man. Brings new meaning to single dad, huh?"

I release a soft laugh. "Is that why you came up to Thorne and Aurora like it was nothing?"

Aiko laughs in turn. "Don't let my size fool you. Thorne's dad has wanted good relations with the US military for years, and not even Thorne is stupid enough to screw that up."

"Does that happen a lot? Adults using their kids as pawns?"

Malcolm's domineering presence in my childhood home floats to the surface, and his immediate threat to have me removed from the home. During his entire speech, I didn't think he was saying anything out of love. It was more like he'd lost a piece of his property and wanted it back. His expression was flat, and his resounding voice of a man used to being obeyed.

My mom's tears and my dad's trembling grip on my shoulder —*that* was emotion. Terrible, ragged awareness.

We can't lose her. Please, you can't take our Ember away ...

He did.

"The power plays of our parents happen in classrooms, the courtyard, the gardens, *and* the playground out back," Aiko says.

I murmur, "I'll be wise to remember that."

"Omigod, I'm so sorry. I'm the worst student guide on the planet." Aiko pulls me to an abrupt halt. "Here I am, instilling the fear of God in you, and I haven't even introduced myself. I'm Aiko. And just so I can tell Headmistress Dupris I plucked the correct new girl from the salivating jaws of Winthorpe's elite, you're Ember Weatherby."

"Call me Ember Beckett." It comes out with a hard edge, and I deliberately soften my jaw. "Don't worry, I caught your name before, and I love how you're being so open." So different from *me*. "It's good to be aware of this stuff."

Aiko wrinkles her nose. "Yeah, but probably not in the first five seconds of being at Winthorpe. Just ignore the cool crowd, and you'll come out fine. Or you could be like me and don't show fear. They *hate* it when they're not terrifying. Really bites them on their gonads."

More students filter around us and through the entrance, most pausing and staring at me before taking the stairs. I stiffen, not quite sure it's my imagination anymore.

"I don't plan to make waves," I say distractedly, eyeing a particularly obvious girl leaning conspiratorially close to her friend. "Aiko, can I ask you something?"

"You mean, I haven't made you want to run for the hills or go deaf? Brilliant! What's up?"

"Why is everyone staring at me?"

Aiko follows my gaze before giving a knowing nod. "Oh, yeah. That."

"What's going on?"

"Well ..." Aiko rubs her lips together before glancing up at me. "Not to give you *more* of a reason to be wary of Winthorpe High, but ... you kinda took someone's place when you enrolled at this school."

"Okay." I draw out the word, waiting for more information.

"Don't get me wrong. When there's an opening at Winthorpe, parents break the internet trying to get their kid accepted."

"So, you're saying I filled a vacancy, and those don't happen very often." I purse my lips in thought, trying to find the hole that would make the other students want to take a closer look.

"More like never. And you took the spot immediately. No interview, no application, just your father's word."

"He's not my father." But I do concede his power. "I'm not surprised he pulled strings to get me enrolled. Malcolm tends to strong-arm people into doing what he wants."

Aiko adds, "You also kinda ... look like her. Not in a creepy way, but your hair color ..." Aiko traces a circle in the air near my face. "Your nose. Maybe your chin."

"You mean she was an albino blonde?" When Aiko doesn't laugh, I ask softly, "Why did she leave?"

"Her name is Savannah Merricourt. She didn't leave." Aiko grimaces as she forces the rest of her sentence out. "She went missing last year."

CHAPTER 5
THORNE

er eyes are different.

Last night, while I huddled under an umbrella and smoked a joint down to the roach, I figured the best I'd get was a nice high before sitting down to a so-called family dinner and pretending we were the people my father liked to peddle us as—wholesome mother, bright young son, and ruthless yet benevolent entrepreneur.

Instead, I spied Malcolm Weatherby escorting a girl out of his car. Spotting her across the road, pelted with rain and highlighted by a crack of lightning, I almost lost my footing and slammed into one of our driveway's pillars, causing the stone raven to topple on my damn head.

It would serve me right to be killed by that bird.

But ... fuck. I thought it was Savannah. That Weatherby found her and was taking her to his place to recover until the police got there, and word got out she survived ...

Until I sucked the spent roach into my throat during my stumble, and ash coated my mouth, allowing reality to choke its way in and her face to take better shape in the storm.

I blame my over-the-top reaction on the weed Jaxon imported from Hawaii.

It wasn't her. Couldn't be. That gut-wrenching swirl of recognition dissipated as soon as I stepped up to the girl this morning and looked into her eyes. Molten brown, like Savannah's, but without the guileless shimmer she always seemed to carry, like her soul was using her vision as more than a window and demanding greater goodness from those around her.

Ember, however, has shadows flitting behind the bronze. Up close, they're slightly bloodshot and red-rimmed, most likely from the toll Malcolm Weatherby has already taken on her. Fear, anxiety, separation, and unwelcome surprise. All those ghostly critters that take up valuable headspace in most, but help me see better at night.

Ember, poor thing, still thinks she'll be able to sleep during those quiet, watchful hours.

Shouts and towel slaps draw my mind back to the present, clouds of steam rising in the heated locker room from the guys who've taken advantage of the pool during morning orientation. It's basically a mass invitation to ditch, a lot of us pretending to set up for our athletics for the year then fucking off to the rec center to toss balls around or actually get in some fitness training. I plan to head to the sauna for a few minutes, then jump back in the pool and do more laps.

"Dude, did you see the new chick?" Jaxon asks me as he slams his locker shut.

I sling a towel around my neck, chlorinated water droplets still clinging to my bare chest. When I turn, my half-lowered stare gives him the answer he's looking for.

Jaxon, obviously, doesn't heed the silent warning. "What's she like up close? Her tits nice?"

Very, actually. Perfect C-cups, but I'm not about to goad him into more idiocy. "Does it matter?"

"Kinda."

Jaxon follows me into the sauna area, freshmen and sophomores leaping out of our way as we glide through with the air of royals. In this school, we are. With Jaxon's midnight skin and my pale pallor and even lighter eyes, we're like a moonlit night swallowing a dull, tedious day.

"She moved into Weatherby Manor last night," I reluctantly add. "I'm guessing she's here to stay."

"Well, what do we do about it? That's Savannah's spot."

Jaxon pulls the door open to the sauna. We're the only ones entering the stifling cedar-soaked heat. Everyone else figured shooting the shit for a while was enough before heading to the mandatory assembly after orientation, but for us, as captain and co-captain of the swim team, we always have the excuse of the next dive into the deep. Winthorpe positively *thrives* on their stellar swim champion reputation.

As Jaxon settles on the bench across from me, I mull over his question until I come to an answer. "We have to get her to leave."

"Your father's orders?" Jaxon muses.

I shrug. "My father and I differ in opinion when it comes to her."

Jaxon's brows jump in surprise, but I dismiss the interest. Instead, I take a swig from my sports bottle as Jaxon ladles water over the heating stones and the resulting steam hisses.

His voice comes out quiet and unsure. "Thorne, you know what it means if your father allowed her in here." Then he adds, as if I don't already know, "She's a legacy."

I tongue my cheek, staring at the wall but not focusing on it. I'm reaching inward, pondering what it'll take to keep my father happy while still pursuing my goals. "I'll leave that up to Aurora and the girls."

"You sure that's a good idea?" Jaxon's skin glistens with

sweat. His breathing has become labored, but like a good soldier, he's not about to leave until I do.

"We don't interfere with their hazings." I savor the words, deviant thoughts filling the spaces between. "But you've given me an idea."

I rise to pour more water over the rocks, considering Jaxon's wimped out. I don't miss the wariness in Jaxon's stare as he watches me.

I like it hot. Uncomfortably so. Almost like we could suffocate while still going through the motions of drawing in air.

"What are you planning?" he asks, his voice turning into rasps.

Though I'm confident we're alone, I scan the small room. One can't be too careful, especially at Winthorpe. Someone's always doing someone else's bidding. I save the frosted glass door for last but detect no lingering shadow nearby.

"You're correct that she's a legacy," I answer in a low tone. "We can't prevent a Weatherby heir from joining the Societies, but maybe you're right, and we can influence what kind of hazing—or initiation—she receives."

"I never said—"

"Enough to make her second-guess her attendance here. *Definitely* enough to piss off my father."

Jaxon snorts. "You won't have to beg. Aurora will be up for it."

I make a sound of agreement. "*Enthusiastic* doesn't even cover it. She was all over the new girl before I'd stepped out of my car." Steam rises between us as the stones hiss and spurt. I smile through the haze, and I have no doubts what I resemble.

"Are you sure *you're* up for it?" Jaxon dares to ask, then coughs, sweat coming down his forehead in rivulets now.

I toss the ladle next to the heater. "Why wouldn't I be?"

"Well, because of who she's replacing."

"Totally irrelevant."

"Uh, I'm pretty sure that's the most important—"

"It's one more thing I can use to make Ember Weatherby hate it here. For reasons I've yet to figure out, my father refuses to make immediate moves against the Weatherbys, and until I find out why, I will."

"I dunno. She seems pretty harmless to me."

I shoot him a glare, hotter than this room. Jaxon's brows twitch, but he doesn't look away. Good man.

"That's the problem with the Weatherbys," I say softly. I'm treading dangerous ground, and my voice knows it. "They seem innocent and kind until they have you at your most vulnerable. Then they strike. My family nearly lost everything, thanks to Malcolm, and now he conveniently finds a long-lost daughter to enroll into Winthorpe after another girl goes missing? Does that seem innocent to you?" I answer before Jaxon opens his mouth. "No. It's a calculated move, meant to be played against my family. Malcolm's up to something, and if my father, the self-proclaimed omniscient Damion Briar, won't do anything about it, well, he's trained me so I can."

Training is such a subtle word and normally used for innocuous things like swim practice or teaching a pet not to shit on the carpet.

Jaxon's features tighten at my statement. He, of all people, would understand the true meaning behind my father's *training.*

I was taught to avoid allure at all costs. But Ember's quiet beauty ... Malcolm brought a lamb into this twisted, elite castle. Ember's first impression haunts me, her eyes both sad and eager, with a mysterious spark behind them that makes me think she'll have some fight in her. My groin twitches at the thought, and I low-key readjust my junk within the suctioned confines of my swimsuit.

"Dude ..." Jaxon clears his throat, then wobbles to a stand. "I gotta ... I have to get out of here."

"Pussy," I say but allow him to lean on me as we exit the sauna. As soon as the cool air hits him, his chest swells with relief.

"I don't know how you do that," he grits out, remaining heavy against my side as I lead us to the pool. "And then put in more laps on top of it."

"Discipline. Drills. Failure never being an option."

"Buddy, you're sounding more and more like Damion Briar every day."

Jaxon grunts, then stumbles when I leave him to hit the air before crashing into the pool. When he breaks the surface, sputtering and cursing, I tell him mildly, "It's also why I have no problems making little girls cry."

CHAPTER 6

EMBER

I'm thanking the heavens for Aiko.

Not only has she managed to regale me with student rankings, the best and worst teachers, and the areas to avoid being cornered (because, according to her, if you aren't one of the kids who run this school, you *will* be backed into a blind spot eventually) she also leads me through the endless lines to pick up our syllabus, order our textbooks, and confirm our electives.

Once my arms were piled high with papers, handbooks, and brochures, we followed the funnel into the vast auditorium, then chose our seats for the first-day assembly. Aiko picked seats close to the middle, where she waved at a few people and gestured to me with a thumbs-up before plopping down and patting the velvet seat next to her.

"This'll be boring as hell," she says as I make myself comfortable. "I wish I had it in me to blow it off like a lot of others do, but I'm just too terrified of authority."

I laugh. "Me, too. I don't want to do anything to jeopardize my chance at the fellowship."

Surprise flickers across her face. "Are you talking about the Marks Fellowship?"

"That's the one." I twist to face her, glad to have met someone with information. "It's super competitive, but it's the one carrot Malcolm dangled that convinced me to move here."

"You're interested in computers?"

"More than that." I'm aware of how my voice has gone breathy with excitement. "I've loved software development ever since I was a kid. I helped Dad create his own landscaping program when I was nine and have been fascinated with it ever since." Winning the Marks Fellowship means an internship at Marks Edelman Technology and then a full scholarship at the college of your choice with a guaranteed position at the company waiting for you—an achievement dominated by Winthorpe grads for ten consecutive years. "It'd be like a dream come true. An opportunity I *never* thought I'd have the chance to shoot for." As I wait for Aiko's reaction, my face heats with embarrassment. "I've completely nerded out on you, haven't I?"

"Girl, of all people, you *should* be talking to me. I love to geek out. I'm just shocked, is all."

"About what?" I try to brush off her tense scrutiny. "That I'm a girl interested in software engineering?"

"No, not at all. Girl power." Aiko squints at me. "You really don't know?"

I tilt my head in question.

"You faced off with a Marks heir this morning. If you were looking for a good impression ... uh, I think you missed it."

My stomach drops. "Which one? Thorne or Aurora?"

Please say Aurora. I could deal with pointlessly spiteful girls, since they usually don't come with a vendetta larger than making themselves appear more popular. But Thorne? Within two seconds of meeting him, I sensed he was a different breed. A slithering malice coiled within him that he releases with very little conscience. Aiko could tell me he's killed people, and I'd accept it as fact. He hides a serpent I don't ever want to meet.

"Close. Belle Marks," she answers with a grimace. "Aurora's minion."

I fall back into my chair, facing the front. "I can handle that."

"Uh-huh." Aiko's tone sounds like she doesn't believe me.

"The fellowship's supposed to be impartial," I reason, despite the nausea swirling in my gut. "There's no way their instant dislike of me could influence my application. Right?"

Again, Aiko responds with a pained grimace. I don't think it ever went away. "Welcome to Winthorpe High, where bribes, influence, and pay-offs are the most coveted currency, inside and outside the school halls."

As if our conversation summoned him, the auditorium's main doors swing open, and Thorne strolls through.

The entire assembly falls silent. Another boy keeps pace beside him, broad-shouldered, satin dark skin, and filling out his uniform with lithe, graceful perfection. A panther flanking the lion. My focus falls on him for only a moment before I'm pulled in by Thorne, the black fabric of his blazer standing out against his bloodless complexion. His inky, chestnut hair curls damply against his ears and forehead, but there's nothing boyish about it. Thorne looks like he just had a quick dip in the Rivers Styx, toying with the Underworld shores before joining us mortals again.

"There he is, the demon himself," Aiko mutters but doesn't shrink in her seat like many others surrounding us do.

I lean forward, curious as they walk in front of the stage to get to the second aisle, then take the stairs all the way to the back of the auditorium. My eyes never leave him, but my other senses are attuned to the students' reactions—the whispers, the murmurs, the sighs, and giggles.

I ask Aiko out of the side of my mouth, "Do they always incite this kind of reaction?"

"When they decide to make an appearance. I'm surprised they've made it before the start of the assembly. Headmistress Dupris must need him for the speech."

Aiko's voice fades as Thorne passes by. His too-pale eyes slide over to mine, and though he doesn't pause, the ice in his stare causes my breath to freeze in my lungs.

My neck, acting of its own accord, twists around to follow him all the way to his seat. Aurora waves him over, and students clutch their knees to their chests to make room for him and his friend to cut across to her. He sits by Aurora, slinging an arm around the back of her chair while his friend takes the seat opposite him.

Aurora turns to smile at him, but her gaze snags on mine midway. Her eyes grow catty and small, her lip curling as she says something to Thorne.

Thorne glances over, the impact of his attention just as severe as it was when I was feet away from him. He smiles, beautiful and malicious, then responds to Aurora. She laughs, her eyes still on me.

Their mocking is enough to break me out of my trance. Cheeks hot, I swivel around to the front.

"They have that effect." Aiko pats my shoulder reassuringly. "Don't worry, it wears off once you realize what douchebags they are."

"Can you even call someone evil a douchebag?"

Aiko jolts, seemingly taken aback by my question. "What makes you think that? Privileged asshats, yes. But evil? Nah."

I risk another glance over my shoulder and find Thorne still staring. I blink, spinning back around again and whispering, "You don't see it?"

"All I see is a life of wealth and zero consequences. That's most of the people here, including me. But I'm happy to report I've inherited a work ethic."

Chills cascade down my arms, despite being covered by my blouse and blazer. I agree with Aiko that the popular crowd believes they're a cut above the rest, but I sense an added dormancy with this crew as though something's waiting to be awakened. I felt it when I saw Thorne across the road, hidden by an umbrella but monitoring me carefully. Then again in my new bedroom, it was as if I were under surveillance, a kind of watchful test. But for what? Maybe it's the old bones I'm now surrounded by, these ancient buildings, crumbling stone, and ghost-filled rooms, but I'm finding it hard to shake the instinct to *run*. Run from Winthorpe, from Raven's Bluff, from Malcolm, and go home to my parents, damn the punishment.

Yet as serious as that instinct is, I can't form it into an adequate explanation for Aiko. I'd rather sit here in silence than tell her I'm scared.

Aiko leans into my periphery, squeezing my shoulder. "You okay?"

I open my mouth to voice an automatic *fine*, but we're interrupted by movement on the stage.

An older woman comes to a stop in front of the center podium, dressed in a calf-length tweed skirt and a blazer buttoned over a tight-fitting bodice. The skin at her temple shines from how tightly her ebony hair is combed back into a bun.

"Welcome to a brand-new year, students," she says into the microphone, her words curving with a slight French accent. "I trust you all had a lovely summer break."

Hard no to that, but I straighten in my seat, eager to hear any nuggets of wisdom. I've been dreaming about going to this school for years, an out-of-reach goal that wouldn't leave my brain no matter how hard I tried to rationalize the impossibility of it. Seeing the headmistress makes it all real, and her regal stare and cultured voice almost make me forget how I got here.

She begins with a list of expectations: pressed uniforms, no cell phones during class hours, limited cussing, and the respect due to all teachers and fellow classmates—

When I feel it.

A tickle at the back of my neck. I subtly rub my hand over the spot, then get back to listening.

It happens again.

This time, I turn around and notice a student sitting directly behind me who wasn't there before. Baby-faced with a tangle of brown hair. A freshman, probably. He catches my eye and smirks.

There's not much I can do with a smirk, so I give him a side-long glance before swiveling back to the front, but not before I cast my gaze over his head at Thorne, who's watching our exchange with a strange, blank expression.

"As our last task, it's time to address the most coveted award at Winthorpe that involves healthy competition between our top-level seniors: The Marks Fellowship."

Any hold Thorne or the weird freshman have on me dissipates with that sentence. My hands clench against the armrests as Headmistress Dupris continues.

"Sadly, only one out of the fifty of you may win. That's not to say it won't be beneficial for every student who participates. Winthorpe prides itself on achievement, and for those of you achieving a 3.8 GPA or higher, you are automatically enrolled for consideration. You will then be expected to complete certain projects in addition to your required schoolwork; papers focused on global history, English literature, mathematics, and, most importantly, computer science. It is a lot to ask of students, but nothing our prestigious Winthorpe seniors cannot handle."

My fingers itch to take notes, but no one else seems as eager to record the headmistress's instructions. Most are laid-back, arms and jaws slack while they fight off sleep. Others surreptitiously scroll through their phones. Even Aiko's zoned out, staring aimlessly into a far corner and thinking about anything besides qualifying for the fellowship.

Is this what it's like to be rich and forever cushioned? Most of these kids will inherit their trust funds or be groomed to take over a billion-dollar business. A guaranteed position in one of the most pre-eminent tech companies in the world means as much to them as finding loose change in their couch cushions.

But that can work in my favor. It may be bullshit to them, but to me, it's everything, and the less competition, the better.

However, the last thing I want to do is draw any attention or derision, so I keep my hands where they are and commit the headmistress's speech to memory.

A noise draws my attention, the unscrewing of a jar or canteen behind us, but I pay it little mind when the headmistress states, "For the past four years, one family in particular has achieved the excellence required to obtain the honor." Headmistress Dupris raises her eyes above my head. A blue, studious flash of recognition. "Aurora Emmerson, you have large shoes to fill, but I have no doubt you'll match the accolades of your siblings."

Aurora preens under the praise, but my brows tighten as my gaze bounces from Headmistress Dupris to her and back again.

"Like I said," Aiko mutters near my ear, "bribery, favors, and nothing fair. If you want that fellowship, the odds are *not* in your fav—"

I shriek, shooting up from my seat. The tickle at my nape turns into full-on molestation.

Specks of black drop from my shoulders, to the chair, to the floor. Aiko, once she figures out why I'm flailing, screeches along with me and bats at my arms and shoulders.

"Miss Weatherby!" Headmistress Dupris cries, glaring at me, then Aiko. "Miss Natsumura! Quiet down at once!"

"Spiders! *Spiders!*" Aiko shrieks, but her voice is drowned out by the rising laughter in the auditorium.

I dance into the aisle, flushing out my hair with my fingers, but the crawling along my skin won't stop.

They're everywhere. Hundreds of spiders, slipping under my collar, skittering across my bare skin, arching their legs into my mouth, finding my nostrils...

"*Get them off!*" I sob, picturing myself covered, *covered*, by black, furry eight-legged insects.

Pressure digs into my shoulder blades. Something hooks my blazer at the lapels, yanking the fabric down my arms, then off.

Freed from the heated confines of the jacket, I blindly pull at the buttons of my blouse, wanting them *gone,* shaking with fear and nausea, pulling at the white cotton until I'm bare and the clothes carrying the spiders are no longer near my body—

"Miss *Weatherby.*"

The sharp, unexpected command has me opening my eyes. Gasping, I hold my hands in front of me, seeing nothing but the white of my skin. No black. No skittering legs.

Gone. They're gone.

Just to be sure, I press my hands against my face, then comb my fingers through my hair, my chest heaving with pounding, deafening heartbeats.

But ... oh, god.

I've torn off my shirt.

The auditorium's gone silent, my heartbeat the only sound I can hear thrumming behind my ears until my blazer's tossed against my chest.

Clutching the fabric, I lift my chin, about to thank Aiko for coming to my rescue, but the words stall in my throat ... because it's not Aiko.

Thorne stands one step above me—tall, imposing, and stone-faced. He doesn't blink when he glances down at my heaving chest, then back up to my face.

Lust smokes out his true expression for a few tense seconds before he notches his chin and stares down his nose, his cold mask comfortably re-settling.

Unrepentant. Vicious. Infernal with dirty promises.

My nipples grow hard beneath the thin lace, which is all that separates me from flashing the entire school.

He notices.

"I ... thank you," I manage to croak, my face likely going as red as the tips of my ears. I press the blazer closer to my chest as if that could stop his relentless study.

His lips tighten. "Don't thank me. Simpering bores me almost as much as juvenile school pranks do."

His insult doesn't hit its mark, but the nearby students erupt with mirth nonetheless, though I note the freshman who was sitting behind me is long gone—taking his empty canteen with him.

"Ah. Mr. Briar, thank you for providing some levity to the situation," Headmistress Dupris says, bending close to the mic. "Why don't you come down and finish the Marks Fellowship requirements as you were about to do before we were so rudely interrupted?"

Thorne dips his head in acquiescence at the headmistress, but his attention on me never wavers. He moves to brush past me, bringing with him the crisp scent of chlorine and cologne. As he does, he murmurs, "Keep it off. That's not your uniform. It never will be. You'll need a stronger backbone than that to get through this year."

His voice sends shivers through the shell of my ear and down my neck, but I don't let it show. The premonition that he'd bite off any weakness and savor its taste is too strong to ignore.

"Miss Weatherby."

I jolt at Headmistress Dupris's tone. Thorne doesn't react, taking the rest of the stairs smoothly with his hands in the pockets of his slacks as if he never uttered the threat, never mind tore a blazer off a hysterical girl who was teeming with spiders.

"My chambers. Now," the headmistress says to me.

I swallow, my hands curling into fists around my blazer. I don't dare ignore her, yet the jacket clutched in my hands and my blouse pooled at my feet prevent me from snapping to attention.

I can't heave my infested clothes over a chair and run. I'll have to put them back on. Shake out the remaining spiders, or at the very least, sling them over my arm. The only thing stopping me from tossing the blazer from my chest is the fact that I'm choosing the lesser of two evils right now.

"Are my orders unclear?" the headmistress asks. "I must admit, you are not making the best impression, despite your father's assurances that you do, indeed, deserve to take someone else's reserved spot, one we had planned to keep open in memorial."

"No, I—"

It's not my fault. I didn't know about Savannah ...

Another grim point is added to Malcolm's list of errors. Without my knowledge, he had me interfere with a poor student's tragedy. And now I was paying for it.

Aurora's audible snicker cuts me off. She hides her mouth behind her hand, but her contempt is clear. *If all it takes to rattle the new girl is a few bugs ...*

Like she'd act any better if a morning cup of spiders were poured over *her*.

I glare at her until her hand drifts away from her face, the grin falls from her features, and she matches my disgust.

Aiko shifts, drawing my attention. She perches on her seat,

her expression softened with pity. I don't blame her for staying quiet. We're not friends. I can't expect her to go out on a limb and defend me. But she jerks her head in the direction of the stage as if to say, *do what Dupris says before this gets any worse.*

"Miss Weatherby? Are you quite done being the center of attention?" the headmistress asks.

"Y-yes, ma'am," I say, bending to pick up the blouse and refusing to so much as wince.

"Clean yourself up, and I'll see you in a few minutes."

I hold the blouse at arm's length as I descend the aisle, raising my head high despite the renewed laughter and snorts. I trust the blazer more for some reason, maybe because if Thorne held it, the spiders likely scattered in fear of a larger predator. The exit seems like a mirage I'll never reach, but I keep my eyes on the double doors, my cheeks burning their reminder of how exposed and humiliated I am.

Thorne's voice takes over the room, redirecting the focus to him. "Well, that's one way to introduce myself to you as your new class president."

The auditorium titters, warmed by his syrupy-sweet voice.

Ugh.

"I also have the honor of commenting on the fellowship since our sweet Belle Marks is too shy to take the stage." A chorus of *aw* rings out as Thorne no doubt redirects his stunning smile to Belle.

Yeah, what a *gentleman* he's being.

"Some of you may be wondering, why attempt to win a scholarship since by attending Winthorpe, we're gifted whatever we want, anyway?"

My steps slow. The auditorium applauds, the elite and the privileged ruminating on the future of their combined, unchecked power.

"Let's ponder this notion." My back is to the stage, but I can hear Thorne's slow, compelling smile through his words. "Despite your lack of monetary need, many of you can't resist crushing the competition and gaining the bragging rights of a win."

Hoots and hollers follow his statement, and Thorne continues over the calls, "If you want even a sliver of a chance of the Marks scholarship, you have to personify honor. The demands of the application will expose any flaws, weaknesses, or errors of character. Consider it a resumé of cruelty. This is why so many try, but so few are able to pass. To those who are willing, your life will be completely changed. Isn't that why we're here? Whether it's for finding the good or acknowledging the worst in yourself, it's up to you what is used to win the attention of my good friends, the esteemed Marks family. Good luck."

I don't acknowledge the podium as I pass it, but at that moment, I can't rule out the notion that he's speaking—staring —directly at me as I walk out of the auditorium and the doors fold shut behind me.

CHAPTER 7
EMBER

Dupris's office resembles that of an old stodgy man's with dark mahogany, maroon-colored velvet, and leather-bound books that probably haven't been cracked open in decades.

It makes me wonder how many men came before her and if she had to fight for her position here with strict orders not to touch the antiques.

With dust coating my nostrils, I take a seat in one of the wingback chairs facing the grand desk and resist the urge to fidget with the gold tassels dangling from the stained glass desk lamp perched on the small table between them.

I'm fully clothed and buttoned up, if a little wrinkled, but after a thorough inspection under the bathroom's glaring lights, I couldn't spot any errant spiders clinging to my uniform.

I still dressed with a few squeaks of dread, though.

A rustling sounds out behind me as Headmistress Dupris breezes through the door to her chambers and then shuts it behind her. She waltzes around me without one look, settling herself behind her desk and opening a ledger before poising a pen above it.

"Are you all right?" she asks without glancing up.

I stiffen. "It's ... I'm fine."

"No, you're not." The pen falls, and Dupris leans back in her red leather chair that rises behind her like a throne. Her sharp features are exaggerated up close, the cut of her cheekbones and pointedness of her chin. And while her eyes are small and bookend a sharp, aristocratic nose, they're alert with intelligence. "And I don't expect you to be. That kind of behavior isn't tolerated at Winthorpe, and the party responsible will be dealt with accordingly."

I school my features enough to disguise my shock. "But in the assembly, you didn't call anyone out. I figured you thought I was hallucinating—or lying." I press my lips together before I become more informal with her. I've never been to the principal's office before, so I'm not sure how honest to be or how offended.

I'm learning fast it's better to be silent than choosing either one.

"As part of your enrollment, we've been given complete access to your files," Dupris says instead of answering. "You are a Weatherby, part of one of the wealthiest families in the United States. Indeed, you carry the line where it was once thought dead." Dupris lifts her pen, idly stroking it. Her stare bores into me. "Yet you come from nothing. A low-income household and a below-average high school."

"My parents earned every cent they made." I fold my hands into my lap, hiding the instinctual fists. "And I grew up comfortable. Happy."

"I am not disputing that." Dupris straightens in her seat. "Despite your census background, you hold steady at a 3.9 GPA, have a vast amount of experience with extracurriculars, and you are, without a doubt, a candidate for a Winthorpe diploma regardless of your newfound Weatherby status."

"I-I prefer Beckett, actually." Her compliments throw me. If I'm honest, this entire *school* damn well throws me.

"Noted. Just as I'm noting to you that on paper, you are a perfect fit."

She pauses, likely waiting for me to comprehend what she's not saying. I do. "You don't think I'm cut out to claim a spot here."

"This morning's adventure was but a taste of the ideas your peers think up. The faculty and I do what we can to monitor the bad deeds, but we do not deal with average student misbehavior. Many of their miscreant activities can be bought off—not by myself, mind you—so usually, it's made nonexistent before it ever reaches me. I'm not being dishonest in telling you we don't tolerate bullying, but I am admitting that most of the time, it never reaches my ears. This morning's stunt was particularly bold. You are an outsider, my dear, and more than that, you are an unwelcome curiosity. That alone leads to malcontent."

"Because I'm a Weatherby, or because I took the missing girl's place here?"

The headmistress starts at my statement but covers it well when she presses her elbows onto the desk and folds her hands beneath her chin. "Both, child. I will do what I can to protect you, but with Weatherby as your last name—all right, with Weatherby as your *inheritance*," she amends after my bold look, "your limits will be tested with these students. They were brought up in this world and are very familiar with all the ins, outs, and hideaways, unlike yourself. And many operate under the surface."

Thorne comes to mind, and I chew on my lip in thought. This isn't the way I thought my trip to the headmistress's chambers would go. Yes, she's doling out punishment, but not to me, and she's ensuring it isn't made public. In front of everyone, she sided with the prankster. It makes me wonder ... is she in charge of this place, or has she learned to duck and weave around the students here to survive alongside them?

I nod, my focus returning to the headmistress. "I'll keep all of that in mind. But I'd like to stay. A diploma from Winthorpe would be ..."

"Life-changing." She repeats the sentiment Thorne used. "I understand."

"And I'd like to apply for the Marks Fellowship." I sit back, stifling the smugness that wriggles inside me at surprising her a second time. "It's one of the main reasons I'm here."

Dupris clears her throat. "Well, you do have the qualifications to be considered. Though, I have to ask, are you—?"

"I'm sure," I cut in.

Dupris studies me for a beat, then gives a single nod. "Very well. Off to sixth period you go, then. You'll be late, so I'll write out a slip."

I doubt there's a teacher or student who doesn't know why I'm in her chambers and not in class, but I allow her to go through the motions, like this is any other meeting other than me flashing my bra to the whole school.

She hands me the pink slip, which I tuck into the inside pocket of my blazer, then exit into the soundless hallway.

Winthorpe High is almost as creepy and hollow as my new home, and I swallow back the scream at the back of my throat as I navigate the soulless halls and try to find the one room I'm scheduled to belong in.

WITH MOST OF my first day consisting of orientation and assembly, sixth period is the first class I take a seat in and one of my favorites. Math.

Or it used to be.

After knocking quietly, I'm halfway in the door, but my subtle announcement does nothing to prevent more than a dozen pairs of eyes from swiveling in my direction.

Everyone's seated, including the teacher, who spins in his chair once I'm visible.

I'm given enough time to spot Aurora and Thorne toward the back, their focus stronger than the rest. It's like I can feel their beams of scathing interest against my skin.

"Ah. Ember Weatherby, is it?" the teacher asks, pushing his glasses higher up on his nose.

I sigh at the repeated use of Malcolm's name, which the teacher must take as acknowledgment. He pushes to his feet and scuttles over to me, his small stature made more pronounced by a rotund torso.

"I'm Professor Lowell. We're right in the middle of a pop quiz," he says in a not quite whisper. "And there's assigned seating. As a W, I have you placed in the front."

There's no point in arguing B versus W, especially while on display at the front of the class, even if I do have clothes on this time.

As an unexpected bonus, the spot he points at is mere feet away, so I don't have to slink through the aisle and deal with more slitty-eyed stares before I can turn my back and pretend no one's watching me. That *Thorne* isn't continuing to take an interest in the nape of my neck. I take the seat Lowell directs me to and try not to be wowed by the quality of the double desk and chair, but they're more like the wood from a church pew than the warped plastic scoop and vandalized laminate I'm used to.

Lemon-scented polish hits me first, then the subtle woodsy scent of true craftsmanship.

Stained glass windows shine rainbow colors onto the flat wooden surface, where Professor Lowell slides the quiz, taps it, then says, "Do your best. This is mainly to see where the class is at and if the required summer reading was completed. I realize you are a new student, and therefore might not have received said readings, but I'd like to assess your abilities, considering where you've come from."

I pull out a pen from my bag. The guy sharing the desk with me glances up through his shaggy chestnut hair, then goes back to the quiz.

Professor Lowell sputters, "Oh, you may use a pencil for this test."

"A pen is fine." I meet his eyes with an innocent stare, and he doesn't quite seem to know what to do with it.

"If you say so," Lowell says. His expression remains unconvinced as he returns to the front.

I feel more than see the classroom's attention sliding to me again. The skin behind my ear prickles, an instinctual warning that Thorne's study has never wavered.

Silently, I complete the questions, keeping my head down and my mind focused. Eventually, the interest wanes, and the students go back to their own papers.

All except for one, and it's not the person I expect.

Thorne has gone back to his test. It's Aurora's gray, stormy eyes that don't move from the side of my face, and it takes extra effort to focus on the numbers in front of me and not her. My periphery notices enough—that her test is turned over and her pencil laid across it. She's the first to finish, but I'm thinking with the way she's staring me down, she wouldn't have been had I arrived on time.

I'm not worried. Schoolwork has always been more important to me than popularity, and I'm not trying to win points with her. I'd rather be invisible at Winthorpe—one of the ghosts that haunt the halls unnoticed, unbothered.

I wonder if Savannah is now one of those ghosts.

My hand clenches against the pen. Here I am, wanting to be a ghost, and she likely *is* one. The mystery of her disappearance has captured my morbid attention, meaning I'll have to ask Aiko for more information once I see her again.

The bell rings. I lift my head while everyone else leaps from their seat, packs up their things, and rushes out of the classroom after tossing their tests in front of Lowell, who's balefully shuffling them into a pile.

Thorne is one of the last to stand, holding his paper at his side as he idly passes through the aisle. My gaze keeps pace with his unhurried movements, his grace and confidence lifting my chin like I'm under a spell.

No boy walks like him—as if he's stalking Lowell and hasn't eaten for days, but is taking his time before the kill.

Saliva pools in my mouth. I haven't even *swallowed* since he stood.

My awe is too much, even for me, and I shake out of the rapture long enough for my eyes to drift to the test, the loose papers fluttering in his grip. One corner breezes backward more than the rest, enough for me to see that the answers on the first *and* second page are blank.

That's unexpected. From the way Thorne commands a crowded room, I assumed he was one of the top students. Why would he leave an easy pop quiz empty?

Thorne lifts his hand, about to settle the paper on Lowell's stack, but it gives me enough time to notice an inky smudge—no, a drawing. A rose?

A small black rose drawn in the space reserved for the first equation.

Lowell glances down at Thorne's proffered test, and I lean forward, ready for my front row seat. Will Lowell comment on the doodle instead of an answer? Instead of *any* answer on the quiz? Is this Thorne's way of mocking the establishment?

I hold my breath—

"Very well, Mr. Briar," Lowell says as he raises his eyes to Thorne. "Enjoy the rest of your day."

I jerk in my seat.

The floors are just as polished as the wood, and I don't make a sound as my chair scrapes back. I couldn't disguise the reflex, though, and Thorne looks over at my sudden motion.

Our eyes meet across the room, and I wait for him to sneer or notch his chin in contempt. To tell me to stay the hell out of it. Instead, his lips flatline, and he breaks off our stare to prowl to the door without looking back.

Oh. I guess he didn't feel nearly as anchored in a deep ocean as I did when we locked eyes.

Once the room empties, Lowell wanders up to me with a soft expression. "If you weren't given enough time, Miss Weatherby, perhaps we could reschedule you to make up the quiz."

"It's all right. I'm finished." I hand him the paper, which he takes more on instinct than expectation.

"Goodness." He scans the quiz, likely ensuring I've answered all the questions. I wonder what would've happened if I'd drawn flowers, too. "Thank you. Results will be posted tomorrow."

"Posted?" I ask while I rise from my seat.

"Winthorpe thrives on cultivating motivation. A part of that includes everyone knowing exactly where they stand within the rest of their class. No student numbers or anonymity is allowed, I'm afraid. Your ranking is meant to help you succeed, not embarrass you."

"I'm looking forward to it," I respond, though I'm a little

rattled. Competition doesn't scare me. I've worked most of my high school years trying to stay at the top of the class, but it's the blatancy with which Winthorpe High does it that leaves me skittish. First, Thorne's foreboding speech about the fellowship, then his mysterious art as an answer to a math quiz that Lowell doesn't comment on, and now I'm learning about the public rankings of every student in this school. What's next? A swimsuit competition?

"Glad to have you, Miss Weatherby," Lowell says, cutting me away from my confusion. "Good luck with the rest of your classes."

I nod, then toss my backpack over my shoulder and head to the door. It's then I notice Aurora lingering at her desk and pushing to her feet as soon as I'm out of Lowell's earshot. She must've been hovering in my blind spot, much better at staying quiet than I was. Either that, or Thorne somehow managed to dull all my senses except for those focused on him.

My breath stills at the thought.

"You think you're such hot shit, but you're just trash dipped in fake gold," she hisses as she sidles up next to me.

"I haven't done anything to you," I murmur, keeping my head straight, but my grip tightens on my bag's strap as we step into the hallway.

Her hot, minty breath hits my cheek. "You may be content taking the place of my best friend, but don't you dare try to take what's mine as well."

And what would that be? I want to ask. But she peels away before I can, becoming a part of the moving tide of students in the hall, chatting and laughing as though she belongs in this private pocket of the world. Because she does.

I'm not sure what I could take from her that she's so confidently claimed rights to. The top rank in math class? The Marks Fellowship that her family's won for four years straight?

All odds are wildly against me—not that I won't try—yet she's after me like I stand a chance.

An image of Thorne stalking through the classroom aisle pricks at the back of my vision, and how I couldn't take my eyes off him, not even for a second. Unbeknownst to me, Aurora was in the room the whole time. She would've seen it all. My enchantment, my bated breath when he stopped at Lowell's desk ...

It's crazy, but I feel like her warning relates to him.

She doesn't want me to stake a claim on *Thorne.*

CHAPTER 8

THORNE

"She saw me," I admit as I arrange the tight-fitting Speedo around my junk, adjust my cap and goggles, then knife into the pool with a perfect dive.

I breach the surface, and Jaxon pops up in the lane beside mine. He doesn't reply while we swim our laps, both of us choosing the vicious expectations of a butterfly stroke and instantly trying to beat each other.

Chlorinated water sloshes against my body, turning into white froth in the air before bucketing down into the pool. My muscles burn with power, my shoulders circling with graceful cutting upsweeps before curving into a rolling tuck and spearing my feet off the opposite wall to do it all again.

In the clogged distance, I hear Coach's whistle, but I don't stop. My arms chop into the water, my thighs burning and my lungs bursting, but I suck in air and exhale at regular intervals—the same pattern I've maintained since I started.

"Briar!" Coach's voice echoes across the indoor pool's tiles. Another lengthy whistle follows.

I keep going.

"Briar, goddammit!"

I can't listen, so attuned am I with the water, the splash, the *speed*, despite my body begging for relief. But I know from enough experience that I'll burst through that pain barrier shortly, going numb and performing the movements with *more* power, more grace.

My heart ricochets against my rib cage, but nobody can see that weakened part of me. All they witness is stealth, perseverance, the killing for the win.

"*Boy*, I swear I'll have someone jump on your back—"

I crash against the wall, my fingers slamming against the touchpad that records my time, and stop.

The other five swimmers float in their lanes, including Jaxon, clinging to the wall, goggles off, staring.

Coach's sneakers squeak and stomp until they halt at my eye level. "I said one *leg*, Briar, not race as if you're in a heat. What are you doing? You could've injured yourself, all before our first meet."

He's red-faced and all bared teeth, but I regard him blandly, despite my heaving chest. I wait for him to look up at the scoreboard.

"Jesus," he says once he does exactly what I predicted.

"Beat my seed time?" I ask, the answer already well-solidified in his expression.

"Shaved off a good second." Coach Albright lowers his head, gazing at me as if I'm some mythical water beast set upon his pool. Maybe I am. "Save that kind of enthusiasm for your actual heats instead of wasting them on your team, for god's sake."

"You're the boss."

His eyes turn into slits, and closed-mouth muttering comes out of his throat. He tucks his clipboard under his arm and stomps off the pool deck, barking orders at the other swimmers before slamming into his office.

"How do you have the energy for that shit, man?" Jaxon says as he bobs in the lane next to mine. "We train twice a day already. You putting extra stress on yourself for a reason?"

Bracing my hands, I push out of the pool while Jaxon gasps for breath and practically doggy-paddles to the ladder, lifting the lane dividers as he goes.

"I told you," I say as I head to the bench and grab one of the rolled towels. "She saw me."

"And that merits a spontaneous 200 Fly?"

"It helps clear my head."

"This is about the new girl," Jaxon concludes as he lifts a neighboring towel, swiping at his face and mirroring my movements. "You failed to tell me she was hot as fuck, dude."

"Fine. She's hot as fuck."

Jaxon pauses in his toweling off. "I can't take you seriously when you talk like a quiet serial killer."

I raise a wry eyebrow. "Allow me to talk about what's *actually* important, then. She saw the rose on my quiz."

Jaxon matches my one eyebrow with two. "Oh."

"Not a big deal. She hasn't been here long enough to ask questions about it, but it's piqued her curiosity."

"Meaning we have to accelerate our plans for her."

I clap him on the shoulder. "I knew you had the title of my second-in-command for a reason."

We gather our things, tying our towels around our waists and padding barefoot to the locker rooms.

"She's not prepared," Jaxon says. "Ember Weatherby is a special exception already, being a senior. We can't initiate her with the freshmen this week."

"We're not going to. She'll go through the trials alone."

Jaxon hooks my arm. I halt, glancing down at his hand, then back at him.

He lifts his hold with a surrendering gesture but still has the balls to add, "Malcolm won't allow it."

"*Malcolm* doesn't have a say in how his daughter is folded into our ranks. Unless he wants to go against those in charge, which I doubt he does. Not after what happened to Savannah."

Jaxon hisses in a breath. "It's not smart. You're too close to it. Choose someone else."

This time, I nail him with a dry look, though internally, I'm bombarded with images of Ember—white-gray hair cascading over her pillow, and her dark, impenetrable eyes when they fluttered open and almost caught me.

She resembles Savannah, yes, but there's an ethereal quality to Ember. An aura that formed itself in the shape of a sharpened, silver hook that plunged into my middle and poked itself out on the other side, tying me to her the moment I spotted her in the rain.

I respond to Jaxon in the most unaffected tone I can muster. "What do you take me for? I've already chosen someone else."

"Who?"

"Aurora."

Jaxon expels a breath. "Aurora won't be easy on her."

"Blame the Weatherby last name for that."

Stifled laughter and whispers draw my attention away from Jaxon and to the door of the girls' locker room, splayed open as the female swim team filters out. Their practice occurs after ours, and at this point, we should be used to the admiring gazes cast our way. It goes both ways; I can appreciate tits in a swimsuit just as much as they appreciate my crotch, even as a blush creeps along their cheeks and their lashes flutter adoringly as their eyes scrape along my torso and bounce away when I catch them. I'm a hard-won prize. Not many girls can claim their conquest of me, but with the sighed exclamations and licking of lips, it's not a far reach to figure out I've starred in a lot of wet dreams.

I work hard for my physique and have no problems displaying it. Same goes for Jaxon, who preens under the appreciative whispers behind hands before the girls' coach shouts at them to take their positions.

Coach Albright whacks Jaxon upside the head with his clipboard as he passes, telling him to keep his hands to himself. I laugh under my breath while Jaxon rubs the back of his head, cursing. It's enough of a distraction that I almost miss the last girl to exit the locker room.

Ember holds the door open with enough of a crack to slip through, but as soon as she hits the pool deck, all the echoing noise turns to sunder in my head.

Her fairy-like hair is well out of sight, tucked into a swim cap with goggles strapped to her forehead. She's wearing the school-regulated black one-piece that crisscrosses at her back, nothing special. Definitely not something that should have my jaw loosening and my mind going blank as the day I was born.

Delicious is the first word I'd use to describe her. She fills out the swimsuit like a vixen yet glances around like a lost fawn. Her legs, pale and long, flex with muscle as she moves, and while she folds her arms across her chest, her impressive cleavage can't be disguised.

"Dude, I know you admitted she was hot as fuck," Jaxon whispers close, "but she's hot as *fuuuuuuuuuck.*"

I slam my forearm into his stomach, and he doubles over, hacking up a lung.

"So dramatic," I drawl at his reaction, but my focus doesn't shift from Ember, who glances over at the sight. She's close enough that I can't resist saying to her, "You're on the swim team."

"Nice line," Jaxon wheezes, and I almost kick him into the pool.

"There weren't any other athletic openings available," she

says. Now that we're not in a classroom during a quiz, she's speaking above a whisper, and her voice is as sweet and airy as it was in the courtyard. "And since sports involvement is mandatory for the fellowship ..." She shrugs.

My shoulders stiffen. "You're after the Marks Fellowship?"

"Dude, keep going," Jaxon mutters while straightening. "You're doing great."

This time, I really do shove him into the pool, much to the girls' coach's dismay.

Ember's eyes widen as Jaxon goes in, but she doesn't comment. Instead, she comes back to me, angling her head to size me up.

My lips curve. "Do I pass the test?"

She jolts. "What test?"

"Whatever you have going on in your mind when you look at me. Am I coming up to standard?"

Her mouth opens and closes, a delicate flush creeping into her cheeks. "I'm not—I wasn't—you pushed your friend into the pool."

"He interrupted our conversation."

We both watch as Jaxon splashes back out, glaring a look of death at me. "You got my towel wet, asshole."

Ember barely notices his sputters. She says to me, "You call this a conversation?"

"It's a back and forth, at least." This time, my smile shows my teeth. It's the type of grin that's truly stopped hearts, my mother's closest friend being the first.

Ember faces me head-on, expressionless.

Interesting. I wonder how much it would take to break through that fresh layer of ice. "I'd wish you well on the swim team, but we're one of the best in the country. You may have been given an open spot, but not many qualify. And if you want to be eligible for the Marks Fellowship ..." I let the meaning sink in.

She straightens her spine and lifts her chin as if she could become taller than me. "I'm aware," she says, then steps past us to find her assigned lane.

"All right, ladies!" the girls' coach, Mayberry, calls out. "As this is the first practice, we'll start with some qualifiers. Let's see how well you do in a 100 freestyle. I'll record the times, and we'll make cuts from there."

"Are we leaving?" Jaxon asks, dripping puddles beside me.

"Let's wait," I say, resting my back against the wall and crossing my arms.

The girls at each of the six lanes stop their warm-ups and get into position to dive, including Ember. I note her form—solid—and focus in on her with more interest.

Mayberry blows her whistle, and the scoreboard starts the counts of each lane. The girls dive, but I only have eyes for one.

Ember is in the end lane closest to us, and she slices through the water with surprising ease. She splashes past us, tucks and rolls at the other end, then comes back, all without fumbling or gasping. In fact, she hits her touchpad almost in time with everyone else, girls who've been training all summer.

Mayberry's whistle shrieks again, and I look up at the scoreboard, noting Lane 6's time. Ember's come in third place, which isn't bad. Not bad at all.

Ember hangs at the edge of the pool, peeling off her goggles and smiling.

"If she shows strength like that," Jaxon observes, "she'll do just fine in the Society's trials."

Impressed at his own obvious nugget of wisdom, Jaxon pushes into the locker room and disappears.

And after a few more seconds of careful study, I follow him.

CHAPTER 9
EMBER

The sideways glances and snide remarks as I shower off actually make me look forward to ending my day at Malcolm's crumbling, empty estate.

Thinks she's all that ...

Came from a piss-poor part of Boston ...

Trying so hard to be one of us ...

Such a loser.

She should go back to eating out of cans.

Whore.

Slut.

Fake-ass bitch.

Not a lot of the insults are that applicable, but do they need to be when the intent is to slice and dice, regardless?

Luckily, each shower is in its own spacious cubicle with complimentary top-shelf soap and lotions. I'd normally stick to the soap shoved in my gym bag, but the whispers leaking under the gaps between the stall and the floor motivate me to linger in the steam.

When goose bumps trail my bare skin, I can't delay any

longer. I push the shower curtain aside and move into the small private section where I can get changed before unlocking the door.

Bare hooks greet me.

"What...?" I whisper, my eyes checking the space in sections as if all the white staring back at me isn't enough indication that my things are gone.

"Looking for something?" a sweet voice asks on the other side of the stall door.

I step up to it, demanding through the wood, "Where are my clothes?"

Multiple giggles sound out in reply. "You'll have to come out and get them."

There are a bunch of them out there, a gaggle of ducks, and I smack my palms against the door at the audacity. And my entrapment. "On a scale of one to five, how mature do you think this is? Elementary? Preschool level?"

"Call it whatever you want. The result will be the same."

The voice, rising in confidence, becomes familiar in my ears. I lower my forehead to the wood on a sigh. *Aurora.* She's not on the swim team, but the girl living my dream is—Belle Marks— and I beat her time by two seconds. "I won the practice heat fair and square. I'm sorry your friend's so butt-hurt you need to steal my clothes in petty revenge."

Snide laughter follows. "Then why are you still hiding in there? Come out, come *out*, Ember ..." Aurora trills. "Or should I just chuck your clothes outside and be done with it?"

I breathe through my nose, calling for calm beside my racing heart. There's no choice—I have to step out or stay here, naked and cold, until a janitor or some other pitying soul finds me. I'm sure she's switched the cleaning schedules, and no one will find me for a while.

"We promise, no cameras."

A resounding snort tells me the opposite is true. I'm not ashamed of my body, but I'm not eager to show it off, either. *Again.* Closing my eyes, I count to ten.

My hand curls on the door's lever.

"I'm getting *impatient* ..." Aurora sings.

I press down and open the stall, forcing my eyes open so I can meet Aurora head-on and unaffected. *Yes, here are my boobs. And yup, you can see my snatch, too, since you clearly asked for it.*

She stands, arms crossed and in full uniform, with a couple of girls flanking her on each side—her butt-hurt best friend included. A few hold their hands to their mouths and another covers her eyes as if dramatically scalded.

Aurora remains steadfast, a smirk painting her flushed, pink lips.

But I'm the first to break our stare, scanning their empty hands and the gaps between their feet. My stomach plummets. Where's my stuff?

I ask on a sigh, disguising my fear, "Can you at least hand me a towel?"

"Did I forget to mention that your clothes are in the boys' locker room?" Aurora says, her gray eyes simply swirling with glee. "Damn. Silly me."

"This is harassment."

"It is," Aurora agrees. "Winthorpe has a zero-tolerance policy against bullying. As class president, Thorne enforces it." Another malevolent grin follows her words. "Care to go to the head-mistress and tell her what a bad girl I am, or would you rather just get your clothes and scamper on back to the cess-filled hole you crawled out of?"

My heart beats so hard, I'm surprised Aurora can't see it through my skin, but I can't buckle at her words. I can save my tears and humiliation for later when I'm alone. But right now, I'm cold, exposed, and practically begging for more mockery.

The faster I move, the quicker it'll end.

"What's wrong, new girl? Winthorpe not what you expected?" Aurora purses her lips on a fake pout. "You're nothing but a cheap carbon copy of Savannah Merricourt, first taking her spot as a senior, and now trying to convince Thorne you're a *legacy*, just like her? Who gave you the right? What diamond vagina did you get spat out of?"

The shower has long since dried on my skin. Prickles of cold raise the hair on my arms, goose bump my thighs, and harden my nipples. I'm heaving with adrenaline and shivers, her words hitting home more than I'd like. "I have no idea what you're talking about. Anything Malcolm's done was on his beliefs, not mine—"

"Oh, so he's *Malcolm* to you? What, are you trying to fuck him, too?"

I screw up my face in disgust. "What's *wrong* with you? Just give me my clothes so I can go back to trying to get through this year unnoticed. I don't want anything from you, Aurora, or anyone else around you. *Including* Thorne and whatever legacy you think I took from Savannah. Leave me alone, and I'll leave you alone, too."

Aurora lifts her face to the ceiling and laughs. "Leave *me* alone? Bitch, I have all the legroom here, so you might as well—"

She doesn't see it coming, and neither do her friends.

My parents didn't leave me completely unprepared for opponents like her. Dad enrolled me in self-defense classes as soon as I started understanding what "sexual assault" could mean. We also lived in a delicate balance between a high-crime neighborhood and a gentrifying district, and I was left alone too often to stay defenseless.

And so, Aurora gets a jab to the throat.

She doubles over, and while she's limply gasping for breath, I drag her blazer down her arms and off as she stumbles around. Her friends screech and retreat as I whirl on them, Belle being the only one brave enough to dive past me to help Aurora.

Wrapping the blazer around myself and keeping my hands fisted at the lapels, I push through the locker room exit, take in a deep breath, and then do a U into the boys' next door.

Lucky for me, it's crowded with the end of football practice.

I count only one guy who shrieks and covers up his junk with a towel when he spots me. The others? They crow their joy, some grabbing their dicks in invitation while others smack their lockers repeatedly in a drummer-like welcome.

I wait for a gap between the noise to ask loudly, "Where are my clothes?"

"Do you need 'em?"

"Hey, fresh meat!"

"Come say hello to my little friend!"

"Do all the new girls make shaved debuts like this?"

"*Show us your titties!*"

I grit my teeth at the lewd comments and try again. "Aurora must've given one of you my bag. Where'd you put it? Tell me, or first guy to approach me gets a kick in the sack."

"Need I remind you," some beefy guy says nearby, "*you* came on to *our* turf. A new clit, no matter how hot and swollen for us, doesn't get to make demands in this room."

"How very chauvinistic of you to say," I purr. "And I see you're the closest to me."

"Leave her."

The command comes from the back of the room, yet crests like a wave over the sweaty, testosterone-fueled heads. The torn silk of it is all too familiar.

Thorne parts the crowd by merely stepping forward into one of the aisles, dressed in full uniform with his hands tucked in his pants' pockets. A duffel—*my* gym bag—hangs off one of his shoulders. His swim practice has long since ended, so he must have stayed back just for this.

For me.

Just like that, the importance of the other boys falls away, and my attention is solely focused on Thorne's approach. He doesn't stop until his shoes nearly hit my toes, and I have to lift my chin to keep my eyes on his. When they do, his lips tilt in a one-sided smirk. "Nice blazer."

"Thanks. It's your girlfriend's." My eyes flick to the black strap on his shoulder. "Give it to me."

"I'm disappointed, little pretty. I was hoping you'd come in here naked and give us all a show."

A round of agreement meets his statement, instantly stifled by a searing look from Thorne.

I don't bother to shift my gaze to the other, lesser guys in this room. It's clear who runs things, both inside and out of the Winthorpe halls. I'd be an idiot not to constantly watch Thorne for the moment he'll pounce.

Because stealing clothes? Child's play. He's just getting started.

Temper flares my lips, but I say, "It's not my fault you underestimated Aurora's ability to follow your instructions."

He inclines his head, those ethereal eyes seeming to study not only my features, but my soul. "What makes you think I asked her to do anything?"

"Because you have my stuff."

"Which she gave me to take good care of until you came to retrieve it."

I snort, though underneath the thin blazer, I'm trembling. "And you didn't think to ask why?"

"It's not my business what Aurora does, as she's not my girlfriend."

My heart rate kicks up at the confession until I wrangle it

back into submission. It doesn't matter whether Thorne is single or engaged to be married since birth. "I'd like my clothes back."

This time, his smile shows his perfect rows of teeth. "Say pretty please."

"I did say the closest guy to me will get a kick to the sack, and like you, I don't like to go back on my promises."

Chuckling, he lifts his shoulder the strap slides down his arm. He holds it out to me. "I hate to admit it, but Jaxon may be right."

Yanking my duffel from his proffered hand, I retort, "Oh yeah, about what? That he chose a degenerate trussed up as a gentleman to be his friend? What are you going to do next, spike my drink?"

Thorne's gaze shutters, and all mirth leaves his face. It happens so fast—in a blink—that I almost, *almost* gasp at the cold-blooded murder flattening his features to stone. "On second thought," he replies in a toneless murmur, "you won't last the week."

My grip tightens on my bag as I spin on my heel, away from his destructive gaze, and give my heart full permission to grip my rib cage and flail against the bars.

CHAPTER 10

EMBER

The girls' locker room is deserted when I return, but I change, dump Aurora's overly fragrant blazer on a bench, and hightail it out of there as soon as I can, tying my wet hair back before anyone tries to come for me again.

Malcolm's butler and driver, Nash, waits for me at the edge of the rec center, and I slip inside the vehicle as unnoticeably as I can.

I hadn't come to this school to make friends, but I never considered I'd be an immediate outcast.

I'm mulling over the word—*outcast*—as we drive through the rest of the pristine campus, slivers of golden light clinging to the buildings in the waning sun.

My family no longer belongs to me, not as it once did, and I'm now living in an ancient, ornamental mansion, wandering the halls and studying my new surroundings as my footsteps echo to the ceilings. The one friend I had is a two-hour ferry ride and drive away, and I'm forbidden from talking to my parents for the entire year. Now, on top of all that, I've earned Thorne's painted target.

I'm not sure why, of all the moments we've run into each other, he decided to speak to me while we were both in swimsuits. He was dripping wet, beads of water cascading down his sculpted pecs and abs, pooling at the deep V leading to what was barely contained in a simple black Speedo.

Thorne waxes, as swimmers do, and therefore he *gleamed* under the indoor pool's lighting, a shining god deigning to cast his sapphire-rimmed gaze upon my exposed form.

I have to admit, I almost fell for it.

The hush this boy draws, the literal freezing of nearby students when he appears, isn't something I should dismiss, but I couldn't help my sharp tongue when he reviewed me as if I were an intriguing new entrée he hadn't yet tried and had every right to taste.

A shiver wraps along my lower spine at the thought of being his dinner. It's too foreign of a feeling to understand whether it's dread coating my bones or temptation. Either one anchors my feet and braces my hands for a fight.

If Thorne Briar thinks I'll just lay down for him and submit to his whims, then he's in for a big surprise.

Winthorpe's sprawling campus disappears, and we wind along the coast. Clusters of trees border one side and the open, crashing sea on the other. Dash doesn't speak the entire way, nor does his gaze flicker in the rearview mirror to sneak quick studies of his passenger in the back seat. He must've been given strict orders to leave me alone, and while part of me is relieved, the other, lonelier section wishes to have *someone* at Weatherby Mansion to make conversation with. I curse my lack of foresight to ask Aiko for her number before we parted ways. Maybe I can wander into the kitchen before dinner tonight and meet the cook, Marta, to see if she'd like some company, too.

It'd be nice to have someone help take my mind off what

happened in the locker room and the price I might have to pay for it. From Aurora, or Thorne—or both.

I've definitely pissed both of them off.

But seriously? They've pissed *me* off.

I'm simmering away in the back seat when Dash glides through the gates, then to a stop in front of Weatherby Manor. I don't wait for him to open my door, and with both my school and gym bag hiked up on either shoulder, I climb the stairs into the home.

It takes a moment for my eyesight to adjust to the cold, dark tones of the foyer, but after a few blinks, I'm able to make out the looming staircase and then go by memory on which door my new bedroom lies behind.

The bags fall at my feet as I flick on the light, my scowl now made obvious in the far mirror, until my gaze falls upon the bed and I find a new laptop, textbooks, and a cell phone.

Unable to contain myself, I race to the side of the bed, lifting the laptop first. A MacBook Pro, a computer I've literally died in my dreams to try to get, over and over again.

The ordered stack of textbooks topples across the duvet as I hop onto the bed, sit cross-legged, and open the computer. It's fully charged, and that *ding* of acknowledgment is like opening the gates of heaven.

I can't believe this is mine. My fingers stroke the keys as it loads for the first time, and that new tech smell stimulates my nostrils. I'm immediately calmed by its benign cool presence, running off electricity and circuit boards instead of cruelty.

The fact that it comes from Malcolm adds an unwelcome pall to the moment, but I can't begrudge the gift, not when I saw all of Winthorpe High carrying around MacBooks or Alienware. At home, I mainly used Dad's clunky desktop for my homework.

The screen flares to life, and I do a giddy wiggle on the bed, thinking of all the tasks I can complete on this baby—not to mention, its connection to the outside world. A quick check of the screen's top corner shows I'm connected to the manor's Wi-Fi (thank god Malcolm spared no expense on that), and I immediately open the browser.

My email's first. I'm hoping my friend Kinsey has dropped a note telling me all about her first day of senior year. Part of Malcolm's deal meant agreeing to relinquish my old phone to him, which meant no texting from friends. Well, my one friend. I didn't mind handing the dead thing over; it was a pay-as-you-go screen, a sore spot I had to carry around when all I wanted to do was explore and dissect the latest tech.

I don't think Dad's ever forgiven me for that time when I was ten and took apart his vintage 90's Nintendo console to try to find Mario. In my defense, it only took me three months to painstakingly put it back together again.

The memory has me looking at the clock on my nightstand, trying to time what my parents would be doing right now. Mom would be getting ready for her night shift, and Dad is probably just setting his feet on our welcome mat, loudly brushing off the soles, followed by his booming statement that he's come home a starving man who needs a good meal and a hard hug.

To think these are people who consented to a black market adoption, the stealing of a child, of *me*, doesn't resonate properly in my brain. Not this couple who works so hard and made every effort to give me a loving home. Not my mom and dad.

I've been staring off so long, it takes me a while to register the few bolded emails in my inbox. There's one from Kinsey, as expected, the preview showing her all-black, emoji-themed enthusiasm for school, and the second one's from ...

Mom.

Before I can rethink it, I click to open the email.

· · ·

Baby, I know I'm not supposed to contact you, but I need to know if you're ok. I love you so much. I'm so sorry. Daddy and I are so, so sorry.

I STARE at the words until tears pool in the corner of my eyes, and they blur. My trembling fingers hover over the keyboard, my mind egging them on to respond and tell her I want to come home and that this isn't worth it, not after today and being forced to parade around naked as some sort of brutal penance for a missing girl whose disappearance I had no involvement with.

But she has a name. Savannah Merricourt.

Her mystery is almost enough to pull me out of the potent homesickness engulfing my heart. If Malcolm found out I communicated with Mom—if he gets any inkling, the deal's off, and my parents will be brought up on charges. The same goes if I decide to tuck my tail between my legs and go home because the kids are too mean at Winthorpe.

It's not only my future that is affected by my staying here, but my parents', too.

"Know thy enemies" is a warning as old as time, and it helps redirect my thoughts away from my old life, from Mom.

I have a lot of research to do, and I've just been given a snazzy new computer.

And I feel like I should start with Savannah.

CHAPTER II
EMBER

When the dusty, wood-carved grandfather clock on the first floor begins its mournful toll for eight in the evening, I'm halfway down the curving staircase, my fingers trailing along the cool, smooth stone of the railing.

It's the perfect staircase for Prince Charming to be waiting at the bottom, if the dust were wiped clean and the cobwebs lifted from the arched windows in the entryway. Maybe at some point, this house was meant for romantic gestures and boisterous parties, but all that awaits me is neglected, ancestral furniture, stone statues lined up against the walls that will likely become my only friends, and frigid air.

I wasn't sure what to dress in for dinner, but Malcolm is stoic enough to expect formality. I erred on the side of caution, opting for a simple black cap-sleeved dress with my hair down and brushed into waves.

Malcolm and his wife's portrait comes into view as I swing around the balustrade. He's so somber in that painting, grim lines bordering his pressed together mouth. Malcolm's wife is tucked into his side, subdued as well, but she exudes an inner light, with a flush to her cheeks and a twinkle to her brown eyes as though she's holding back a giggle.

It couldn't have been fun painting such a bleak couple. I wonder if the artist decided to be cheeky and added some life into her face, or if she actually was internally laughing about something out of view.

The small brass plate below it flashes as I move closer. It reads, **Malcolm and Julie Weatherby, 2003.**

"Dinner is ready to be served, Miss Ember."

A squeal catches in my throat, and I jump from the painting as if the late Mrs. Weatherby tried to reach for me from the confines of her afterlife.

"I didn't mean to startle you." Dash steps out from the shadows.

"It's just so quiet," I say, a little breathless as my heartbeat gets itself under control. "I didn't expect anyone to be so close by."

"I have the footsteps of a field mouse, I'm afraid. You'll rarely hear my approach." He says this with a straight face, one hand tucked into the lapel of his jacket in an incredibly butler-like manner. "Are you ready to be escorted?"

"That's all right. I know where the atrium is."

"You'll be in the dining room this evening."

"Oh."

He untucks his hand and gestures me forward. "After you."

Sneaking one more glance at the portrait, I turn to follow him deeper into the manor.

Dash takes me behind the staircase to an unfamiliar dark hallway. The ceiling isn't arched back here the way it is in the front, and it feels smaller, made more cramped with the heavily framed paintings and sculptures of various mediums and body parts. Bronze, marble, and stone ... heads and headless torsos. There really doesn't seem to be a pattern to Malcolm's art.

Dash hangs a right, and I keep at his heels, afraid to be left behind and watched by sightless eyes. He then opens double doors decorated by gilded flowers, and enters first inside a grand dining room, complete with a three-tiered crystal chandelier hanging above the middle of a long, cherrywood table.

Malcolm is already seated at the head, lowering the drink from his lips at my arrival. "You're late. Again."

Shamed not by his admonishment but by the fact I was staring so openly at his dead wife's portrait, I start to apologize—

"I found Miss Ember in the West Wing. I'm afraid she was a little turned around."

Darting a glance at Dash, I close my mouth and give him a small nod, thankful he didn't call me out on my distraction. He has to know Malcolm better than most and yeah, probably likes him a lot more than me. Dash's stern expression in response gives me another clue into my mysterious biological father. Mentioning his wife, however brief, must hurt Malcolm dearly.

I file that fact away while taking my seat to the left of Malcolm, which has the only other place setting.

Eight different pieces of silverware shine under the chandelier's diamond light, and the three golden plates stacked on top of one another between aren't any less intimidating.

Malcolm's rumbling voice tickles my ear. I haven't looked up at him and really don't plan to for most of the meal. "For your first dinner here, I thought it'd be nice to give you a formal welcome."

Dash clears our top two plates, then takes his place in the corner, draping a hand towel across his forearm and awaiting further instruction. I follow his movements, my fingers curling into my lap. "This really isn't necessary. I'm fine with a Big Mac, honestly."

Malcolm's brows quirk in my periphery. I wonder if he knows where a Big Mac comes from. "I insist. You look lovely tonight, by the way."

It seems I chose the right outfit, yet I still shift in my chair like ants are crawling all over my butt. It reminds me of the spiders that *actually* climbed my body. Desperate to change the tune of my thoughts, I say, "Thank you for the computer."

Malcolm nods, reaching for his drink. "I want you to be equipped with everything you need to excel at Winthorpe. If you require anything else, please let me know. It didn't seem like you had proper materials at ..." He drifts off, covering up his faux pas by taking a long sip of brown liquor.

Malcolm's made it clear that talk of my former life isn't welcome in his presence, and I bite back a retort, my mind churning against the unfathomable gifts he gives versus what he takes away.

A thought takes root, and I hide my smile behind my water glass. If he doesn't want to talk about my old life, perhaps I'll bring up *this* one.

"I learned a lot on my first day," I say, setting down my glass.

Malcolm's shoulders stiffen as if he didn't expect me to make such open-ended conversation. "Yes? That's wonderful to hear."

I sit back in my seat, wagering how blunt I should be. "The first thing someone said to me was that I looked like Savannah Merricourt."

Malcolm almost chokes on his third sip in less than a minute, recovering with a louder than normal clearing of his throat. "Well, that didn't take long."

"No, it didn't." I angle my head, staring at him head-on for the first time since stepping into the dining room. "They also said I took her place."

Malcolm lifts his napkin from his lap, refolds it, then sets it back down. "That's the more macabre way to look at it. The fact is, Winthorpe opens its doors very rarely, yet it still makes exceptions for promising students such as yourself. Your legacy with me also helped nudge those doors open a crack, but I promise you, you are not at Winthorpe solely because of a vacancy from a tragic disappearance."

"But it's part of it." I don't bother asking him what happened to Savannah. I learned all that upstairs. The daughter of a senator, she went to school one day, sickly and distracted, yet kept up with her class presentations and attended her after-school extracurriculars, one being swimming. Once practice ended, a classmate saw her get into an unfamiliar black luxury car, and that was the last anyone saw of her.

"I can't lie to you and say it isn't," Malcolm responds. "But you are also there because you were *meant* to be at Winthorpe. If it weren't for your kidnap—" Malcolm clears his throat again, schooling his face away from an outburst. He takes a deep inhale, then meets my eye again. "Just know you belong there. No one has the right to say otherwise."

I take another refreshing drink of water, then say, "Not to worry, I throat-punched the girl who said it."

Malcolm blinks at me, but we're interrupted by Dash, who'd somehow slunk through the walls and fetched our dinner. He comes between Malcolm and me, placing a whole roast chicken surrounded by rosemary-scented carrots and potatoes, browned and steaming.

My mouth waters at the sight.

"Shall I cut you a particular piece of the chicken, Miss Ember?" Dash holds up a long-bladed knife, polished like a sword.

I'm perfectly capable of cutting my own meat, but Dash has a blade the size of my head. I gesture toward the leg and the thigh, and Dash separates it with a few swipes, then sets it on my plate.

He does the same for Malcolm, who sits back until Dash is finished plating and disappears again.

"I didn't get any phone calls about a scuffle," Malcolm says as he leans forward.

I pause with my fork halfway to my mouth. It takes me a minute to figure out the smile playing across his lips.

"Who was it?" he asks.

I hesitate before I answer. "Aurora."

"Aurora ... Emmerson?" Malcolm isn't looking at me, he's busy cutting into his dinner, but I swear I hear a deep chuckle in this throat, and my lips can't help but twitch in return.

No. I will not become close with this man.

"I sometimes play squash with her father. An intolerable asshole, which I'm told he's imparted to his children. Did you actually throat-punch her, or was it more of a verbal lashing?"

It would be so easy to wipe the amusement from his face. I could tell him about how they stole my clothes, and I had to confront Aurora naked. I could also explain how I needed her blazer to get into the boys' locker room to retrieve my clothes, my ass still hanging out for all to see and comment on.

But I don't want to tell him my story or how I've fought and earned every part of my history, including the parts he wants to delete. I don't want him to get to know me, either. I want him to get bored with me, to consider me another expensive piece of art he no longer sees until I can leave this estate, unnoticed and free.

So instead, I answer, "More of a verbal head-to-head. I've pretty much solidified her dislike of me, though."

"Don't sweat it too much. The Emmersons are a mean, opportunistic bunch. They'd as soon cut down their friends as they would their enemies."

"Is that why they keep winning the Marks Fellowship?"

Malcolm's eyes lift from his place and lock on mine.

Dammit. The last thing I want is for him to be interested.

"Is that something you're aiming for?" he asks, slowly working his jaw. "Because you must understand you have every opportunity available now that I—"

"I want to earn my spot at an Ivy League, thank you, and an internship at the Marks Edelson company would be an unstoppable force on my application."

His throat bobs. "You don't need it, Ember."

"I want it." Then I add, with weighted meaning behind my words, "It's one of the main reasons I'm *here*, Malcolm."

Malcolm raises his napkin again, delicately folding it in fours. His careful movements send a warning bell ringing through my head.

He responds, too softly, "Facing off with the Emmerson girl is one thing, but you are not to associate with them, the Marks, or the Briars. Do you understand me?"

"Because they're your rivals? Why?"

Malcolm flicks his gaze to me, long enough to show me the fire he's attempting to bank. "It's too lengthy of a discussion to be of a concern to you. Suffice it to say, Damion Briar and I have known each other a long time and have had plenty of years to cultivate our mutual dislike. I don't trust him, and I certainly don't trust his son, who is essentially his carbon copy."

"Carbon copy. That's the second time I've heard that today. Aurora said I was Savannah's cheaper one."

I'm pushing Malcolm to the edge of his temper, but I can't seem to help it. My frustration of the day seems to have culminated over a roast chicken dinner in a grandeur room with a man I have nothing in common with.

Malcolm answers through gritted teeth, "Savannah was blonde, like you, with delicate features, as you have, but I see nothing more than surface-level similarities. Kids will be cruel, especially Winthorpe legacies who believe their position at the school is a right, not a privilege."

"You knew Savannah?"

Sadness glazes over his features for a moment, overtaking his anger. "Her father, Senator Merricourt, was a dear friend of mine. News of his scandal was heartbreaking to the entire town."

I read about that, too. Unsubstantiated rumors of Senator Merricourt's relationship with an underaged intern still swirl around today. "Was?"

"It ... we parted ways after my wife's ..."

The mention of the bright woman in the painting creates fractures in his expression I don't want to see. I'm not supposed to empathize with a man who rips me from everything familiar, then expects me to take up a new life on a blank slate or he'll send my parents to prison.

Yet the broken lines around his mouth and eyes squeeze my heart. In retaliation to its sympathy, I veer back to what's clearly making Malcolm leash his temper. "Aurora called me that, too, a legacy, and Thorne mentioned it. But the way they said it, it's like they didn't mean Winthorpe High."

Malcolm's silverware clatters to his plate. Fists take their place in his palms, visibly trembling as he stares me down. It takes everything in me not to shrivel in my seat at his unexpected vitriol.

"You spoke to Thorne Briar?" Malcolm asks, but his burning stare tells me he doesn't require an answer. "You are to avoid him at all costs. And if he so much as mentions a legacy to you, or something to do with a Society, you are to turn around and walk in the other direction. Am I making myself clear?"

I swallow. "Perfectly," I whisper.

"Good." Tossing his napkin across his unfinished meal, he rises, smoothing down his jacket. A signet ring on his pinky finger flashes. All I can make out is the silver head of a raven before he pushes away from the table and stalks around my chair. "You may finish your dinner, but I find I no longer have an appetite."

The double doors shut behind him.

Surrounded in silence, I set my fork and knife on top of my plate, then lean back in my chair, settling my hands on my thighs.

I no longer have much of an appetite, either.

LATER THAT NIGHT, I have such a difficult time sleeping that I turn on my lamp, open my computer, and stalk social media—both Thorne's and Aurora's accounts.

I found them through Aiko, and I found *her* through the Winthorpe database a few hours ago. We've been instant messaging ever since. She was more than happy to inform me that Winthorpe frowns on any use of social media outside their surveillance, but students are savvy, and most have made secret accounts the academy can't trace. It didn't take much prodding to get both Aurora's and Thorne's handles on their TikTok and Instagram, and I've been prowling ever since.

To my disappointment, I'm not gleaning a whole lot.

Parties, cars, mansions, and some expert sports shots like Thorne's perfect butterfly form, water foaming around him as he slashes through the pool. Aurora pouts at the camera often while Thorne never looks at it straight on, always focused on someone or something just outside the lens, his mouth half-cocked, standing close enough to be in the picture but consciously spaced apart from everyone else.

Photos of them around a bonfire surrounded by the rocky crevices of a cave capture my attention, sand and crumbling stone the background to their entwined arms around their friends.

That's what draws me in. Thorne has his arm around a fair blonde with a smile that lights up her face more than the orange flames. I peer closer. She looks up at him like she sees the true prince behind the monster.

My eyes dart to the caption: *fun with friends and at home with my girl.*

Thorne's account is devoid of emojis and cutesy captions. He prefers a straight-up description, harking back to the old days when he'd be writing it on the back of an old photograph before storing it in an album.

An odd feeling creeps along my shoulders and down my back after reading *my girl.* Savannah's the sole person he's deigned to touch in over a year of photos, instinctually loose with her, his head tipped toward her and the bare brush of a grin tickling his lips. It's the kind of caring attitude that comes with ...

Realization shoots through my core.

Savannah was Thorne's girlfriend.

Sighing, I push the laptop off my legs and stare off to the side. Why this affects me, I'm not sure, since he's been nothing but contemptuous and judgmental the few times we've spoken. He's a jerk who draws flowers for grades and orders bitchy girls to strip innocent ones of their dignity.

Thorne Briar is not my friend and *certainly* not a guy I should be crushing on. Considering Malcolm's reaction, I'm better off avoiding Thorne entirely. Not that I don't enjoy pissing Malcolm off, but the sheer, numbed rage on his expression when I admitted Thorne approached me ... that's not natural. The Briar and Weatherby rivalry runs deep in their veins, and I want the Marks Fellowship more than goading Malcolm to a place he may not come back from.

An outside *creeeaaaack* draws my chin up, my attention

shifting to the bay windows. I'm getting used to the moans and aching cries of the house, but I've never heard this one before. Not at this time of night.

Flipping the laptop shut, I slide off the bed and head to the window, blackened with night. To see the outside better, I flick off my lamp on the way.

A made-up image of Thorne sneaking onto Malcolm's property and finding a hidden door into my room drifts into my mind, but I shake it off, both in the hopes of deleting such a stupid hope and forgetting I ever had it in the first place. The *last* thing I want is to give that guy unlimited access to my imagination.

The windowpane's cold to the touch, my palms pressing against the clear glass as I peer out through the ivy clawing across the wood trim. It's through the tangled leaves I spot Malcolm, still in his suit, pulling the iron front gate shut behind him as he exits the manor, another doleful creak following his movements before it clangs shut.

He glances up at my window, but I duck to the side, shadowing myself while keeping one eye on him. A stern expression cloaks his face as he pauses for a moment, thoughtful cogs that I can't read whirring inside his head as he studies my window. Once he's seemingly satisfied, he moves to the sidewalk, then across the street.

When he clears the stone pillars on the other side and prowls up the raised driveway, I suck in a breath.

After viciously warning me away, Malcolm has snuck out to visit the Briars.

CHAPTER 12

THORNE

K udos to the English teacher for coming up with an original essay topic, but I was done in an hour and stared out of my bedroom window for the rest of the evening. A lot of girls call me broody for this habit—choosing to glower at nature instead of burying my face in a screen. If they knew what was going on in my head while I was doing it, they'd whimper and call me a bastard, instead.

It helps to visualize triumph, first of confronting my father, this time with *me* holding the knife, and another of me coming in first in the 200 Fly, Freestyle, and every single class I'm forced to take to get through senior year. I don't care who I step on in these visuals, male, female, teacher, headmistress. The result is always the same. I win.

Getting ahead with readings during the summer leaves me with too much free time to reenact these shrewd scenarios in my head, and my expression really does turn into a glower as I stare out into the night, visualizing what's on the other side even though I can't see it.

The new girl, my latest fascination, is likely fast asleep by now and ready for a visit. I wonder if she knows about the first time I snuck into her room and leaned over her bed, watching her expressions stumble through dreams. Or nightmares, by the looks of it. She's a mystery, this one, both in timing and in heritage. This little scavenger must've seen an opportunity and pounced, wringing the poor old man dry with her big, black-brown eyes and crazy-pale hair. Malcolm must've been astonished by her presence, demanding a DNA test which I suppose she passed since she's here, yet she looks nothing like him. She resembles a creature crawling out of the caves below Winthorpe, white-blond hair trailing behind her as the waves crash forward, her face more akin to a mythical Siren than a Weatherby.

Her existence is too sudden to be a coincidence and too dangerous to ignore. I have to keep watch on her and ensure she's not here to wreak havoc on a strategy my father's employed against the Weatherbys for years.

I didn't witness Father's first reaction to the discovery of Ember Weatherby, but I can imagine. Malcolm Weatherby has a teenaged daughter, who happens to enroll at Winthorpe the moment news of Savannah went deathly quiet. No updates, no sightings, no indication she's still alive.

My gut churns as the last image I have of Sav takes shape in my mind's eye. To distract myself, I swivel in my desk chair, barking, "What have you found?"

Jaxon is splayed out on my California king, a laptop half-cocked on his stomach. He snorts awake at my question. "Shit, man, that Purple Haze you got completely knocked me out."

"Then knock back in and tell me if you've found Ember's records."

"Yeah. Sure," he grumbles, shifting to sit against the carved wooden headboard of broncos locking hooves.

Pretty sure the same carvings were displayed on my crib. Gotta love my father's sense of humor.

"Found her under Beckett," Jaxon says, his fingers flying across the keyboard. "And her grades are stellar, despite having gone to a shit school. Lots of student participation, no suspensions or other slaps on the wrist. Not even an open container charge for drinking in public. In other words, boring AF." Jaxon makes a face, but at my stern expression, he goes on, "She's as advertised, man. Decent competition for the Marks Fellowship. Aurora's rightfully pissed, especially if Belle's dad decides to polish his image by awarding the prize to a poor kid underdog instead of her bestie."

"Give me a fucking break," I scoff. "She's a Weatherby now. The sole heir to his fortune. She's fine."

Jaxon shrugs. "Girl's got goals. You want to read her early decision essays?"

I jerk my chin in assent, and Jaxon passes over the computer. As he does, a shadow flickers in my peripheral vision, and I cast my gaze back to the window.

A stiff-backed figure stalks up our driveway.

"Your dad expecting visitors?" Jaxon asks. The figure disappears at the same time the sound of our front door opens, then thumps shut. "Or is your stepmom trying to escape again?"

He laughs at his own joke, but my lips stay flat. "She learned her lesson the last time. She's not about to do it again."

Jaxon sobers.

The laptop's hot on my thighs, but I can't seem to focus on the screen. I'm too interested in who could be paying us a visit after midnight on a weekday. My father entertains all sorts of clientele, but the nocturnal ones intrigue me the most.

Without a word, I set the laptop on my desk and head to my door. Jaxon knows better than to ask where I'm going. Instead, he sighs theatrically, flicking on Netflix on my fifty-inch flat screen, then folds his arms behind his head.

"You fall asleep in my bed, I'm punching you in the kidneys

and rolling you to your guest room," I say before I depart. Jaxon acknowledges with a grunt.

The hallway's almost pitch-black. All the bedrooms are on this floor and not much else. I drift toward the middle but take a sharp right and press on a painting that catches on hidden hinges before opening wide. Stepping through, I feel along the walls for the flashlight I keep hanging there, find it, and turn it on. The painting shuts quietly behind me.

The Briar estate has upward of thirty hidden passages. I found most of them as a boy, my buddies and I daring each other to go deeper, stay longer, and do it all in the blinding dark. Cobwebs brushing against our faces used to cause shrieks so high, the staff thought the place was haunted with banshees.

Nowadays, what used to be harrowing hide-and-seek games have turned into ways to gain currency on my father. For all his egotistic excesses, Damion Briar has never bothered to learn the secret corridors of the Briar mansion, despite it being built by our cutthroat, paranoid ancestors.

As I take the small set of stairs curving to the ground floor, the flashlight bounces against the crumbling stonework. There aren't any paintings or other art forms adorning these spaces, not even those Father purchases at black market auctions. He displays those in his office as subtle *fuck yous* to the legal establishment. In here, it's just the spiders and me.

Spiders. Remembering Ember, screaming as she peeled off her blouse, makes me smile.

I come to a halt at a dead end, my fingers pressing against a stone button on the wall. The Renault painting opens on the other side. On silent feet, I press forward into the hallway.

An arc of golden light across the floorboards carves the path to my father's office, the door shut and the voices muffled.

I stick to the shadows, slinking closer, the cuffs of my sweatpants catching on my bare heels until I come to a stop just short of the door. Pressing my back to the wall, I angle my head until my ear's cocked, and eavesdropping is at an optimal level.

"Your boy can't approach her again."

Malcolm's growling voice comes through the thick wood as if he were standing right beside me.

"I doubt he did," Father responds, leisurely and unhurried. "Not this soon."

"She *mentioned* it to me, Damion!"

"If you don't want to draw Thorne's interest—or my wife's—I suggest you keep your voice down."

Malcolm emits another sound, this one pained and impatient. I lift my chin, concurring with him.

"Then why has Ember asked me about the Societies? About her legacy? We agreed she would be kept in the dark," Malcolm spits.

"Calm yourself. We made it so she's to have no contact with her parents for the year or *anyone* outside of Winthorpe. She's blind and deaf, Malcolm."

"Is that what you expect me to do? Keep her locked up in my empty manor forever? I refuse to do that to her. We had an agreement, Damion. I don't want her involved in my past. And this fellowship she's after that I'm sure *your son* put into her head, she's not to come close to winning it. You must respect that, or—"

"Or what?" Father drawls.

I stifle an eye roll at the baited question, said in a tone that's eviscerated men a lot crueler than Malcolm, and Malcolm's quite intimidating, indeed. But the mention of preventing Ember from winning the fellowship keys piques my interest. Her own father, ruining any chance she has at winning what she's termed as her dream? I chew on the advantages of being privy to this particular secret.

"You've done enough." Malcolm's response comes out as a

ragged whisper. "You're not to touch my daughter, and you tell your boy to stay far away from her."

"I'll do that," Father says, unconcerned. "But I can't say my son will listen. He's inherited more from his namesake than you'll ever comprehend."

My muscles twitch, bracing for an invisible fight. The fucker's put a Pavlovian response in me, always ready to swing before being swung *at.*

I've never managed to bring my father to his knees, but I've put in a few dents, and my fingers curl into my palms, knuckles raw from his latest dare.

"What you do to your son is none of my concern," Malcolm says, his voice bringing me back to the present. "Nor more than how I choose to raise my daughter, a girl who's just come back into my life, is yours. Your meddling is *done*, Damion."

"I decide when I'm finished." At the tone, I imagine my father inspecting his cuticles as he says it.

"You've won. Is that what you want to hear? You've *won*. Now leave my family out of it."

"How quaint that you believe you've made a family again."

"Damion ..." Malcolm warns.

"I cautioned you not to unleash the Briar curse on yourself and all you love, yet you did it, and you're still paying for it. How you choose to live out the rest of your wretched life is up to you."

"Ember is a part of my life now, but your vendetta should not fall on her."

"Yes, you found an heir. I suppose congratulations are in order, yet I don't see you throwing a welcome party for her. You used to be so wonderful at social engagements. Is it because she wants nothing to do with you?"

My father has always been a cruel bastard, but this is new lengths.

A scuffle ensues, grunts and the shattering of liquor glasses against Father's William IV desk. I'm versed enough in the sounds to understand the wheezing of breath to come from Malcolm. Father's resorted to his usual move—the tip of a blade against the soft spot under his opponent's chin, even if that opponent happens to be his former best friend.

A hand clasps my shoulder, and I whip around, muscles bunched and teeth bared. The whites of Jaxon's eyes come into view in the dark, and the shine of his fingernail as he holds his finger to his lips and mimes, *Shhhh.*

His grip tightens on my shoulder, jostling me slightly, his eyes hard on mine. It takes a minute to figure out I'm breathing through clenched teeth, nostrils flaring, dots of sweat breaking out on my bare chest like I'm readying for battle.

Jaxon sucks in a deep breath, puffing out his chest until I catch on and follow suit. When he exhales, so do I. We do that a few times—two beasts lingering in a hallway of classical art—until Jaxon's satisfied enough to move us deeper into the shadows and through the hidden panel in the wall.

We disappear into a blacker darkness, my breaths slowly coming under control and exhaustion taking its place. I won't last much longer as the spear of adrenaline dissipates with every step.

The lingering effects of bracing for a fight dull my senses for the rest of the trip. As I flop into bed and Jaxon flips my laptop shut, Ember's ethereal face ripples into my mind's eye.

My eyelids grow heavy, weighted by her somber, shielded expression. That last image of her will have to do. I won't be paying a sleeping Ember a nightly visit after all.

CHAPTER 13
EMBER

I suppose breakfast with Malcolm will be a regular thing. When I reach the bottom of the staircase, Dash directs me to the atrium, where Malcolm awaits my presence.

He lowers the paper as I step up to the table. Pastries are piled in the middle with a steaming carafe of coffee as the centerpiece. Unable to resist, I pour myself a mug and perch on the opposite chair.

"The Danishes are from the local bakery in town," Malcolm says as a greeting. I guess we won't be talking about his outburst last night. "I'm told they're divine."

I take note of the pristine, crumb-less plate in front of him. "You're not eating?"

"I'm not particularly hungry this morning."

His statement prompts a closer study, and I spot a flush of red on his jaw. It's covered by day-old stubble but obvious enough to be fresh. Malcolm notices where my attention has gone and snaps his newspaper open, asking, "I apologize for last night. I'm still ... navigating what this is between us. Please know, however, everything I said yesterday evening is for your protection. Are you prepared for your second day?"

"Sure," I say, forcing my gaze away from the bruise. He's deliberately changing the subject. If he doesn't want to talk about it, I'm not about to initiate the discussion. I do wonder if it's all connected to his secret visit across the street, though. "How did you sleep?"

Malcolm's brows jump in surprise. "Very well. You?"

Liar. "Not great. I'm not used to the new environment yet. Sounds like creaking floorboards and swinging gates ... I swear there was movement just outside my window." I wait for him to fill in the blanks and admit he left the house last night.

He doesn't. Simply looks at me blankly and says, "You'll get used to it. I've lived here all my life. Now I can sleep through anything."

My eye twitches at how freely he admits to staying at this manor for decades. I don't see it as an advantage; I see it as imprisonment.

"You don't wander the halls at night or anything?" I ask, aiming for a joke, but it comes out more like an accusation.

He glances up from his newspaper again, holding my stare longer than necessary before answering. "No."

I see we're further solidifying our relationship with lies then. I don't confront him. Instead, I file away this conversation for future use when I have a better handle on how to deal with him and his will to trap me here alongside him.

"I should get going." Pushing to my feet, I snag a Danish before hooking my bag and exiting the atrium.

"Dash is waiting out front."

I don't bother to say goodbye, and neither does he.

MY SECOND DAY at Winthorpe comes with a better understanding of the castle's layout, and I spend less time in the courtyard, where Aurora and her cronies have congregated, and more time lingering in the deserted hallway. No one else is eager to be the first to get to class.

I have a textbook propped open in my hands so I don't look like a complete loser, pretending to do the assigned reading last minute while I wait for the morning bell to ring. I'm a few weeks ahead, having spent most of my summer preparing for a school that makes SAT scores look like Tetris Masters.

That's how Aiko finds me.

"Hey, there!" she says as she bounces to a stop. We're alone, but she glances around conspiratorially, then cups her mouth and asks, "How did the snooping go?"

I smile at her. "Fine. I think I found enough out about my enemies."

"Eesh, don't say that word." Aiko grimaces. "The *last* thing you want is Thorne and crew as your enemy."

"I'm not sure I have a choice in the matter." I relay to her what happened after swim class yesterday since I didn't want to describe it in text, and her mouth gapes open.

"Holy shit, Ember. That's terrible. I'd tell you to go the headmistress, but ..." She trails off, wincing again.

"Yeah. I've figured out the politics around here." Sighing, I hike my bag higher up my shoulder while closing my textbook. "I wanted to ask you ... do you know much about Savannah Merricourt?"

Aiko pales to the point of being green. "You really don't pause in your punches, do you? First Thorne and Aurora, now Savannah. Do you have a death wish? I'm asking you. Honestly."

I chuckle, but Aiko doesn't return the humor. I quickly school my face to match her expression. "I'm serious, and it's horrible, the way she disappeared. I'm not trying to be nosy, but I need to understand *why* Aurora hates me and Thorne wants to scare me off."

"Can't you try to survive without understanding their motives? Because I promise you, they're a superficial bunch. It could be you're not pretty enough—" Aiko's cheeks go bright red. "Which you are *so* pretty, that's not what I mean. Or you're a threat to Aurora's chance at the fellowship, or any number of stupid things that are only important to people like them."

I turn her words over in my mind, but my instincts don't change. "No. There's something deeper going on with them. Malcolm, too."

"Malcolm?" Her expression clears. "Oh. You mean your biological father."

I'd rather not get into *that* conversation. "Have you ever heard of Societies, or anyone mentioning *a* Society?"

A locker bangs nearby, but according to Aiko, the sound deserves a big swivel toward the sound and an exaggerated, "The bell will ring soon. We should get to class."

Squinting at her, I say, "What am I missing here?"

"Nothing. It's just a stupid rumor. Don't worry about it."

I grab her arm before she can scamper but do it gently, reluctant to spook my only friend. "I haven't properly thanked you for your help last night. I really appreciate it."

"You don't have to thank me. It was easy." She relaxes in my hold.

"What rumors?"

Aiko frowns at the dart of a question, hitting her between her brows. But she answers. "Just some dumb hazing that goes on in the catacombs or the caves. Both places are forbidden to access and result in instant expulsion, by the way."

"And they get away with it?"

"Of course. It's them. The quadrant of gods—Aurora, Belle, Jaxon, and Thorne. One of them could commit murder and the faculty would turn a blind eye. Heck, one of them probably did." Aiko turns somber, shuffling her feet uncomfortably.

The name *Savannah* goes unspoken between us.

I don't want to push her, though I'm starting to guess maybe Savannah participated in one of these hazings, and it went wrong. The kind of cover-up families like these could put in place would be similar to thick steel.

"When do these hazings normally happen?" I ask.

"Beginning of the year. You know, to get in their club or cool parties or whatever. Only a handful are chosen. It takes a certain kind of person to even *want* to do what they require. Even then, look at their group. There are only four. There have always only been four or five."

I go quiet, but I'm sensing Aiko's urgent need to finish the conversation, so I ask my final question. "My research last night led me to some pictures of Savannah and Thorne in some cave. The rest of the popular crowd was there, too."

Aiko nods, unsurprised.

"Is that one of the hazing spots?"

"No. That's one of the main party spots and why it's on their feed. Anything they get up to involving the school's underground ... they don't post about it." A loud, piercing sound interrupts our conversation, and Aiko glances up at the loud clanging of the bell. "I'll see you in second period, okay?"

"Sure. And thanks, Aiko."

"You should consider joining the journalism club," she jokes. "I think you'd be real good at it."

I smile, but it's faint around the edges. Then I turn around and enter math class.

"Ah. Miss Beckett," Professor Lowell says as soon as I cross the threshold. "Your files were updated regarding your last name preference. I've altered the seating chart accordingly and shuffled everyone around."

Mortification turns into a hard ball in my gut. "Oh, you didn't have to make everybody move."

"Nonsense. Easy fix. You're in the back row now, next to ... yes, next to Mr. Briar."

That ball of mortification turns into a boulder. "Really, sir, I don't want to cause an inconvenience. I'll stick to my old seat, and—"

"Consider yourself more than an inconvenience," a languid voice drawls behind me. "Wouldn't 'mistake' be a better fit?"

The boulder shatters.

I twist on my heel, coming face-to-face with Thorne wearing a half-cocked grin on his face and all the time in the world to insult me right where it hurts. "Screw you," I hiss.

"Now, now," Lowell warns. "Take your seats before I decide on detention, instead."

Thorne heads down the aisle first, leaving no question that he's *not* a gentleman, and I drag my ass behind. He stops at the double desk and takes out a text and a notebook, the actions indicating he's busy while still keeping an eye on me the whole time.

Sliding into the seat next to him, I'm slammed with his scent of cool water and soap. That combination shouldn't have all olfactory senses tuning in to him, yet my fingers stiffen and my entire body freezes under the scope of the delectable beckoning.

"Problem, little pretty?" Thorne takes his time sitting down while staring straight ahead as he asks the question.

"You stink like chemicals." My books smack against the desk to enunciate my point.

"I snuck into the rec center for an early morning swim. You should try it, if you enjoy swimming with the sharks."

I snort at his lame threat, but he speaks the truth. Thorne and his friends likely take over the pool before school hours, knifing into the water and hunting down anyone who doesn't belong.

The rest of the class wanders in. Aurora comes to an abrupt halt at the sight of me beside Thorne. I straighten my posture, hoping to exude confidence mixed with the type of expression that says, *this was not my idea, and I'd rather set fire to myself.* Even though it was, technically, my wish to stay a Beckett.

My effort isn't reciprocated. Aurora's pointed stare doesn't relent until she falls into the seat in front of me like she's been forced to sit in front of that one kid in kindergarten who always smelled like fart.

"Everybody settled?" Lowell asks as the classroom shuffling continues. He doesn't wait for any confirmation before he says, "Good. I have the results of the pop quiz." Lowell lifts a sheaf of paper from his desk. "It should hit your online portal soon, but I'd like to extend an advanced congratulations to our newest student, Ember Beckett, who inched out Mr. Briar by a hair and received the top marks."

The entire class sucks in a singular breath. All heads swivel in my direction, fear leeching into their colorless faces.

I keep my focus on Lowell, despite the warning itch traveling up my arms and convalescing at the side of my face—right where Thorne's fiery gaze hits.

"Surely, there's a mistake, sir," Thorne says without turning to Lowell.

Lowell sniffs. "No, Mr. Briar. I'm afraid I couldn't ignore Miss Beckett's perfect score compared to yours."

Slowly, Thorne arcs his attention to the professor. I release my breath subtly enough that Thorne doesn't notice. I hope.

"Look again."

"Mr. Briar, it's already been made official. There's nothing more I can do. Congratulations, Miss Beckett."

Thorne doesn't have to pin me in his sights again for me to

understand the pure outrage radiating from his body. I kind of love it. *That's what you get for being an arrogant asshole.* "Thank you, sir."

"And me, Professor?" Aurora, the only person who didn't twist around to witness Thorne's reaction, keeps her tone light and innocent, but her back is rigid. "Where am I?"

"You're third, Miss Emmerson, after Mr. Briar. The rest of you can find your marks on the academy's portal, so let's all turn our heads forward and start today's lesson."

Aurora's exhale hisses out. She tosses an elbow across the back of her seat and turns to us. "One pop quiz at the beginning of the semester is dumb luck. You're not taking this fellowship, Gone Girl."

I'm working hard not to recoil at the utter hatred flushing her cheeks and arch a brow. "Gone Girl?"

She sneers. "You'll be gone soon enough."

I press my lips together, internally reciting all the reasons not to engage, but my impulsive mouth won't listen. "I guess it takes more than a rich kid's floral artwork to get to the top of Lowell's class."

Aurora's eyes turn into slits. She flicks her attention to Thorne, who up until now, was ominously quiet during our exchange. He doesn't acknowledge her attention. Rather, he's copying down Lowell's equation like none of this has anything to do with him.

It gives me pause. With quiet, cautionary hesitation, I side-eye him.

"Miss Emmerson! Turn around, please."

"You are so utterly clueless on how it works around here," Aurora whispers darkly, but she can't resist a last parting shot before doing as the professor asks. "I doubt you're a real Weatherby, and Mr. Weatherby's only keeping you because you're some prize he won during the Soc—"

"Aurora."

Thorne doesn't glance up as he bites out her name, but the tone has lethal consequences. Her chin trembles with rebellion, and it's at that moment Thorne lifts his head and gifts her with a terrible, too-old stare, pen poised above his paper as a writing utensil *or* a weapon.

Aurora shuts her mouth and spins to the front, her back landing hard in her chair.

Her words ring in my head, despite my better attempts to listen to Lowell. These people who have only known me a day are able to find and latch on to the most vulnerable parts of me without batting an eye. How do they *do* that?

My pencil scratches against the paper, not to take notes but to quietly unleash. Aurora's pissed I actually completed the quiz, Thorne's silent and probably furious that his *garden* didn't get him the top score, and to add the final insult, I'm not a Weatherby, but I don't feel like much of a Beckett anymore, either. Thorne was more accurate than I'm sure he realized—I'm adrift. Not in a pool, but in an ocean of sharks.

"Tomorrow night."

Thorne's hushed voice draws me out of my thoughts. I'm scribbling in my notebook, loops of flowers and leaves that apparently give certain students an advantage at this school, having already completed most of Lowell's planned syllabus for this month. I angle my head toward him. "What?"

"Tell Malcolm you have a study session at the library, or a sleepover with a fake friend, or just ditch him outright. You have a meeting to attend."

"I'm not going anywhere with you." I lift my chin slightly to motion to the back of Aurora's head. "Or her."

"You don't have a choice, Ember *Weatherby*."

Thorne's hand snakes out to grab my wrist, and I gasp as he

uses his other hand to crumple the first page of my notebook, then tear it off its bindings.

He was so fast, I'm still uselessly poising my pencil as he holds my wrist hostage. "What the hell?" I whisper. "Those are my notes!"

"Any further mention of our roses," he murmurs, his grip tightening, "or drawings of them, and I'll be forced to do more than just slap your wrist to get you to stop."

Thorne's preternatural stare, made into pale moons by the bright, overhead lights of the classroom, holds mine prisoner. His hold is steady, the cold grip of his fingers sinking into the warmth of my skin and taking it for his own.

Revulsion should be snaking through my veins at his touch, not the thrum of electricity that travels from my arm and blooms in my chest as soon as his palm brushes against the inside of my wrist. My breaths slow, then shorten, the longer we're locked together, but I won't flinch. I refuse to be the first to beg for release.

"If you won't tell me why first-grade drawings will get you close to the top in a senior math class," I say quietly while Lowell prattles on, oblivious to what's going on at the back of his classroom, "why should I care about your threats?"

My arm twitches in his hold, the single clue to the lightning snap of temper shooting through his body.

I deliberately let go of my pencil, sending it clattering onto the desk and drawing Lowell's attention. Thorne's hold disappears, leaving a damp chill in his wake that I can feel all the way into my bones. Resting his arms in his lap, he shifts in his chair as if bored until Lowell is seemingly satisfied with the lack of rebellion occurring back here and resumes his instructions to the class.

Doing my best not to gloat, I pick up my pencil and listen to Lowell, but Thorne's proximity won't let me forget him.

A buzz exists in the air between us. It's imperceptible to the rest of the room but loud and demanding on my senses. I sneak a glance his way to see if he feels it, too, but he's given me his profile, his jaw cutting through his skin and his eyelids lowered as he folds his arms across his chest and stares toward the front.

I remain that way through the duration of the class, achingly tense while he chooses to ignore my presence in the same way as Aurora, as if he didn't clasp my arm and promise to punish me. A closer inspection reveals the muscles in his cheek clenching.

My stomach tightens at the remembrance of the sudden, angry vise-like grip of his hand, coupled with a vision of him grabbing both my wrists and holding them above me until my back hit the classroom wall. I furiously blink it away, horrified at succumbing to such a blatant fantasy. In *math* class.

"All right, students, you have your assignments. Head off to your next period," Lowell says as the bell rings.

Thorne jolts out of his stiff posture and packs up his things. Aurora idly mentions something to him, but too much blood is roaring in my ears for me to hear. I need to get away from them and go someplace where I can breathe.

But Thorne's voice stops me from rising.

"You want your explanations?" Standing, Thorne tucks his schoolbag over his shoulder, and I'm faced with the looming Thorne that controlled my brief fantasy. "Come tomorrow night behind the rec center. Nine sharp."

Aurora frowns. "Thorne, you're not serious."

"You're right. I'm usually a fucking clown." His expression is flat, cold stone.

"Don't invite her. It's members only, and I still have questions about her heritage, obviously." Aurora glances down at me long enough for me to lurch out of my seat and stand with them.

I don't blink from her gaze. "I'll think about it."

"Don't think too hard," Thorne says. "Like I said, little pretty, all your answers to the mysteries of Winthorpe await." While turning on his heel, Thorne adds, "Unless you're not interested in the fellowship anymore."

Damn him.

He doesn't look back as he disappears through the classroom doorway.

Playing dirty is practically a part of the curriculum in this school. If I have any chance at even breathing on the fellowship, never mind claiming it, understanding Thorne Briar is a necessary evil. He holds power at Winthorpe, and if Aurora, my main competition, is sticking close to him, then so must I.

Even if that means entering into Winthorpe's hidden gallows, hewn with ink-drawn roses.

CHAPTER 14
THORNE

Coming face-to-face with Ember is annoyingly difficult.

I'm getting better at tamping down the urge to roar every time her dark eyes find mine, but the uncanny resemblance to Savannah is haunting in its accuracy. Ember has more grit than Savannah's spritely nature, but they both possess that infuriating, flyaway hair that begs me to smooth it down at their temples.

Sitting next to Ember was torture in itself, but having her take the top grade in the class, then draw *my* rose as if it meant nothing but a doodle, sent me over the edge.

"Were we not supposed to jump her in her bedroom, blindfold her, then take her to the initiation?" Aurora whines as we cross the halls, the sixth and final period beckoning. "Why did you just invite her like that? I thought it was my decision on how we treated her."

"Remind me again who is in charge."

Aurora's steps slow while I continue smoothly. She says, "You are."

"Exactly," I toss over my shoulder. "So, why are you questioning my decision?"

"Because you're too close to it. Her."

I draw to a halt. Students who mingled at the sides of the hall or made a beeline through the center to get to class give me a wide berth. In seconds, the south wing is deserted, save for Aurora's incessant complaints. I ask her, "Do you have any idea what I have planned?"

Aurora's lips form into a pout. Answer enough.

"I've changed my mind. Ember's initiation won't come close to Savannah's," I say in a low tone. "What was it that she did? Right, Sav slept overnight in the catacombs with you by her side. Ember won't have that kind of comfort." I stalk closer to Aurora, who shrinks in my shadow. The girl is all bark. "She will be scared, and alone, and made to believe she's coming so close to death, she'll scream for mercy and run out of here, refusing to ever come back."

"It's hard to believe that Ember's looks won't affect your plans."

"*She* is not Savannah, and I'll never treat her as such. I want her out of here just as much as you do." Especially after hearing Malcolm and my father's meeting last night, offering the certainty that if Damion Briar's interested in her, Ember has to go.

I offer none of that to Aurora, however, who is about as trustworthy as an underfed Pomeranian.

"We have to bring her into the fold because she's Malcolm's daughter," I continue. "But we have no instruction whether or not we *keep* her. So do me a favor and let me do what I do best."

"As long as you're keeping your emotions out of it."

I give a light scoff, though my blood boils underneath. "You want to talk emotion? You're afraid she'll take the fellowship from you, aren't you? I've never seen you act so ... beneath yourself. Stealing her clothes after swim practice? How common, Aurora."

"*Fuck* you." Aurora's cheeks blotch with red. "Like you have any idea what it means to work hard for an uncertain future—"

"Say that again."

Aurora's back smacks against the wall, cornered. "I ... that's not what I meant. I know you're deserving of every accolade in this school—"

"Provide some clarification, because all I'm hearing is that my history with Sav and her disappearance is clouding my judgment in who to bring into our special club."

Aurora's eyes spark. Though pressed against the wall, her gaze steadies on mine. "Not only is Ember replacing Savannah's spot in Winthorpe, she's also getting her position in our Society *and* replacing her as your new love interest."

My breath stills, and my body turns to marble. "I am *not* interested in Ember."

"Keep telling yourself that." Aurora juts out her chin.

My fist cracks against the brick next to her head, and her jaw goes slack as her defiance wastes away.

"Question me again, and any chance you have at the fellowship or any other position in this school disappears." I snap my fingers in front of her nose for emphasis. She flinches.

She whispers, "Fine."

As I step back, my shadow follows, clearing the way for sunlight to hit Aurora's pallid face. "Better run, or you'll be late to class."

She mutters something as I turn on my heel, but I don't bother to threaten her again.

Once is always enough.

Swim practice goes long, and I take my time in the showers after, too. I'm never eager to head home and sit at a strained dinner, pretending normalcy over prime rib when we're anything but normal.

Jaxon's dad is back from overseas, so I don't even have him as a buffer between Father's natural discontentment with any subject other than himself.

"See you tomorrow, bro." Jaxon claps me on the back as he heads out of the academy's doors first.

"Last one at the rec center in the morning does fifty laps."

"Fuck, man." Jaxon spins on his heel and walks backward in the parking lot as I tread behind him. "I ain't coming tomorrow. I'm giving this godlike body a break."

"So close to our first meet? Pussy." My sports bag bounces against my hip, aggravating the sore muscle there. It's been bothering me since the start of the semester, but I block it out while in the water, pretending it doesn't exist.

"You gotta let up at some point. Especially with your plans tomorrow night." Jaxon winks before swinging around.

"Keep that to yourself. I have a hard enough time keeping Aurora quiet."

"Yeah, I heard." Lucky for Jaxon, he doesn't expand and instead jumps into his purple Lamborghini.

I dip into my black BMW i8 beside him. Since both our cars' windows are tinted, we can't see each other any longer, but for the sake of consistency, I flip him off before reversing out of the lot.

The winding hills and natural landscape of Raven's Bluff are usually a soothing balm on my withered soul, with the evening light pulling at the trees' shadows and beckoning for high tide below the cliffs. It's a dangerous time when animals meant for daylight scurry into their habitats and panic at the predators just cracking open their eyes. I should be on the lookout for deer, but

I press on the gas, the motor's purr transforming into a roar, and take the turns too tight, the tires flirting with the roadway's edge.

Yet the rush doesn't come. My mind's too wrapped up in Ember and my plans for her. Aurora's observation hit too close to the mark, and I'm stuck mulling over her accusations—that I'm drawn to Ember.

Doesn't Aurora see how different they are? Savannah was the sun ... Ember is the moon. Their resemblance is close, but it's not like we have a piece of Savannah back. Doppelgängers are notorious bad omens, and for once, I believe Aurora agrees with me on that. Ember must be extinguished. I'm not a superstitious guy, but if she's still here, I have the instinct that Savannah can't return.

Fucking myths. I blame the environment. Raven's Bluff is nothing but gloomy rock, salted air, and white-crested waves appearing as skeletal hands to drag you into the deep. It's no surprise that Ember's appearance has everyone feeling like shit.

My headlights flash against my home's gates, the twin stone ravens stark against the light. As I turn into the drive, my attention drifts across the street, where a single window glows in Weatherby Manor, probably Ember and Malcolm sitting down to dinner.

I wonder what they talk about. Are there excited discussions now that father and daughter are reunited at last, or is it as stilted and painful as mine? Malcolm isn't my father. He's a beaten man with less and less to live for, but I've always remembered him as a quiet kind of vicious, kind to children but ruthless to businessmen. Physically *and* mentally. Well. Back in his heyday, he was.

Before my father broke him.

Our driveway is much longer than the Weatherbys, and it takes me some time to crest the hill and come to a stop at the front. I've slowed down substantially—an instinctual reaction to having to step through these doors rather than fly through the cliffside roads.

It's inevitable, though, and I put the car in park and slip out.

Josh, our doorman, butler, and everyman, pushes the thick, wooden door open as my shoes crunch over the gravel drive.

"Welcome home, Junior." His weathered face cracks into a smile. He's the only one allowed to call me that due to his distinguished title of becoming more of a father to me than my own.

"Thanks. Are they in the dining area?"

Rarely, if ever, do I use my stepmother's and father's names.

"Sure are. They're waiting for you."

"Grand." I toss Josh my keys and leave my duffel at the bottom of the staircase. My parents would prefer I change and approach dinner like they do—pointlessly formal—but I prefer subtle, incessant rebellion and stay in my Winthorpe tracksuit.

"Ah. You've arrived at last." Father glances up from the dining room's bar area as I pass through the arched entryway.

Father's dressed in a navy suit that matches the shaded color of his eyes, his graying hair slicked back from a face that will become mine with time. My stepmother is frozen at the table in a simple ice-blue dress, downcast and meek as always, her wineglass lipstick-stained and empty.

I take a seat across from her without deigning to answer my father.

"I assume you're late because you were busy pushing your body to its limits." Father takes his place at the head of the table. "Your first meet of the season is in a week. I expect first place."

"I'm aware of when the race is." I eye his crystal glass of bourbon as he raises it to his lips. He'd never willingly pour me a glass. Not because he wants to enforce the national legal age requirement, but because he enjoys depriving me of the simplest pleasures.

That's fine. It's taught me other ways to get what I want.

I grab my glass of ice water. "You could've started without me."

"That's not how we do things in this house. Is it, sweetheart?" Father looks at his wife.

The prompt makes her blink, but not much else. "Yes, dear."

I stifle a sigh. There's still at least an hour of this.

Josh enters the room carrying three entrée plates, depositing the first in front of my father, then me, then my stepmother.

Father's hierarchy at its finest.

"I assume she'll be initiated soon." Father cuts into the roast with sharp precision, not bothering to glance up as he makes a statement he assumes only idiots would be confused by.

I spear a green bean with my fork. "I think I've convinced Ember to meet me tomorrow night."

"You *think*?"

"She'll do it." I raise my gaze to his. The overheard conversation between him and Malcolm hisses into my mind. "Unless you know of a reason she shouldn't?"

Father's gaze is flat as a crocodile's when he answers, "Not one."

I don't want her involved, Malcolm stated. These days, Malcolm's commands to Father mean little to nothing.

"Then it'll happen tomorrow night," I say between bites.

"You'll inform me if she passes or fails."

It's not a question. I make sure to dab my mouth with a napkin, prolonging his wait before I answer. "My goal is to have her fail."

Father's impassive expression cracks with the slightest tilt to his lips. "Good boy. I hear she's also attempting to be a candidate for the Marks Fellowship. I've studied her qualifications—she'll be difficult to deny, but I'm looking on the bright side. Having

Malcolm's daughter work for the Marks family could be just what I need to wholly pulverize him."

A fork screeches across a plate. Both Father and I stare at my stepmother. Her food has cooled and remains untouched, but she's dragged her fork across the porcelain rim, her knuckles white as she grips the silver utensil.

"Not feeling well, sweetheart?" Father angles his head with zero concern on his face.

"I don't like this," she whispers.

"I agree our supper isn't up to Stella's usual standards, but to be fair, it is still a five-star meal."

No one at this table believes my stepmother's talking about the food. Father patronizes her, pokes at her, and chips away at her soul in all the ways he can.

"Perhaps," he continues, "it's time for your nightcap."

"Yes. Yes, it is." She rises, her forearms trembling as she grips the table until Josh comes to assist her out of the room.

"That woman," Father murmurs into his drink, though I doubt she'd hear him with that medically clouded mind of hers, "is becoming less and less of a priority."

"Because you've broken her spirit, or destroyed her life?" I ask mildly.

Dishes and glasses rattle as his fist hits the table. His expression is one of barely contained rage. "Watch yourself in this house, boy."

I sit resolute. "I'm only asking since I'm about to embark on my own path of destruction. Though I'm wondering, do we want to destroy Ember Weatherby or use her?"

"Mm. That's yet to be decided. Let's see how strong she is first. She may buckle at the first challenge and cause this conversation to be entirely moot." Father leans back in his seat, bringing his tumbler with him and finishing the last of his bourbon in a single tip of the glass. "Consider this an initiation for yourself, as well. If you indeed want my position in the Society, you must prove it to the dukes and duchesses. This is your chance."

I tip my head to the side, feigning interest. "Is Malcolm part of my peer review?"

"Malcolm is no longer relevant when it comes to Societal decisions."

"He was your second-in-command for a while there." I set my silverware on my plate, having lost my appetite as soon as I wandered into this hellhole.

"Consider that a position you may now aim for." Father sets his empty tumbler down and rises. It seems none of us are particularly hungry tonight. Poor Stella. "You being my only son does not entitle you to that role, nor will you inherit my position, despite your legacy. You must prove it. To the dukes, duchesses, and to me."

"Yes, my king."

The bastard is so used to the title, he doesn't notice the sarcasm running through it.

"Good night, son." Father tosses his napkin onto the table, leaving me to receive dessert alone.

As soon as he's gone, I head to the bar trolley and peruse the crystal decanters, deciding to mix up my own nightly treat.

CHAPTER 15
EMBER

"*I warned you ... Stay away ...*"

I roll over, mashing one side of my face into the pillow and swatting at the voice.

The *voice*.

My eyes fly open, and I sit up, the duvet falling from my shoulders. A fast scan of the room has my attention whipping to the wall—*that* wall—where I swore I heard a click.

The duvet falls to the floor as I leap out of bed and scamper toward the source, but everything's gone flat. There's no seam, no lever, nothing to indicate it moved. And it's not raining tonight, leaving the floor around it as clean and polished as it was when I went to sleep.

"Dammit." I smack my palms against the wall as if that would get it to open.

Am I going insane? Or is it some ancestral part of my brain warning me away from this place? I'm thinking the walls have actual ears and someone's paying me visits when all that resides in this dusty manor is a lonely man. I doubt he spends his nights whispering cryptically to his teenaged ward while she slumbers.

Still wishing it was Thorne? my subconscious muses. I give it a figurative slap in the face in response, then stride into the bathroom for an actual splash of cold water.

The faucet spurts with water so frigid, I wouldn't be surprised if Malcolm has plumbing running through the cliffs. The icy spray makes me gasp, but it does as advertised and clears my head of those sticky, unwanted cobwebs in my head.

A check through the window showcases the creeping dawn, and I'm almost dreading the day as much as I fear those eerie visits at night. There's no way I'm falling back to sleep, so I use the extra hour to take a long, soothing shower. Once finished, I dress in my Winthorpe uniform and head downstairs, where Malcolm no doubt waits.

The route has become familiar, and I pass the foyer's portrait without a glance. The atrium is empty when I enter, but the circular table is fully set with a steaming bowl of oatmeal at my usual place setting as if the chef knew I was awake and striding through the manor.

Small bowls filled with fruit and nut toppings decorate the center. Unable to resist, I begin spooning them onto my oatmeal.

"I see manners aren't your forte," Malcolm observes as he strides into the room, a newspaper tucked under his arm.

"I wasn't going to eat it." The defense comes out before I can think better of it, and I clamp my mouth shut. *I don't have to make excuses to him.*

Without a comment, he takes his place at the table. Malcolm's dressed in a beige two-piece suit today, freshly shaven with combed-back hair. At first glance, he appears impeccable, but a closer inspection reveals the dark circles under his eyes and the tense lines around his mouth.

This is the point when I should ask about his work or try to figure out what's wrong, but I'm not the daughter he wants me to be. I just want to do my time and leave.

"Aiko's asked me to stay over tonight." I lower onto my seat, my breakfast overflowing with strawberries, honey, and toasted coconut flakes.

"On a school night?" When Dash places a similar bowl in front of Malcolm, he merely glances at it, then pours himself a cup of coffee from the carafe.

I stifle an eye roll at the fatherly concern. "It's to study. I was surprised by a pop quiz on the first day, and I don't want to be caught unawares like that again."

"I see." Malcolm stares at me over the rim of his mug. "Even though you rose to the top of the class with that test."

My spoonful freezes halfway to my mouth. "How do you know that?"

"Winthorpe is very involved with its students' parents. I'm notified every time you fail, as well as when you excel."

"Oh." My brows lower.

"I'm impressed how you surpassed your classmates."

"It was only the first day. And the first test." And the first time I beat Thorne. The thought makes me smile. I'd like to do it again. "If I want to maintain that ranking, I have to study harder, and Aiko's offered to help me understand how it's done around here. It's pretty cutthroat."

"That it is." A faraway look crosses Malcolm's expression before he schools it back to neutral. "This is Kai Natsumura's daughter."

It's not a question, but I nod anyway with a mouth full of oatmeal.

"I've crossed paths with him a few times. He's a polite, if rigid, man," Malcolm says.

Somewhat like yourself? I want to quip but keep my thoughts silent.

"I'm surprised he'd allow his daughter to entertain company on a school night."

"Uh, well, I think he's out of town." I have no idea where he is and can only hope Malcolm isn't one of those dads who likes to call the friend's parents to make sure his daughter's telling the truth.

My grip clenches around the fork. *His daughter.* I can't believe I thought that. Immediately, I amend it to, *his daughter who's been blackmailed to sit at this table.*

A scowl pulls at my lips. There. That feels better.

"Standard." Malcolm inhales deeply. "I suppose it's lonely for you in this big house. I'm glad you're making friends and think it's a great idea to get to know a girl who's in a similar position."

My scowl fades at the edges. Malcolm's being so understanding. Is he really *empathizing* with me? I've gained an inch of his trust by using Aiko, yet I'm deceiving him. Guilt tickles my shoulders. It's hard to believe I'm acting this way.

Where has the good girl from Boston gone?

"Thank you," I say before going back to my breakfast.

"You're very welcome. I hope I don't get a call from the school tomorrow saying you skipped classes."

I shake my head. "It won't happen."

Perfect attendance is part of the whole fellowship deal, save for emergencies, and I'd be a fool to screw it up. Except I'm not staying over at Aiko's—not initially. I'm meeting Thorne after school hours because I'm curious how a mysterious flower could get him second place in class, and he's threatening my standing with the fellowship.

I've always pursued knowledge and can't resist the clues Thorne's leaving behind. Uncovering the inconsistencies at Winthorpe is quickly becoming a pet project.

The only question is ... what will Thorne want in return?

"It'll be fine. I'm looking forward to it." I spoon the last of the oatmeal into my mouth, then push to my feet, waving farewell to Malcolm.

Famous last words.

CHAPTER 16

EMBER

I find Aiko hanging out on a stone bench in the courtyard garden with a textbook propped open on her thighs.

Her dark hair whips across her face in the wind as I approach. "Good read?"

Aiko peers up at me. "The best. I love some good biology before eight in the morning."

"Science and coffee. My favorite combo." I hand her one of two cups of steaming coffee I'm holding. "I had Dash stop at Raven's Buzz in town."

Aiko straightens and makes grabby hands for one of the cups. "Send Dash my love. This is amazing. Something about this coffee is so much better than what Winthorpe has to offer."

I take a seat next to her, sipping on my caramel latte. "Consider it a thank you for being my alibi tonight."

Aiko swallows her first gulp, wincing at the heat—or the coffee strength, since I like it strong—then says, "No problem. But you promised you'd explain in person."

I nod, staring out at the crowds and cliques of Winthorpe students laughing and pushing at each other, most heading inside due to the dip in temperature. It's cloudy today, a hovering fog obscuring most faces and salting the air more than usual.

"Thorne's asked me to meet him tonight."

Aiko chokes. Coughing, she says, "Excuse me—what?"

Her eyes are huge as she regards me. I try to shrug off her unease and respond, "I saw him in Lowell's class a few days ago, when we had that pop quiz, hand in his paper with nothing but a drawing of a flower. A rose."

In such chilly weather, Aiko's cheeks should be flushed, but I swear I see them turn white as porcelain. "You ... saw that? Are you sure? Maybe he was just scribbling out a wrong equation and decided to doodle over it because he was bored. He does that. They all do."

"I know what I saw. The rest of his quiz was blank."

Aiko stares straight ahead, both hands cupping her coffee. "And this is making you, what? Meet him alone? What about what happened after your first swim practice? Are you sure you want to do this? What if it's something worse?"

"Swim practice was a lesson for both them *and* me. I refuse to bow down or be afraid of that crew. In order to do that, I have to face them head-on and early. They've decided I'm some sort of smear on their missing friend and are dangling my chances at the fellowship like they can take it away. I have no choice."

"Small-town arm wrestling at its finest." Aiko holds her coffee up and cheers the air. "This place finds the tiniest reasons to justify their bullying, I swear."

"If I don't stand up to them, they'll make my year hell."

"They might just do that anyway." Aiko turns her face toward mine, studying closer. "But are you sure ...?"

I shrug, my shoulders so tense they go up to my ears. "I've been pulled out of the life I thought I knew and dumped into this rich, lavish lifestyle I can barely comprehend."

"I get that. But that doesn't change the fact Thorne and his cronies might hate you for taking over Savannah's life while she's ... somewhere. Or dead. Whether you meant to or not."

I acknowledge her point, but how can I properly explain to Aiko that looking into Winthorpe's shady dealings is much more preferable than pondering the blowing up of everything I thought I knew?

"Until I figure out how to beat Thorne, I have to do what he wants."

"I don't know, Ember. I wouldn't trust him with my favorite teddy bear, never mind my life after school."

"Which is why you're coming with me."

Aiko's coffee sloshes. "Huh?"

"Yep." I squeeze her arm, indicating that we should rise as the school bell rings. "I've decided you're coming with me to meet Thorne. He didn't say to come alone."

"Yeah, but—no."

My head swivels her way as we walk. "Why not?"

"I've gone about my time here threatening to bite anyone who comes near me, just how I like it. You're great, Ember, you really are, but the last thing I want is to draw Thorne's attention when I've managed to condition him into avoiding me for the rest of senior year."

I pull my lips in, mulling over her words. I'd never force a new friend into an uncomfortable situation, but... "How about if you hide somewhere and be my witness? Would you do that?"

Aiko slows her steps. "I'll consider it. But *only* because I want you to be safe while you do this stupid thing."

"It's not stupid. Okay," I amend after Aiko's long look, "It's kind of dumb, but it's the only thing I can think of to get him off my back. I can't be like you, but I *can* get more information to survive at this school."

"Fine. I'll watch from the shadows and intervene if I have to

—by calling on my cell for help."

"Aiko," I laugh, nudging her on the shoulder as we pass through Winthorpe's doors. "What is it you think he'll do? Try to kill me?"

Aiko hooks my elbow, halting us in the middle of the hallway while irritated students filter around. "You really don't know?"

"Know what?"

She continues in a low voice meant only for my ears, "Thorne was the last person to see Savannah before she disappeared. He was a suspect in her disappearance, and as far as I'm aware, he still is. His father buried all records and reports of his questioning, but Ember, I *mean* it when I say, be careful."

The warning bell rings, and Aiko releases me, backtracking to her first period. I have to tell my limbs to move, to get my feet to hurry, well before my brain catches up and I process Aiko's revelation.

A sudden image flashes through my mind: of Savannah, broken at the bottom of the cliffs with a black rose drawn on her forehead, so Thorne could get away with murder, too.

THE DAY GOES BY SLOWLY, thickened with my dread and anticipation at meeting Thorne later in the evening. But I *have* to know what that rose means. What a "legacy" has to do with Winthorpe, other than automatic entry into the school.

Would he tell me? Or is Aiko right, and this is just an excuse to hurt me without witnesses?

Except there is a witness now. Aiko will be in the wings, phone in hand. While I don't know her well, the concern etched into her face this morning has me trusting her enough to protect me tonight. Hopefully, we'll end the evening with an actual sleepover, and we can laugh over our drama because my meeting with Thorne would be just that—a meeting where we come to an understanding, I keep my eligibility for the fellowship, and we agree to co-exist this year without bothering the other.

No way will that be the ending, but I try to exude that kind of positive energy, if only to assuage Aiko's fears every time we cross paths today.

There's no swim practice on Wednesdays, so after sixth period, I stop off at the library, planning to get ahead in my subjects before grabbing dinner at the dining hall. It's usually reserved for boarding students, but open to all who stay after school. As the final bell rang, Aiko offered that I stay at her house until it was time, but I'm the worst at waiting and would probably send her anxiety through the roof if she watched me fidget, rattle around, and stare at the clock on my phone until I left. We agreed to meet by the little pond to the east of the academy instead.

I wiled away the hours completing assignments, studying for more potential quizzes, and preparing notes for midterms. Nerd alert, I know, but it keeps my eyes off the time, and it's a stark reminder that I'm not here to fuck around as much as Thorne enjoys fucking with my head. At seven, I collect my stuff and use the marked pathways to get back to the academy.

The sweet, barbecue scent of roasting meat hits me first, followed by notes of garlic and herbs, and I follow my nose through the school until I push through the carved wooden doors and into an alcove of multiple long benches and an open kitchen in the back. A buffet is set up in front of the chefs, grills spitting and pots clanging, and I take my place in the small line to start piling up my plate.

I wile away the wait by staring off and thinking of how to approach this evening, my body language relaxed, the empty plate hanging at my side. Strangers surround me, yet I feel more comfortable here than I do with Malcolm in his manor. There's no pressure for conversation or to be on time; students and teachers working late just want to eat and leave, a lot like me.

"Were you going to pour a Coke?" A student in front of me turns from the soda machine, holding a full cup. She's small, soft-spoken, and definitely a freshman. "I accidentally poured regular instead of diet."

"Oh. Sure." I accept it from her hand, balancing it on my tray.

After my plate's sufficiently weighed down, I find a spot in the corner, sit, and eat as much pulled pork as I can on a nervous stomach.

A prickle of unease skates along my cheek. I lift my head, scanning the dining hall. Maybe thirty students and five teachers are eating dinner, talking among themselves and ignoring me. But *someone* has eyes on me. I can feel it.

After another thorough scan, I find nothing, though, and resume eating.

Until a tray lands across from me. I snap back, my heart thundering as Thorne leans into my view and takes a seat.

"Evening, little pretty." Thorne's mouth flashes white. His friend who's always with him sits down beside him. "Want company?"

My gaze bounces back and forth between the two of them. "No."

"Too bad." Thorne picks up his fork and digs into his meal, keeping his flat-eyed stare on mine as he chews thoughtfully.

I bet he expects me to wither under his supreme focus. I don't. "Aren't you supposed to be growing scales in a body of water somewhere?"

Thorne swallows his bite. "Cute. I don't believe you've met Jaxon. Jax, this is our fresh meat."

Jaxon nods my way but is otherwise too focused on inhaling his food. His shaved head sparkles under the overhead lights. I guarantee they've just come from the pool, like always.

"She'll be joining us tonight," Thorne says with enough undertone to have Jaxon straightening from his crouch and eyeing me with interest.

"Right. Tonight," I emphasize. "As in, not now."

Thorne unleashes another heart-stopping smile, his pale gaze catching the moonlight streaming in from the windows. "I beg to differ."

Sitting back, I fold my arms, ensuring an impressive stiffness remains in my expression. "Nine o'clock. That was the deal."

"Timetable's been moved up, little pretty."

"I still have studying to do." Miraculously, I keep the panic from skittering across my face. Aiko won't be here yet. I'll be accompanying these two into the dark without any rein- forcements.

Mouth suddenly dry, I take a sip of my soda, feigning bore- dom. Thorne isn't somebody who's used to hearing no, and even though I plan on doing it anyway, I'd rather not defy him while coughing or stuttering. "I'm not just going to go off campus with you, a boy I barely know."

"On the contrary." Thorne doesn't miss a beat. His lids lower, a dark crescent of lashes shadowing those eerie blues. "We won't be moving off campus, and I'm not taking you anywhere alone." He gestures to Jaxon.

"I trust Jaxon about as much as I trust that you're not up to something."

Thorne laughs softly, tipping his drink to his lips while eyeing me over the rim with that infuriating, lazy bedroom-sex look. "We're also meeting a group of people by the cliffs. Class- mates. About twenty of them. You're walking into the open air, Ember, not a lion's den."

Says you. Lions hunt in prairies, I think but cover my retort with another sip.

"Consider it a party." For the first time, Jaxon pipes up, and

I'm surprised to hear an accent there. South African, maybe. "There's an old lighthouse the girls decorate, and we kick off the start of the year. It's private, exclusive, and fun. Rarely do we invite a newbie, but my buddy here insists."

Jaxon's eyes twinkle, his dark orbs reflecting the sconces on the wall behind me. They turn into twin flames, belying his friendly, easygoing tone.

Throughout the exchange, all Thorne does is watch.

"Like I said, nine … nina…" Frowning, I stick out my tongue. It feels too swollen for my mouth. "Niiiiine … oh … cluck."

"Trouble, little pretty?" Thorne inclines his head.

His movement blurs in and out of focus. I blink hard. *"Whudyudotame?"*

After peering over his shoulder, Thorne pushes to his feet, motioning for Jaxon to do the same. "Nothing you won't be able to recover from. Just relax. There you go. Relax, little Weatherby …"

Spots frame Thorne's movement toward me. My scream curdles in my throat, so I use my arms instead. I swat at his approach and kick out at Jaxon coming in from the other side, but they bat away my attempts with little effort.

"Not feeling well? Don't worry, we got you." Thorne's voice tunnels into my ear. As he lifts me in his arms, I hear Jaxon calling across the dining hall that I'm fine, just dizzy, and Thorne will carry me to the nurse.

"N-no … lemme … lemme *go*." My demand comes out as a clogged whisper, and my eyelids grow heavy as I try to see in the dark.

"Pro tip," Thorne says into my ear. "Never accept a drink from a Winthorpe female freshman. They love me."

It's the last thing I hear before his hold tightens around me, and I tilt into the abyss.

CHAPTER 17
EMBER

Thick, brine-soaked air coats my lips. I lick them, tasting enough salt to turn my stomach, and I roll over onto my side, dry heaving until the taste leaves my tongue.

"She's awake."

"No shit."

I don't recognize the first voice, but I *absolutely* pinpoint the second. "You *drugged* me, asshole."

My growl kicks off another fit of coughs, and I move to get on all fours for relief, but I'm stuck.

"I'm afraid you're caught in that position for a while yet," Thorne says from somewhere above. "Why don't you open your eyes, Ember, and adjust to your surroundings."

"How...?" I scrunch my eyes *shut* because every time I try to open them all the way, it hurts. Like blinking through dry sand. *Water. I need water.* "How long have I been unconscious?"

"An hour or so." He says it like he's talking about the weather. Like Thorne didn't just spike my drink like a spoiled asshole rich boy and try to ... try to ...

Oh, god.

I force my eyes to open despite the pain. Am I clothed? Is there blood between my legs? Did he ...?

"Relax." Absurdly, his voice comes out soothing. "You're in your school blouse, skirt, and underwear. We took your blazer, shoes, and socks. And didn't touch anything else."

Breathing heavily through my nose, I try to yank my arms forward. Wet grit coats one side of my face, a trickle of water playing against my lips. I'm lying on my side, but it's so dark, I'm having trouble seeing even with my eyes open.

A giggle sounds out nearby, echoing through and around my ears, fucking up my internal compass. I jerk this way and that, trying to track it. "You're rather tied up at the moment. It's better to stop fighting."

Aurora?

"Untie me." My back arches for a fight, but a burning fire where my wrists are bound behind my back and around my ankles stops me. Some sort of rope.

"Not yet." Thorne again, his deep voice thriving in such a black-veiled place. "Light your torches."

The *snick* of matches tickles my hearing, and I squint as, one by one, the torches light up into an arc around my body. Hands gripping the handles come into view, then the lower half of their faces. The top halves stay obscured by ... hoods?

Yes. Heavy, flowing hoods—some white, some black—are attached to cloaks that obscure the bodies beneath.

"What ... what is this?" I whisper, struggling to sit. "Another bullshit prank? In a—" The little fires let me see more of the rocky, dank space, stifling now that I see it ends near their backs, and my own is nearly flush against a sharp, granite wall... "—in a *cave?*"

"Gosh, she's *so* smart." A cackle follows, cloaks fluttering with shaking shoulders.

"Get me out of here." I jut out my chin. "This is so fucked up.

You drug me, tie me up, then trap me in a cave. What's the matter with you people?"

"Is she really meant to be one of us?" someone mutters. Probably the girl who offered me a spiked Coke. What ever happened to a sisterhood? "Because she has no goddamn clue."

"*Enough.*" Thorne's voice snakes out, startling the rest into submission.

I follow the source, finding him in the middle, wearing a black cloak and an arrogant smile. "Ember Weatherby, as the only living legacy to Malcolm James Robert Weatherby, you have the privilege of being initiated into the Virtues."

"The what?" Wetness slicks my wrists, followed by a coppery tang hitting the air. I'm bleeding from my struggles.

"Those of us in black call ourselves the Nobles." Thorne sweeps his arm to encompass the group. "And the Virtues, our girls, are in white. We communicate in roses, dominate in pushing our bodies to their limits, and excel at academics. We are the privileged, the rulers, the influencers, the *takers.* The havoc we wreak lives long after our time at Winthorpe is complete, and if we continue to abide by our Society's rules, we will live the rest of our lives lavishly, every dream realized and all enemies turned to ash in our wake. Our invitations are few and given only to those deserving of such a future. Do you wish to pledge to the Noble and Virtue Societies?"

"Uh ..." The singular flames flicker against the ten or so faces, all regarding me like a fish just flapped on shore. "No."

Hoods jerk with surprised whispers to their neighbors, some torches tilting precariously.

All but Thorne. He tips his chin until the sheen of his eyes comes through the shadows of his hood. "I suppose that's my fault. I haven't adequately described to you the consequences if you *don't* accept." His chest rises and falls with a sigh, the fire of his torch dancing with his breath. "You're here because Malcolm plucked you out of obscurity after discovering you existed. He gave you every privilege by enrolling you at Winthorpe, provided you with a mansion, has you fattening up with professional chefs, and oiled you with the latest, most expensive designer products." Thorne pauses. "Do you think that doesn't come with a price? He may think he can protect you from his heritage, but tonight proves he cannot. Just as your denial to enter into the Societies proves how utterly unqualified you are for the Marks Fellowship."

I inhale through clenched teeth and pull at my bindings. All self-defense instruction flies out of my head as my pounding heart takes over. "I'm pretty sure it's a rigged system, anyway." My eyes dart through the crowd, searching for Aurora. "Is this how you'll get it?" I ask her, though I can't find her through the cloaks. "By literally tying me up and preventing me from competing with you?"

"While addressing the Society, you talk to *me*." Thorne's voice cracks out, practically fracturing the stones of the cave. "Not her. If you want answers, ask the prince of the Nobles."

The prince of the...? Dear god, these rich pricks are more prickish than I ever could've believed. But I set my jaw and ask, "Is this how Savannah felt?"

The resulting hush is so sudden, its thickness envelops the cavern.

"Huh?" I prompt. "Did she have to go through this to be a part of your cool kids club, or is this how she went missing? Did you trap her in a cave, waiting for the ocean to obliterate the evidence—"

"Shut the *fuck* up." Thorne shoves his torch in my face. So close, I wince away from the flames searing my eyebrows. "You have no idea what kind of shit you're starting with that talk. Sav was one of us, but we would never hurt her. *I* would never hurt her."

My mind latches on to his nickname for her—*Sav*—so familiar it rolled off his tongue different from the rest of his sentence. Softer. Sweeter.

There's a nudge at the base of my brain, a poke of jealousy that I work to stifle while being chained and cornered by this guy. I shouldn't feel twinges for him right now. I shouldn't feel *anything* but the consuming desire to escape.

He's a suspect in her disappearance.

"If I say yes," I murmur between the small fingers of flames, "will you let me go?"

Thorne's lips curve, his cold warning dissolving at my small question. "Certainly. After you complete your initiation, I'll personally untie you and see you home."

I weigh my options. The whole point of capitulating to Malcolm's demands was to have a chance at my dream—to be the daughter my parents always wanted and make something of myself. To use my affinity for coding and numbers to enter the technology field and become one of the few female software developers in the country. It's a competitive landscape even with every qualification. Cutthroat and tiresome, a constant test of will. The Marks Fellowship was meant to ease that barrier to entry and get me the resumé to top all others—as an intern at the number one technological empire in the United States. If I don't have that, my dream could still be possible, but it might take years of sweat, tears, taunts, and rejections. And I may never end up proving myself while fighting it out in the trenches where so many others want it, too.

I don't know if I could handle any more heartache.

Yet here Thorne is, swinging this once-in-a-lifetime opportunity like it's his to dole out, and perhaps it is. Maybe getting what I want means having to make him believe I'm under his control. If I do what he wants, I can give him enough power to choke on.

I wonder if Savannah wanted the Marks Fellowship, too. It's clear what Aurora is willing to do to get it. Would she allow herself to be tied up? Would she say *yes* to Thorne's every bidding?

Am *I*?

"Fine," I breathe out.

Thorne's lips curve in triumph. He steps back into the fold. "The pledge has agreed to her initiation."

"Fan-fucking-tastic." Aurora separates from the line of cloaks, glimmering with white and gold. "I suggest she—"

"Stand down, Aurora. I'm taking charge of her."

Aurora starts at Thorne's demand. "It's always the princess of the Virtues who gets to initiate fledglings. What gives you the right?"

"Because I have founder blood running through my veins, unlike yourself, and I've been given express orders from the king to take control of the Weatherby initiation. Are you questioning it? *Again*?"

No high school senior should have such authority in their tone, yet Thorne wields it as if he were born with a deep, raspy husk that sends shivers down lessers' bones. Including my own.

Aurora responds with a whine, but my focus switches to the water sloshing at their feet, soaking the cloaks' hems. The waves trickling into the cave have become audible and lap against my bare feet.

An uneasy nausea coats my stomach.

"Can we decide on who gets to initiate me outside of the cave?" I ask through the bickering. "Even better, can I be untied now?"

Aurora's head snaps in my direction. "Dumb bitch, you're not going anywhere."

"But *you* are."

Thorne's warning ricochets through the small cave before

being absorbed by the cloaks. Thorne continues, "Everyone who's not me or the pledge, leave before the water gets too high."

I knew it. High tide is coming.

"You sure, bro?" A cloak neighboring Thorne, who has to be Jaxon, clasps Thorne on the shoulder. "I could stay, make sure everything ..."

"It'll be fine. Make sure Aurora exits the cave with you. Count heads when you get to the top."

"Your rules, boss." Jaxon, still hooded, beckons to the rest of the group while he navigates to the mouth of the cave. They follow him without question.

Who's all in there? Why aren't any of you concerned for the girl in bindings? I hope my question is written all over my face as they pass, and that I wrack them with guilt tonight because of it.

Wishful thinking on my part. I doubt they care. It's like they'd rather I drown than defy Thorne. *What kind of punishment could he inflict that's worse than drowning?*

Thorne stays, stiff-backed and unmoving, in the middle of the cave, his recruits, or cult followers, or whatever they are, filtering around his unnervingly still form.

Footsteps slide and crunch against sand and rocks until nothing but the white-noise rush of waves remains.

And a single flame illuminates us.

"Are you ready?" he asks, his smile stretching past the fire.

CHAPTER 18

THORNE

"For what? What do you have planned for me?" Ember retorts. Her voice is ravaged, though she hasn't unleashed one scream.

The ocean's freezing waters inch closer, its foaming edges washing over my shoes before being dragged away, then coming back stronger.

Ember's disheveled and tangled form curls up on a crescent of sand on the cave's floor, the force of the waves starting to push at her body and forcing her to brace.

In a blink, she turns into Savannah, stripped, bruised, and rabid as she claws at the sand to get away. I blink again, and she's gone, replaced by a confused and wary Ember.

Fuck. I can't take much more of this.

"The tide's coming in," Ember says, her eyes not on me but at the mouth of the cave. Her profile glows orange in the single torch's light. "Fast. Do you really plan on drowning me?"

"Not if you can make it out."

Her eyes snap back to mine. "What's that supposed to mean?"

The bottomless darkness of her irises simply gleams in the flames. Her ash-blond hair is a mess, tangled on one side and hanging in damp, sandy clumps, but fuck if she doesn't look like a mermaid washed up on my shores.

I hadn't allowed anyone to touch her when the drug took hold and she slumped over in the dining hall. She was mine— even unconscious, she was *mine*. Not because she resembles Savannah, though that's uncontested, but because in such a vulnerable state, I didn't want anyone close to her. I couldn't save Savannah, but I could protect this one.

Ember's slim body fit against mine perfectly but ran so much hotter, her sweet strawberry scent made stronger with her pulsing panic before she succumbed. I carried her across campus to the lighthouse as promised, then laid her down gently while I peeled off her jacket, knee socks, and shoes. I'd caressed her calf —couldn't resist—those delicate ankles coming close enough to my mouth to dart out my tongue and taste. But I stayed in control, requesting that Jaxon get the rope, and watched my little pretty sleep until everyone else arrived.

I carried her down the perilous hidden staircase carved into the side of Winthorpe's highest cliff before we hit the shores and the caves below. One can't see the way down from any true angle, not with a helicopter or a drone, but instead must go by feel and experience. Considering I've been indoctrinated into the Nobles for well over ten years, I could take these rock-strewn stairs in my sleep.

Ember was pliable in my grip. Docile. It's a great memory to reflect on as she tries to melt me with her mind alone, staring up from the ground, frightened yet furious.

"If you're so concerned about getting splashed," I say, "then go ahead and stand up."

Her attention strays to her feet, where her ankles are knotted together with rope.

"This is a test of communication." I cross my arms, the heavy, outdated robe crimping at my inner elbows. "Will you work with me to stay, or against me to escape? Remember the three traits I mentioned. Communication, domination, and superiority. If you can't handle a bit of salt water, how will you handle the demands of Winthorpe? Or the Marks—"

"Your manipulation tactic is getting tiring." Ember sits up straighter, bending her knees and flashing a slip of white cotton underwear. My gaze drops at the same time my balls tighten. But I raise my eyes almost as fast as they fell, schooling my expression flat and pretending this girl has no effect on me.

"Is it? From my vantage point, you're still a victim of my whims."

Ember hisses out a curse, and I smile. She wriggles her ass against the hard sand, finding her balance and pushing up on her fists tied behind her. After a few shoves in that position, she manages to stand, wobbling on unsteady, bound feet.

"Look at that. My mermaid's learning to walk."

"Fuck you," she spits, damp strands of hair flying in front of her eyes. It only makes my grin stretch wider. "What now, huh? Am I supposed to bunny hop out of here?"

Oh, but I love her fire. Mostly because it'll be so sweet when I staunch it out permanently. "Now, we wait."

Ember's chin trembles as she looks down at the water as it hits our ankles. "For what?"

"For the ocean to try to claim us."

Her shoulders jerk back. "Are you *insane*? You can swim out of here. I can't! Untie me, Thorne. This has been super fun, but don't play with my life like this. *Free* me."

"You keep saying that like I'm actually going to do it."

Her chest heaves with haggard breaths, her blouse long ago made translucent, the white of her bra glaring through like twin beacons guiding me to shore. Her nipples have turned into pebbles. She's freezing, and I should offer her my cloak, but my father's talk with Malcolm ripples into my mind.

Keep her in the dark, they said.

I idle closer, drawn in by the golden sparkle on her skin left behind by the illuminating flames and granules of sand. She shudders with panicked breaths. *Such a trapped, beautiful creature.* It weakens me enough to say, "If you can withstand this, you can withstand anything."

"Communication doesn't lie in surviving high tide. It lies in dealing with your stupid *shit* and Aurora's pointless mocking and this school's ridiculous lack of supervision when it comes to night security."

Her plump lips are reddened by the cold. I stare at them as she hisses and spits while I draw closer.

"We rule the school, not the faculty or the tenured teachers, little pretty. We become the alumni, the donators, the benefactors of all Winthorpe holds dear: Money. That's what you want, too, isn't it? A high-ranking career, female empowerment, shit like that?" I step up until we're toe-to-toe, cocking my head as she raises her chin and meets me, eye to eye.

The water hits our knees. She has more trouble staying upright with the pushing tide. I tuck my free hand behind my back, watching her struggle.

"Isn't that why you jumped at the chance to become the sole Weatherby heir?"

"You don't know *anything* about me," she rasps. Her cheeks flush red, and I have the sudden urge to dig my fingers into her tangled hair and pull her head back until I have full access to her mouth.

My cock twitches, the icy water doing little to stop my throbbing need for her.

"I'd ask you to elaborate, but I don't think we have the time," I muse, glancing down at the black water at our thighs. Our feet have disappeared. With the small light we have, only broken ripples of our reflections bounce back at us.

"Thorne ..." This time, my name comes out as a tremulous whisper. "Please. Whatever this is, I want no part in it."

My heart thunders in my ears, her proximity almost too lethal to survive. It's like her fear is tangible, vibrating against my chest. My sodden cloak grows as heavy with watery hands, and I imagine them as *her* hands, toying with my legs, stroking up my thighs, saltwater swirling.

I have to touch her.

I move until our chests hit, hers soft and mine hard. She gasps, terror sparking in her eyes, but she holds steady. Reaching around her, I dip my chin near her nape, her pulse a flutter of a dying butterfly that calls to my mouth. I lay my lips at that spot against her skin, and I feel her shiver, goose bumps forming, her pulse skittering against my tongue.

My smile bares my teeth, pressing against her skin. She buckles, sighs, maybe tries to think of a proper insult, but can't seem to speak.

Inhaling deeply, nestling into the warmth of her damp skin, I find her bound wrists, and with a flick of my fingers, I untie her.

She jolts against my body, her hands flying forward. She starts to bend to untie her feet—

I hook her under her jaw, forcing her eyes on mine. "Not until I say so."

She struggles in my hold, but with tied-up feet, she can't do much but scratch at my forearm. "Let me *go!*"

The water is at our stomachs now. I should be numb from the waist down, but I'm all fire, the torch I'm holding resembling a spurt of what burns in my veins. "You liked what I did just then. Kissed you. Licked you. *Bit* you." I brush my nose against hers, which she tries to bite.

Still holding her at the neck, I jerk back just in time with a smile. "Yes. You liked it *very* much."

"Unless you want to kill us both, you can't hold me here forever."

"I don't plan to. Not here, anyway. Here, I'm giving you an offer."

Her eyes go wide with disbelief. I'm not cutting off her airway, so she inhales and cries, "What the *hell* could you offer me right now, other than my escape?"

"The best orgasm of your life."

That shuts her up for a few seconds, at least. "What the —*what*? You're a psycho. A bona fide sociopath."

This goes against every command, every order, but dammit, she's so close, so impassioned and fluttering against her cage like a rare bird. I need to have her.

"You want me," I say simply. "If I touched you between the legs right now, you'd be wet, all for me."

"I'm wet because of the ocean creeping up on our bodies, you son of a—"

"Are you? Should I check?"

Ember tries to pull out of my hold, but of course, my thumb and index finger stay around her neck like a helpful, balancing vise that prevents her from toppling over.

"If I let you go right this moment, you'll fall underwater, and there's no guarantee you'll get back up."

"You'd watch me struggle?"

"I would, but I'd prefer to watch you come."

She stiffens. Flabbergasted, horrified ... but her lashes lower in intrigue.

Ah. I wasn't imagining her shivers for me, then.

"Have you ever played with death and pleasure?" I ask quietly. "Bringing yourself to the brink of both? I promise, once you do it, you'll never want vanilla again."

"You ... you—"

"Touch yourself, little pretty."

Cold water sloshes against our elbows, our entire lower halves submerged. She's steady in my grip, her jaw tilted up by my hand, and I feel her muscles working in thought.

I lay the torch on a jutting piece of rock just above our heads, spotlighting her face like we're in a theater, and pop the button at my collar, shedding my cloak.

Let the ocean take it. I'm ready to claim *her*.

"Do it, Ember," I murmur close to her lips. "It's not like I can see through the black water. You can have your privacy."

"Is this a joke?" But she searches my eyes for honesty.

"No." I stifle the moan that crawls up my throat as I dip my hand underwater to undo the top button of my pants and palm my hard, aching dick. I start to stroke, picturing her hands, imagining her mouth instead of the ocean jerking me off. "See? I'm doing it right now."

She pauses at the grit in my voice, her head angling in my grip as if in intrigue. Then her eyes turn as black as the night water surrounding us.

"Are you doing it?" I ask softly.

She starts swaying against my palm on her neck, her eyes never leaving mine, but her lips part with a gasp. "Yes."

Though my body ignites with that fucking image, her perfect, slim fingers dipping into her folds, I calmly state, "Good girl."

My strokes turn faster, the water near our necks now, both our heads tilting up to maintain our breaths. She floats in my hold, my hand never leaving her throat, but her feet must've left the ground quite some time ago.

"Oh my ... oh my god," she whispers, her exhales growing harsher. Her knees smack into my thighs as she spreads hers. For better access, I'm guessing, and I nearly spill my load at the thought of her exposed in front of me, open for my dick.

"Are you there yet?" I rasp out the question, my strokes fast and hard, our foreheads almost hitting the cave ceiling as the water flows inside, taking the cave as part of its murky, midnight depths.

"Thorne, I-I'm scared. I'm scared, but I—oh, fuck. I ... I—"

Her voice echoes in the small space of cave we have left, but I don't rush her to finish. A part of the ecstasy is flirting with danger—I wasn't lying about that. Instead, I tell her to wait. Wait for our mouths to be underwater. Wait for that last breath.

Save it for the ultimate pleasure.

Saltwater hits my lips, its presence tickling under my nose.

And just before the water covers our heads ... "Now exhale."

Incredibly, she listens. Ember must be so immersed in the throes of her pleasure, her better sense has taken off. My upper lip curls in the submerged silence as I pump, then hold, my balls bursting with need, then pump again, hold.

On a grunt of an exhale, I sink, my body spasming with an underwater orgasm that holds me rigid until it's damn ready to let me go.

Releasing Ember's throat, I cup her ass instead, bringing her core to mine, giving her soft skin the last of my come as she thrashes with her own orgasm.

Her hands grip my shoulders. A clogged cry bubbles against my ear. She humps me underwater, grinding against my still-hard shaft, flat against my stomach, to extend her breathless pleasure.

My heart lurches in warning. My chest starts to ache. It becomes force over instinct as I hold my mouth closed so as not to inhale water, but we're at the brink.

Ember goes slack in my grip.

We're blind. The torch was snuffed out however many

minutes ago, but I dig into my pocket, find my phone, and hit the flashlight setting.

Grabbing her hand, I swim us out of the mouth of the cave. My lungs and burning limbs are used to this kind of deprivation, my relentless laps in the pool doing their job by keeping me alive.

Once out, my head breaks the surface first. Ember's comes next, coughing and spluttering, her hair slicked back like a seal.

I duck back underwater and find the rope at her ankles, loosening the knot with another flick of my hand, then swim to the surface again.

"This way." I maintain a firm grip on her hand and swim us to the hidden steps illuminated by a spill of firelight Jaxon left there. We drag ourselves out of the water, our clothes clinging to our bodies. Ember falls against my side, gasping for breath, her legs unable to hold her up.

I take some of her weight, and when she's fully settled, I lift Jaxon's torch and navigate us to the top of the cliff, her shivers becoming mine. "Congratulations. You passed your first initiation."

"F-f-first?" Her teeth chatter with the question. "That sh-should've been all three combined."

The old lighthouse flashes on once we reach the grassy hill, and Society members begin to filter out. Jaxon takes the lead, carrying towels, and a newer initiate behind him holds two steaming mugs. Though I'm trembling as much as Ember, from both the temperature and what we did, I hold myself upright as if this task was the easiest thing in the world and pleasuring myself in front of her was always in the plan.

"She passed?" Jaxon asks as he approaches us, cloak on, but his hood is flipped back. He throws a towel over Ember, then hands one to me.

"With flying colors."

Ember glances at me, her look assessing as though she's wondering if I'm about to trumpet what we did—the sick thing I *made* her do—but all I offer her in response is a closed-mouth, promising smile.

More members gather around us, some applauding, others muttering and questioning, but I draw Ember in close one more time, making sure the shell of her ear is against my lips when I whisper, "Your penchant for choking off is our dirty secret, little pretty."

CHAPTER 19
EMBER

My heart rattles like a small bird trapped in a gilded cage for the next few weeks, slamming against those bone-hard bars every time I sit through class with Thorne, and every morning when I rise, wondering if this is the day my next trial into the Virtues will begin.

Sitting down with Malcolm at breakfast and dinner has become more difficult. Each time I do, I don't utter a word of what went down the night I was supposed to stay over at Aiko's. It's not because I'm bending to Thorne's demands to keep that night a secret. It's more because honesty and open-mindedness are not what defines Malcolm's and my relationship. He'd commanded I stay far away from Thorne, legacies, Societies, and look what I've done instead. I've willingly taken their first test, consciously stripped myself of mental barriers, and discovered a hidden part of myself I didn't know existed.

When Malcolm stares at me strangely over a plate of eggs three weeks later, I burn the thought of choking while rubbing all over Thorne's soaked body from my memories. I was only doing it to get out of there. To pretend obedience so he'd fucking swim us *out*.

Yeah, that's what I tell myself.

That isn't me. It *can't* be. I've never had sex before, but I have fooled around, and that kind of foreplay has never been in my fantasies, never mind a realistic maneuver in my repertoire. Cutting off air supply the instant my body heats and stiffens with pleasure somehow amplified the ecstasy to the point I grabbed the closest thing underwater—Thorne.

Not to save me. I held on to him to prolong the pleasure, my throat closing off and burning for air the instant my core flashed fire through my veins. Two vastly different flames battled for release. One white-hot, the other red as Hell.

My cheeks heat at the same time my fork scrapes across the plate, drawing Malcolm's attention again. "Everything okay?"

"Sure. Fine." I swallow the clump of eggs that can't seem to pass the embarrassed swell of my throat.

"If this is your way of ... look, I'm sorry I haven't been here on the weekends. Business overseas is picking up in a way that forces me to be present. Sending a lesser employee would only insult the investors my company aims for."

"No, I get it." Giving up on breakfast, I sit back and reach for my lukewarm coffee instead. "I've been spending most of my weekends getting ahead in class. It's worked out for both of us."

Malcolm's lips thin. "While I'll never begrudge your drive for success, I wish you'd reach for an achievement other than that scholarship."

"Fellowship," I correct. "And it'll change my parents' and my lives."

It slips out before I can catch myself. I didn't mean for it to land between Malcolm and me that way, yet the ceramic mug almost cracks under Malcolm's grip.

"Your life has already transformed extensively," Malcolm

says, storm clouds darkening his eyes. "You'll never want for anything, so I'm failing to understand why you continue to pursue this goal."

I set my mug down. It hits the rim of my plate, but I pretend the sound doesn't clang against my ears. "Because it's mine to win."

"You're a Weatherby. From now on, you'll always win."

"Like you?" I twist to face him fully. "In this empty manor with cobwebs in every corner? With no one around, ever? You may have the money and possibly the power in your company, but personally? Personally, I don't think you've won anything."

One corner of Malcolm's mouth tics, his only sign of hurt, and my stomach lurches at the sight. I'm taking out my frustration with Thorne, the Societies, and *my* actions on him. I'm ashamed, and Malcolm doesn't even know it.

Then Malcolm extracts all the guilt from my body by taking a sip of his coffee, dabbing the corner of his mouth with a linen napkin, then murmuring, "I won you, didn't I?"

My chair topples backward with the force of my stand. "I'm not your prized horse. I'm a *person* whose life you stole by crashing into my childhood home and roaring that none of it was real. You couldn't do it gently, could you? You were so absorbed in the insult that somebody defied you, deceived you for years, that you never considered the *adult* daughter at the other end."

"Adult," Malcolm scoffs. "You're still a child."

"Is that what you thought when you were eighteen?"

He visibly pales. "I wish I did. My life would've turned out for the better had I realized I still had many more years to grow."

"I'm not you. I'm a good person. Student. *Daughter.*" My voice wobbles, a vivid reminder of who I'm trying to convince of my innocence. Me or him?

Malcolm tilts his head to regard me from above, but he doesn't rise. "That's how you perceive me? A bad man?"

"You eviscerated my parents in front of my eyes. Demanded I come with you or they'd go to jail and live the rest of their lives behind bars. Prohibited me from speaking to them for the entirety of my stay here. How do you *think* you came across?"

Malcolm's hands clench against the tablecloth, wrinkling the pristine ivory fabric. "You were stolen from me, my *blood*, and they—those 'parents' of yours—knew it. I may not have given myself time to properly think about my approach, but *goddammit, Ember*, I didn't know I had a child!"

His voice crests to a rise as he stands, pulling the tablecloth with him and sending the dishes shattering, the sterling silver clattering against the marble tiles of the atrium. I startle, but I can't back down. "You're angry and hurt, which I understand. But you didn't give me the courtesy to be angry and hurt as well. There's another half to this story, Malcolm. And you've refused to see it—to acknowledge *my* devastation."

"I never got to name you," he says hoarsely. "Was never able to hold you."

For a moment, our heavy breaths intermingle in the air.

I break the silence. "Yet you keep me here in this empty house like a porcelain doll, part of your collection. We have these formal dinners and breakfasts where neither of us talks much, and then you disappear. You don't support my academic goals and refuse to tell me why. You prohibit me from doing things rather than encourage me to do *anything*. You won't tell me about my birth mother, only that she's long dead. How is this getting to know me? How is it making me a part of your life?"

Malcolm's expression shutters. "I am doing this the best way I know how. You may not understand, but protecting you is my ultimate goal."

It's the wrong thing to say. Here, he could've explained, told me more about himself, his relationship with my birth mother, or the reason for refusing to support my run for the Marks

Fellowship. He could've talked about the rivalry between him and Damion Briar or told me why the Weatherbys have no business mingling with the family across the street.

He could've made a step toward having me trust him. Then maybe I would've confessed my own wrongs.

Yet Malcolm does none of those things.

I say quietly, "You were a victim in this, too, and I'm sorry. I'm sorry you missed the eighteen years I had with Barbara and Gene Beckett. But you must understand, with the way you yanked me out of my life, you've stolen me from them the same way my parents took me from you."

He doesn't argue as I turn and storm through the atrium into the too-wide hallway where my footsteps echo and my heartbeat throbs in my ears.

CHAPTER 20
EMBER

"Wait, is this another situation where you allegedly come to my house yet are secretly meeting with Thorne and giving me the type of panic attack where I pass out under a tree while waiting for a text from you that never comes?" Aiko finally finishes and takes a deep breath.

I manage a smile while closing my biology textbook, and Aiko waits beside my desk. "It's for real this time. I could use a place to stay tonight."

The argument with Malcolm juts into my mind, and I shove my text into my bag harder than necessary. Both of us said harsh things. It's hard to believe he let me walk away without consequence, considering his penchant for control. I hit him harder than he expected, my issues taking shape in my mouth with more emotion than I wanted. I've been adrift these past weeks, confused by pleasure and pain. I can't separate the two as easily anymore, even when I think about the past and my parents versus him. My life now versus then ... and Thorne versus all the other boys I've come across.

"Ember? Hellooooo." Aiko waves a hand in front of my face.

"Yeah, so could I stay over tonight?" I ask as if I hadn't just spaced out in front of her.

She shrugs, hitching her bag higher on her shoulder. "Sure. Dad's out of town, so it'll be just the two of us."

"That's cool." It'd be fun to get to know Aiko better, outside of texting and the academy walls. She's sweet in nature with a fierce loyalty I sensed the night of high tide when I rolled up in front of her, soaking wet and off-balance. She'd caught me under the arms and screamed into the night, "Thorne Briar, you have *a lot* to answer for, you slimy coward!"

"What'd he do to you?" she then whispered into my neck as she attempted to hold me, a girl almost twice her size. "Do you need to go to the hospital?"

"No ... nothing. Init ... initiation," I think I'd muttered, but my tongue felt dry and cracked, my head cloudy with images of scraping my nails down Thorne's unbuttoned shirt as we floated down ...

"Fucking hazing," she'd muttered, then dragged me to her car where she let me sleep it off until I was decent enough to enter Winthorpe's rec center showers and pretend I hadn't been drowning in the ocean mere hours ago. They'd wanted me to stay for the party, this cloaked club, but all I asked to do was leave. Thorne carried me over the hill, likely spotting Aiko's idling car, then released me into the night with a quiet promise. "See you soon, little pretty."

I drifted in and out of sleep in Aiko's back seat. Every time I opened my eyes, Aiko was in the driver's seat, staring out the windows with her mouth in a grim line as if she were keeping watch. What she was looking out for, I didn't dare ask. These students at Winthorpe are way more attuned to manipulative tactics than I gave them credit for. Aiko could be one of them, but at that moment, I was too busy fighting off dreams where Thorne slammed me against the cave walls, spread my legs, and took me with ferocious, rough possession. Sometimes I wanted it; other times, I screamed for him to stop.

To say I tossed and turned is an understatement.

Even then, Aiko had the wherewithal not to drop me off at home—another mark in her favor—because Malcolm would've had a ton of questions and demands for both of us. Dash would've *for sure* roused him as soon as a damp and rumpled Ember showed up.

She later admitted she was also terrified of her father's ire in addition to Malcolm's, and if he ever found out about the Winthorpe hijinks and her participation, even if peripheral, he'd send her to the same boot camp he sends all his recruits. I get the sense he's an Army man I do *not* want to tangle with.

Going to her house and playing at a Friday night sleepover seems innocent enough not to raise his or Malcolm's suspicions of what I went through. The most Malcolm will get is a curt text stating where I am so he doesn't send the Raven's Bluff police after me.

Aiko and I stride into the hallway on our way to our next class. I haven't mentioned what the initiation was for or the names "Nobles" or "Virtues." Aiko called it *hazing* as if she knows the Winthorpe elite enjoy recruiting potential candidates into their popular crew but not much else. I figure tonight could be used to question her further and see if she knows more details.

I don't want to get her in trouble. Thorne's warning is at the forefront of my mind—to keep the Societies a secret or face the consequences. Considering Aiko's so open, I can pry without being obvious or involving her further. Her unyielding watchfulness that fateful night also battles for my time and attention.

I'm determined to figure *something* out before my next trial. The thought of Aiko or any other pledge doing what I did with Thorne makes me want to scratch out their eyeballs and know every part of him they touched, so I can rebrand his skin with my tongue. At the same time, I want to shroud and protect Aiko from all of it—to keep every innocent girl away from the Society and *him* if they want to preserve their soul.

It's a defensive dichotomy that has my conscience squirming against my skull.

"This is you," Aiko says as we slow in front of Lowell's classroom.

"Yep." My stomach plunges into the depths of my core. However many days later, and I still dread sitting next to him or being close to him. Neither he nor Aurora has given any indication of what's coming next. In fact, they've been suspiciously silent and have worked hard to ignore me every time I'm forced to enter their orbit, whether in class, swim, or the dining hall. But I passed the first initiation—Jaxon asked, and Thorne answered in the affirmative.

What are they waiting for? That question alone has my spine stiffening, my ears tuning in, and my heart racing every time I'm within their proximity.

"I'll see you after school, okay?" Aiko pats me on the shoulder. "Chin up. We haven't even made it to October yet."

"Don't remind me." I offer her a wane smile before she disappears around the corner, her bag slapping against her back with her cheery steps.

So different from the Aiko who guarded me in the car that night. I linger in the doorway, staring at the spot she recently vacated.

My forehead nearly smacks against the wooden frame as I'm shoved forward.

"You're blocking the entrance, Gone Girl."

Aurora's sneer lands like pellets against the back of my neck. I turn. "There's plenty of space for two in the doorway. Unless you're wider than average?"

God, it feels good to fling an insult. I was beginning to think

Aurora had written me off as not worth her time. If she was that confident, it meant my chances at the fellowship were smaller than when this competition started.

"You wish you had this body, you fucking skeleton," she spits, then shoulders the rest of the way in.

I follow her, mostly because there is a cluster of less violent students waiting to be let in.

Aurora plops into her seat, deliberately crossing her legs in the aisle. I hop to the side at the last minute, close to breaking my nose on the marble floors in front of the entire class.

And in front of Thorne.

"Clumsy-ass whore," Aurora mumbles. Some nearby students overhear and laugh with amusement.

"Yep. Still a bitch," I say on a breathy sigh, then slide into my seat.

A crisp, soapy scent envelops me as soon as I'm seated. If I wasn't already hyper-aware of Thorne's presence, his addictive smell would've clued me in. I do my best not to angle into it as he sits, straight-backed and unaffected, while the rest of the class settles.

My body may be listening, but my mind won't fall in line. It coaxes the image of me rubbing up on him forward, the feeling of his hard length between my legs as we both choked on salt water and forced our bodies to a deadly climax.

And while my better sense wags a chastising finger at the memory, I doubt Thorne even blinks when he thinks about it or ponders on our mutual masturbation at all. The few peeks I risk show a stoic profile, the hard line of a closed jaw, and the heavy-lidded stare of a bored senior forced to attend afternoon classes. I can't picture him writhing in his bed, sheets soaked in his sweat as he replays our dirty actions, again and again as his fingers run slow circles around his dick. I'm sure he's not wondering why there aren't any more nightly visits after a clash like that, why he's not slipping in bed with me instead of whispering wet warnings while I sleep.

Going so long without strange creaks in the night or the pushing open of secret doors ... I'm starting to realize my nightly visitor might've all been in my head. Especially after facing off with Malcolm and realizing how deeply rooted my issues have become. I'm entombed in hurt and lost without my family. Perhaps I did make up a friend who's sending me warnings and watching over me while I sleep.

Heat circles my center. My attention keeps darting to Thorne.

"I assume everyone completed their assignments?"

I jerk back into reality as Lowell launches into his lecture, noticing that my hands are clenched into fists on top of my binder.

"You're staring at me," Thorne says out of the corner of his lips.

Those are the first words he's uttered in days. He's feigning vague interest in Lowell at the front of the class but angles his head in my direction.

"He deigns to speak," I respond sarcastically, loosening my hands and opening the binder to last night's assignment. "Do I kiss your ring now or later?"

"Watch your mouth." His hand snaps out, flattening my wrist to the desk and holding it there. "You're meant to be on your best behavior until I summon you again."

My core throbs at his last words until my heart hammers a warning—*you do not want to obey him again. You may not make it out a second time.*

I breathe through a swollen throat, my pulse pounding up into my ears. Yet my voice comes out as indolently as his. "From what I understand, there's a boys' club and a girls' club. Why do you have interest in the girls' side of things?" I notch my chin to include the back of Aurora's head. "Isn't she in charge of my summons, as you call it?"

"You're different." He squeezes my wrist hard enough to leave marks. "Addictive. Strange. Too similar to Sav—"

"Don't say her name." My voice comes out as a harsh, primeval whisper that surprises even me. I shouldn't feel possessive over Thorne. We only had one confusing, questionable night together. And he *drugged* me. Let's not forget about that, Ember.

He chuckles, low enough for only me to hear. "Jealous, little pretty?"

"Get your hand off me."

Thorne's grip only becomes harder.

"I'll scream."

"Oh, a warning from the submissive little mouse. Feel me quaking next to you."

I jerk my hand, but my arm barely moves.

"Tradition demands I pay you a small favor after the first initiation," he muses gently despite his vise-like grip on my delicate bones. "After all, you're a fledgling, the lowest in our ranks. Not even achieving baroness status. I can't stop thinking of you, however. Of your soaked clothes. How your nipples went hard for me. How wet you must've been around your own fingers despite the ocean lapping at your thighs."

Thorne says all this as if he's reciting a calculus equation. Despite my hand being nailed down, I scan the classroom frantically, desperate that no one overhears. My survey showcases some scrolling through their phones under the desks, others writing down notes as Lowell drones on, and one or two drifting to sleep with their chins in their hands. My attention moves to Aurora in front of me, posture-perfect in her seat and facing forward.

Of course she'd be that way. She has the fellowship to think of. *I* should be dedicating all my attention to Lowell, too, if it weren't for Thorne and his inflammatory words doing crazy, tingling things to my insides—

"Are you wet for me right now?"

I have to open my mouth to breathe. My nose isn't doing a well enough job releasing my pent-up breaths.

Thorne leans closer, his scent drifting. "Mind if I make sure?"

No way. My eyes widen in horror at the public implications Thorne dares to play with. He wouldn't—he would never—

The grip on my wrist lessens until it releases entirely, throbbing where Thorne once held it. I'm limp with shock as that godlike grip moves to my bare thigh, then up.

"Don't you dare," I whisper, boring holes into the back of Aurora's head as I force myself to keep straight.

"I figure three weeks of resistance is enough. It's time to remind you who's in charge."

"Big deal, you're the leader of a secret club in high school." I seethe his words right back at him. "I'm *so* terrified. Feel me quaking."

His answer is to scrape two of his fingers up my folds, pressing into my underwear. "Mouthy girl."

I nearly choke when I try to stifle my gasp. I snap my focus to my neighbor one desk over. We're in the back row, but he must be able to see this, see Thorne's hand working under my skirt. *See us so Thorne stops this!*

Unfortunately, he's one of the two people snoozing into his hand.

My breath hitches as Thorne continues to stroke, leaving sizzling electricity in his wake. His fingers dance to the side, pulling at the hem of my underwear.

Thorne groans deep in his throat when he slips under the fabric. "Fuck, you're practically bare."

Tipping my head back, I force my exhales out as normal as I

can make them while Thorne slides against my wetness, pets against my folds, then plunges in.

He starts with one finger, and my head falls forward, my pleasure-ridden stare snagging on Lowell as I try to ground myself into the reality that I'm in a classroom.

Thorne decides on two.

I grip the edge of the desk, my hips swaying to his pumps.

Three.

"F ..." I can't even *whisper* a curse.

He curls them into a C-shape, stroking against my G-spot. My thighs clench in warning.

Oh, my god. I'm about to come.

"Say you'll be a good girl from now on." Thorne's strokes slow, baiting the orgasm.

I turn my head, mouthing, "*Fuck you*," as I curl over my desk, inching my butt closer to his fingers, internally begging for a release.

His obscenely beautiful eyes shine with mischief. "I do enjoy a bad girl, but not one who I deem worthy of joining my 'secret club,' as you put it. Do it. Nod your head. Agree to obeying my every command, and I'll approve the next trial."

"Miss Beckett!"

I startle so much, I almost leap from the desk at Lowell's summons. I clench around Thorne's fingers inside me, who wiggles them deviously.

Horror, pure mortification, heats up my entire face.

"I trust you completed the assignment and can give me the full formula to question five."

"Y—" Fuck, even my voice sounds like it's being stroked by Thorne. "Yes, sir. I have the answer ... right here."

I flip the page in the workbook until I find the question at the same time Thorne finds my clit with his thumb and circles.

The *zing* hits all borders of my body, and I snap a look at him.

He simply leans forward, his free forearm on the desk as he peruses his own workbook with a cocked head, awaiting my answer.

Bastard. Fucking prick to end all pricks.

While he spreads me, strokes me, and explores my walls, I rattle off the answer to Lowell in a shaking voice.

"Excellent!" he crows, then turns back to the electronic whiteboard.

My shoulders sag as the class's attention leaves this iniquitous corner until Aurora twists in her seat to level me with a glare.

"You got lucky," she says.

I'm crouched so low against my desk, and I'm two seconds away from moaning, but I can't alert her. "Don't be upset I'm as good at numbers as you are at faking them."

I breathe out. Breathe in. Thorne plays.

Pure wrath twists Aurora's features like she wishes she could just light me on fire and watch me die. "She doesn't deserve any of this, Thorne. She doesn't give a shit she's a Weatherby. We should end the legacy while we—"

"Miss Emmerson! I trust you have something to share with the rest of the class?"

Aurora's nose scrunches at being caught, but she nails one more death glare on me before she swivels around. "No, sir. I was only asking Ember how she's so *smart* and *amazing* at math."

"Indeed. It seems you have some healthy competition for the Marks Fellowship, despite your friends and family discount," Lowell responds with completely flat affect before returning to his lesson.

I'd laugh. At the very least, I'd grin at Lowell's well-timed undercut, but I can't do much but hold in my cries as Thorne swoops and curves along my edges, prodding me back to the brink.

"Where were we?" he croons somewhere nearby. My senses are fading, collecting to the one necessary point in my body. "Oh, yes. Tell me you're mine to do as you're told."

"N-never."

His thumb presses into my clit, causing that bundle of nerves to become so sensitive, it hurts. "Do I need to add pain to our foreplay? Is that what gets you off? I'm thinking it does."

Thorne bends his thumb until the sharp tip of his nail cuts into my center.

I cough back a cry, drawing a few stares, but when they dart over to Thorne, they quickly avert their eyes.

"Remember who decides the fellowship. Who controls you. I *own* you, Ember. Admit it so I can feel you come all over my hand, and I can lick up every drop."

The centered pain isn't making me recoil. My stomach tightens, my thigh muscles grow taut. I'm at the cusp of the most potent orgasm of my life, and I'm about to do it in public.

"Say it," he whispers.

"I'm ..."

"Yes?"

"I'm yours. Fuck, I'm yours. Just end this torture. Please."

After a cunning smile, he does.

Pleasure rockets through me, spasming my muscles. Ribbons of nerves crackle and heat under my skin, short-circuiting my mind. I almost swallow my tongue to stop from screaming out the energy that binds me to Thorne.

Lowell glances over with a concerned draw to his brows. "Are you all right, Miss Beckett?"

"Uh ... uh-huh. Just. Just a little light-headed," I pant, my forehead close to hitting the desk.

"Do you need to go to a nurse?"

"I ... maybe." Anything to get away from Thorne and lessen his power.

"You're excused. Do you need assistance?"

Shaking my head, I stand at the same time Thorne withdraws his fingers, an aching hollowness replacing where he once filled.

As I slide my books into my bag with weak, floppy arms, Thorne sits back in his seat and brings his slick fingers to his nose. He breathes deep, his stare holding mine, then parts his lips and sucks on each one slowly. Knuckle by knuckle. Savoring my taste.

Trembling, I swing my strap over my shoulder and wobble down the aisle, Aurora's glare nothing but a tiny sewing needle pricking my arm. The rest of me is focused on Thorne and how he clocks my every move.

I don't look back, but I don't need to. I can fully picture the arrogance crossing his features as he witnesses his effects on me while I leave.

It's only when I reach the deserted hallway that I can breathe clean air. Lifting my chin to the arched ceiling, I do just that, closing my eyes to the solace.

But an unwanted thought tickles my brain. One that won't go away no matter how hard I nudge it back.

I'm starting to think Savannah may not be missing, but that she had to make it out before too many pieces of her were claimed by Thorne Briar.

CHAPTER 21

THORNE

Damn that girl for getting into my head.

Showers from behind the row of lockers hiss and steam as I spin my combination lock. A towel is slung over my shoulder, used once. The rest of me remains damp and bare. Any more thoughts of Ember, and my desire to own her will be made known to the entire boys' swim team in mere seconds.

"Fuck, that was a harsh practice." Jaxon drips beside me, more modest with a towel wrapped around his hips as he opens the locker beside mine. If he sees my hard, bobbing dick, he doesn't comment. "You see the girls, though? I think half of them almost drowned under their coach's sprints."

Drowning. A purr escapes my throat, my hand twitching near my cock to stroke and remember. I'd been reluctant to dive into the pool for practice, then shower. It meant washing Ember's scent from my fingers, and I'd been getting high off that sweetness all day.

Ember had done well in our first swim meet, though. As she's been doing for her initiation, too. I expected no less. "I'm moving up the next trial."

Jaxon pauses, reaching into his locker. I don't have to expand for him to understand what I'm referring to. "You sure, man? That's not following protocol."

"*Protocol* is a word initiated by my father. It doesn't have to stay as gospel."

At one time, my father was my age—an incredible feat for my brain to acknowledge, but it was true. He ruled Winthorpe's halls as well as I did and ran the Nobles just the same. Back then, there were concrete procedures in place to initiate pledges into our secret society and gift them with perfect grades for the rest of their time here, capped off with entry into any top college they wanted. Such a guarantee demanded sacrifice, and Damion Briar usually had them admitting their greatest fears, to which he made them face. Fear of darkness? Sit in a hole in the catacombs for a week. Terrified of burning? He'll brand you in places you most protect, including those you love. Can't stomach the idea of drowning? He'll hold you underwater until you pass out, revive you, then do it again. And you can't even make the most of it and jerk off while repeatedly choking on the water.

Damion spread those trials across an entire freshman semester, following the guidelines of the founding chapter in Briarcliff, Rhode Island. Those Nobles are incredibly by the book with their teachings, harkening back to the nineteenth century when the Nobles and Virtues were created, using soul-mate bindings and blood vows.

My father preferred that line of thinking, too, up until the Briarcliff chapter imploded. It turns out, their fossilized views and strict supervision weren't enough to keep out the poison, and now the weakest are left to pick up the pieces.

"I prefer a more modern take to our initiates." I pull on my briefs. "Specifically, a senior. I'm expediting her last two trials back-to-back."

Jaxon dresses faster than I do but lingers and towels off his scalp. "Is that wise? I thought your dad wanted her to fail the first trial."

"That'd be too easy. She's rebellious, stubborn, and a Weatherby," I say by way of explanation. "Ember needs to be leashed, not freed."

"Yeah, 'cause it's not like she's hot and fun to kick around."

I spin, my eyes burning. "What did you say?"

"Relax, man." Jaxon says it mildly, but he lifts his hands. "I'm not about to touch her. It's clear to the entire school she's yours."

"Good." I pull on a Winthorpe T-shirt and slam my locker door shut. A nearby sophomore winces, then scurries away. "And for those not in the know, spread the word."

"Aurora has a point, though." Jaxon waits for me to pull on my sweatpants and shoes before we exit the locker room. "She's the daughter of your father's adversary, so it makes sense to put an end to the legacy now. Wouldn't your dad be proud? Why would he want to run a chapter with the blood of his enemy inside?"

My strides are careful, wholly controlled, but I doubt Jaxon notices the serpent slithering underneath, anxious to strangle him. "Because, you idiot, Malcolm Weatherby *wants* his legacy to end. Ask yourself, why would my father allow Malcolm's suffering to stop and his daughter to walk free?"

"Shit," Jaxon mutters, kicking at a loose pebble as we step outside. "I didn't think about that. Hey, can I get a ride?"

"Just stay the night."

Jaxon doesn't comment, and I don't ask anything more of him. It's Friday evening, a night his father hits the bottle like clockwork. Jaxon, while strong enough to beat his father to death, most especially after my teachings, would rather not put himself in the position to do so. He was smacked around by his dad enough as a slim, gentle, prepubescent soul, and his reluctance to become a rabid revenge killer is obvious to someone like me, his most trusted friend.

There's also the small problem of his father being a Count, a trusted adviser and regent member of the Nobles. As vassals in a society whose regents run the most important companies and governments to the economic infrastructure in the United States, the younger ones are expected to fall in line, regardless of the situation.

Another archaic rule I aim to snuff out.

I press the key fob, and the headlights to my car flash in the dusky gray of the surrounding stone. As we walk toward it, Jaxon says, "So, you're going to allow Ember Weatherby to become a baroness of our Virtues, then? Disregard your dad's orders like a rebel son?" Jaxon snorts. "Fuck if that's the truth. Tell it to me for real, bro."

How can I explain the unearthly draw of that girl? At first, I blamed it on her resemblance to the girl who laid my heart bare, then strangled it with my own dick. Even when she disappeared, Sav wouldn't go away. The cops came to my door, demanding access to my phone and my computer, asking for an alibi and generally ruining any chance I had at getting back to normal.

Ember was meant to be an assignment. Find her weakness, exploit it, and get her to do whatever we Briars needed to keep Malcolm Weatherby under control. It was disgustingly easy, too. The girl was practically wet for the Marks Fellowship, a bonus, considering Belle's father, Norris Marks, owes my father many favors. All I had to do was fake the power to take her candidacy away, and she's willingly become a Virtue initiate. If I were a nicer guy, I would've pondered why she became so pliable beneath that threat. Being torn from her family, or who she thought were her parents by blood, must've really done a number on the poor, sweet thing. And realizing Malcolm was your true blood? The man who's wasting away in a decrepit mansion and who can hardly summon the means to keep his company running? How anticlimactic.

The man was weakened. Destroyed. Crumbled to nothing by a swipe of my father's hand. Yeah, that'd get me wanting an independent future, too.

Not my problem.

However ... I've tasted her. Scented her. Held her by the throat and pushed her under, only to witness her eyes widen with pleasure as they landed on mine, her body bucking, begging to come closer to the man who holds her life in his hands.

Asking to stay under.

How could I give someone like that the cold shoulder? Well, I could and will, but I'd rather be cold to her face and watch her plead for punishment while I pumped my dick, readying for her.

"I want to keep her close," I say to Jaxon as I slide into the driver's seat.

Jaxon comes in the other side, tossing his bag in the back seat and shimmying until he's comfortable. "Fine. I won't say a word about your quick-fire initiation."

And he won't. We've done a lot of favors for each other, tonight notwithstanding.

"I assume this'll all be in private, and you're refusing to allow the rest of the Nobles and Virtues to bear witness."

I give him a nod as my baby in black roars to life, and I reverse out of the parking spot.

Jaxon folds his arms at the back of his head, the mother-fucker enjoying his chauffeur moment to the Briar mansion. "At least tell me your plans so I can live vicariously."

"Easy," I say as I turn out of the academy and hit the narrow, public roads. I press harder on the gas. "First, I'm going to kidnap her."

CHAPTER 22

EMBER

A delicious burning occurs between my thighs every time I move. Doing laps and practicing my front stroke has never been such aching torture before, yet I scissor my legs in the water, delighting in the zings of pleasure Thorne left behind.

That is, until my mind catches up and beats me with a mental stick.

I shouldn't have let Thorne finger me during class, let alone enjoy it. And I shouldn't *still* be loving it as my lungs swell with effort, my throat burns, and my limbs contract and ache, lap after lap. Coach's directions ended long ago, but I can't seem to stop the combination of a swollen clit and the need for air. If my hands weren't so busy with the front stroke ...

Damn you, Thorne Briar.

I hear the echoes of a whistle underwater and pop up.

"Beckett! I do enjoy an enthusiastic athlete, but our practice ended ten minutes ago. Out you go."

"Sorry, Coach!" I push up my goggles and breaststroke to the ladder, swinging up and out. As I walk across the pool deck, I pull off my swim cap and goggles, drop them on the bench, and scrub my face with an available towel.

I haven't stopped throbbing. Clenching my thighs, I hope that's enough to stop the need. Otherwise, I'll have to circumspectly rub one out in the showers before I meet Aiko.

"Your form needs work," a girl sneers behind me.

Turning, I notice Aurora's bestie and the Marks heir, Belle, and another girl I sometimes see with them. "Yeah, but my timing doesn't."

Those doe eyes of hers grow small. I've beaten her by a second every time we've raced other academies, and I can't wait to do it again. One second in the swim world is like a half hour in the real world. I tie my towel around my chest, wink at her, then head to the locker room.

I'd be nicer to her if I thought she had sway with her family's fellowship, but with her constant capitulations to either Thorne or Aurora, it's clear she's not the one I have to impress.

"You think you're something special, huh, bitch?"

This is said by the girl next to Belle, so pale the blue veins under her skin resemble rivers flowing toward pitch-black hair.

I halt halfway to the door. "Let me guess, you're the Snow White of the bunch."

The Disney princess observation goes straight over her head. "Delaney, actually. And one of the members you're trying to be."

"I'm not trying to do anything."

"A part of the problem." Belle places her hands on her hips, chlorinated droplets beading on her muscled thighs. "You don't even care about the privilege you're being given, but that's fine with me. Thorne may be paying attention to you now, but he gets bored easily. Think about what happened to the last girl he singled out."

I lift a brow. "Isn't Savannah Merricourt supposed to be your friend? Nice loyalty you have going there."

Belle gasps at the same time Delaney snarls.

"You know," Belle says, "I felt sorry for you originally. Looking so much like our friend and being the center of unwanted attention because of it. Then dealing with Aurora's automatic hatred to taking Savvy's place. And on top of that, gaining Thorne's attention. A guy who'd rather make a clingy girlfriend disappear than break up with her." Belle taps a finger to her chin, pretending to mull over her words. "That's a lot of weight for a new girl. Except your attitude sucks, and you don't deserve our fellowship. You have this unearned confidence that's a real turn-off. I can't wait to see what Aurora has planned for you next. I'm even *more* excited to see if you survive Thorne. He's a beastly one."

I don't deign to respond. Pursing my lips, I turn on my heel, my feet slapping against the tiles before I push the locker room door open and let it swing behind me.

"You'll never make it past the trials!" Delaney calls out before the door clicks shut.

The showers are deserted, but Belle and Delaney aren't far behind. I rush through a spray-down and towel off with jerky movements, conscious that at any moment, I could be cornered.

At my locker, I hear Belle and Delaney's muted voices. I pull out my phone to send Aiko a quick text. I asked her to meet me outside by her car, but I'm thinking she should come in here instead. Safety in numbers and all.

A shadow covers half my form as I'm digging through my locker for my clothes.

"How'd the finger-fucking go?" Aurora's voice purrs.

With a sigh and my cheeks burning, I pull out my folded jeans and sweater, dropping them on the bench so I can face her. "I didn't take you for a voyeur."

"You think I couldn't hear you moaning?" Aurora crosses her

arms. "Don't take pride in it like you're the first. He's fucked me in classrooms, too."

Jealousy pitches in my gut. It's so leveling, I put a hand up to the lockers for balance. I never thought I'd be Thorne's first, but to know he's fooled around with Aurora, a girl I can't stand, the one chick who wants to mutilate me before she ever sees me triumph over her ... it makes me sick. Sick with protective rage.

Which is ridiculous. Thorne is more of an enemy than she is.

But he brings you so much illicit pleasure ...

"Tell me, has Thorne stuck his dick in you yet? No?" she asks, then cocks her head with a slow smile. In my periphery, I notice Belle and Delaney flanking her, malicious grins in place. "Do you want me to describe it to you?"

"I can think on it just fine, thanks." I pull my towel tighter around me. Against my better judgment, I flick a wishful glance at my clothes lying on the bench.

Aurora's expression turns into a cat who's just received her cream. "Afraid I'll take those, too?"

It takes effort to keep my voice level. "What do you want?"

She steps up to me so fast, my back hits the lockers. At my instability, she reaches for my towel, yanking it out of my grip and exposing my entire body.

Aurora doesn't back off. She stares down at my pebbled nipples, then goes lower.

"Hmm. Nice upkeep."

"Step the fuck off me," I whisper, "or I'll knee you in the cooch."

"Brave words." Aurora breathes near my mouth, collecting my oxygen. "How about I finger you, too? Do you want that to be your next trial?"

"Thorne's in charge of my trials." I maintain my stare on hers, refusing to cross my legs, though my instincts beg me to.

"Are you willing to go against him? Or is it sexual assault that gets you off?"

She huffs out a dark laugh. "You may be in the running for the fellowship, but you'll never get my seat on the Virtues, no matter how much you fuck the Noble prince. Got it?"

I swallow, my fingers curling against my palms at my sides. I'm outnumbered, so it's best to play dead. Unless they touch me. Fire swirls in my throat at the thought. *If they touch me—*

Aurora scrapes a finger across her lips, assessing. She's still much too close. "Membership with us requires cost. Consider it equal to selling your soul to the devil. You should reconsider your desire to be one of us before it's too late." Aurora darts her face forward, and to my horror, I wince.

She chuckles. "It's not only Thorne who will own you. He's in charge of the Nobles at Winthorpe and likes to think he runs the whole Society. But the Virtues? That's all me, sweetheart."

"Hey! Back off!"

Aiko's yell echoes off the surrounding tiles. Aurora turns toward the sound, and I take my chance, pushing her and ducking out of the half-circle they'd formed around me.

Aurora nearly tumbles over the bench, Belle and Delaney breaking away from their intimidation to help her.

Aiko's small form steps between the row of lockers, her dark eyes burning. "Did you not hear me? Get away from her, you rabid bitches."

Aurora rights herself, smoothing down her skirt and batting away Delaney's ministrations. Belle steps aside, working her jaw as she notices Aiko.

"We were simply issuing a friendly warning," Aurora says, ensuring a venomous look in my direction before she backs off completely.

Aiko pauses her stare down enough to glance in my direction. Her gaze softens at my nakedness. "Get dressed, Ember. You're okay now."

Am I? With my gaze bouncing among all four girls, I carefully pull on my jeans and sweater, forgoing underwear due to the severely uncomfortable time constraint. I don't bother to do anything with my damp hair, either.

Aiko maintains a defensive stance as I sidle up to her. Her focus is on Aurora, summoning the type of death glare that has Aurora blinking rapidly, then falling back.

"I'd rather not waste any more time on you," Aurora says to me. "Turn your brain on, Ember, and stop ingratiating yourself into Winthorpe. You don't belong here. And you'll never be Savannah."

I speak, despite the warning tug on my arm from Aiko. "Can you stop, already? I never said I wanted to be her. I never even *knew* her. All I want to do is survive this year and have the future I've been planning for years." I don't tell her it's more important than ever since my comfortable life exploded and there's nothing left but my carefully crafted future. It's all I have that's under my control, but she doesn't deserve to hear my reasons. "I don't want any trouble with you, Aurora. If you stay in your lane, I'll stay in mine."

She folds her arms across her chest. "Give up your application to the Marks Fellowship, and I will."

"No can do." I mimic her posture.

Aiko steps forward. "Aurora. Leave."

Aurora's upper lip twitches like she's ready to defy Aiko. And why wouldn't she? Aiko reaches her shoulders, is as thin as a piece of paper, and has the tinkly voice of a fairy. If Aurora could corner me, she could certainly intimidate Aiko.

Yet, for some reason, she doesn't.

"Let's go, girls," Aurora says to her crew.

Like good little doggies, they follow, Delaney and Belle dragging their gear with them instead of getting dressed.

I suppose that's another taste of Aurora's power. She can make you step into a crisp autumn night in a wet bathing suit if she so chooses.

What she did to me, how she directs her "friends" ... it doesn't sit well. I'm starting to second-guess the whole secret society thing. I'd wanted to match Aurora— with academics, in extracurriculars, and any other goddamn token she's gained to get her closer to the fellowship. But with this, and Thorne's demands, and the way my body's reacting to his fetishes ...

Maybe I should stop.

My thoughts must be written all over my face because Aiko takes my hand and squeezes gently. "Their bark is worse than their bite. Whatever they're making you endure, just remember why you're here."

I look down at her, thoughts whirring behind my vision. I'd love to confide in Aiko and get her take on the Society that seems to run Winthorpe more than the faculty, but Thorne's warnings keep reaching up and strangling my voice. If *this* is what I have to endure, the last thing I want is to make Aiko go through it, too.

"You seem to have found a nice spot in Winthorpe's social hierarchy," I observe as we turn and head out of the locker room. "Aurora and her minions don't look like they trouble you much."

"I had to work for it."

Aiko forges ahead as she says it. From this angle, I can't see her expression, but the flatness of her tone explains enough. Was she forced into the type of uncomfortable situations that I've had to work through? I want to ask—I'm desperate to, actually, but her voice leaves no room for questions, and I don't know her well enough to pry. Not yet.

"Here's my ride." Aiko's voice rises with chirpiness as she points at a fire engine red Volkswagon Beetle.

"Really trying to blend in, huh?" I say, a smile crossing my lips as I poke her. I don't tell her this feels like the first time I'm seeing her car. When we'd hobbled over the hill to where she parked, I don't remember a blur of red in front of a line of trees. All I recall is the sharp smell of leather, the warmth of a blanket, and the security of Aiko watching over me.

Aiko unlocks the doors. As I fold into the passenger seat and she gets into the driver's side, I sneak another look at her. She *must* know more about Winthorpe than she's letting on.

Because if she didn't, why would she be helping me?

CHAPTER 23
EMBER

Aiko lives on the opposite side of town than I do. Trees and small rock formations rush past us as we cruise downhill, the odd scurrying squirrel rushing for a tree trunk as we fly by. The sky, normally a drab blue at this time, has darkened to a stormy gray, warning of an impending squall. Aiko seems nonplussed by it as she wheels around curves, the Beetle surprisingly nimble in her hands.

Her smooth driving lulls me into a sense of complacency. I lean against the window, watching the patches of forest blur by while the clouds cloak the treetops and the sky rolls over into night.

My eyelids flutter when the tires crunch on gravel. I straighten, peering out the windshield at the approaching home.

Aiko's family house doesn't have the haunting gloom of Weatherby Manor or the darkened mystery of the Briar's house. A two-story gray farmhouse meets me instead. When I step out, I hear the gentle lapping of water.

"We're near the shore?" I ask as I push the passenger door shut.

"Beachfront access." Aiko rounds the hood of the car, motioning for me to follow her. "It's a pain in the butt to navigate out of Winthorpe and downhill, but worth it when you arrive. Dad says this was built in the mid-1800s." Our shoes crunch against loose stones as we walk, but I'm enjoying the lazy, saltwater haze rolling onto the shores and half-obscuring the house in fog. Aiko kicks a larger rock out of the way. "Oh, yeah ... plumbing's a bitch, and we pretty much rely on fireplaces for our heat. Thought I'd warn you."

I tear my gaze away from the stretch of beach behind her home, studying the backdrop of rocky cliffs to the left instead. "I don't mind. It's like this spot has been carved out of the cliffs just for your home." Glancing around, I don't see any neighbors.

"The privacy is nice." Aiko steps up to the small porch, the painted gray wood creaking under her weight. "It can get lonely, though. Dad isn't here much."

Aiko unlocks the door. She hasn't described her dad much, but her stories of his strict nature and rank in the military are enough to put me on edge.

Tremors follow me over the threshold. I cross my arms over my chest, claiming as much warmth as I can. My wet hair doesn't make it any easier.

"I'll light the fireplace." Aiko takes my bags from me and sets them down beside the staircase directly in front of us. "Hungry? Shoot. We should've picked something up on the way. I could make us a pizza?"

I hope my smile puts Aiko's sudden nervousness at ease, though it's becoming clear I'm her first visitor in a while. "I'm easy. Whatever you feel like. But ... could you direct me to the fireplace? I'm freezing."

"I'm such a noob." Aiko mimes smacking her forehead. "That whole debacle with Aurora must've seriously messed with your after-swim routine. You kinda look like a wet cat."

"Feel like one, too."

She grins, her lips finally relaxing in the corners. "Meet me upstairs. There's a fireplace in my bedroom, and it'll heat the room faster than the one down here. Hang a left at the top of the stairs. Last door on the right."

Aiko disappears through the archway and around the corner. She didn't explain where she was going, but I assume it's to the kitchen to grab us something to eat. I do as she instructs, lifting our bags and carting them up the stairs. Her nerves are cute. She must not have many friends who stay over.

Shame lays itself over my skin as I navigate the staircase and remember how I'd asked to stay at her place for a cover to meet Thorne. She'd lit up when I suggested it, then waited for me on campus in case my meeting with Thorne went sideways and I needed to turn the cover into a reality, when all the while, I never came. Not until I had to.

God, I don't deserve her. With what I'm doing and who I'm toying with, my sweet friend continues to wait on the sidelines, hoping I'll need her. Yet ... Aurora feared Aiko tonight. I can't place the exact moment I realized it, but Aurora bent to Aiko's will almost immediately, heeding Aiko's warning and releasing me from her hold. Not that I couldn't have handled it, but it would've been messier had I fought and the consequences much higher had Aiko not stepped in and halted Aurora with words alone.

Would Aurora have assaulted me? She clearly wants to get me back for the throat punch. But I have Aiko, sweet on one side and wily on the other, to thank for keeping that question an uncertainty instead of an eventuality.

My steps are hollow on the wide-paneled flooring, and I can't find a light switch in the hallway. Unlike the first floor with large windows and high ceilings, it's more cramped up here, the narrow hall with only four doors adorning the righthand wall.

One of them is open, a warm arc of light filtering onto the wood floor. I follow it, pushing the door open farther to reveal dusky-rose walls, a four-poster bed with plush, light pink sheets and pillows, and off-white furniture.

My footsteps are suddenly silent as I wander in, peering at the fiction books stacked on a nightstand, then the vanity with all kinds of cosmetics, creams, and makeup brushes. The soft light I noticed in the hallway comes from an old-fashioned lamp perched on the dresser, its gold fringes swinging as if someone has just pulled the string to the light bulb. Then vanished.

Another door is cracked open beside the vanity table, but this switch is easy to find as I hook an arm around, flick it on, and illuminate a walk-in closet filled with a rainbow of fabrics.

Literally, a rainbow. All are neatly hung in order of hue.

Brushing a hand along the buttery soft dresses, cardigans, and coats, I'm hit with the stale fragrance of gardenia as if my rustling has unleashed a long-dormant scent.

Jewels glimmer near the back, and I bend low, ogling the diamond-crusted watches and thin gold chains. Diamond pendants shine as I move in and out of the closet's overhead light. A simple wooden jewelry box rests on a shelf below the exquisite accessories, similar to the one I had as a child. I open it to soft lullaby music and a tiny spinning ballerina. Delighted, I bend closer. I lost mine years ago, and the music reminds me of happier moments of unclaimed innocence, when I still believed in fairies and good luck charms.

Plastic jewelry adorns the inside, the kind that you used to win at arcades or pay 25 cents for at a grocery store. Smiling, I finger a scratched plastic ring, then on a whim, press on the ballerina's head for the hidden compartment a lot of these kids' music boxes used to have. The secret shelf pops out halfway. I have to use my nail to coax it open, but when I do, I pause.

A single golden pendant gleams against the red velvet lining. I reach for it.

"What are you doing in here?"

Yelping, I spin around, dropping the heart pendant I picked up. It lands on the floor with a quiet *ping*.

Aiko stands in the closet's doorframe, her arms laden down with chip and candy bags, peering over them with suspicion.

"I ... the light was on. When I saw the room, I thought it was yours ..." *Lame.* Even I don't believe myself.

"I told you where my room was. Last on the right."

"Yep. You did say that." Like a child caught with the cookie jar, I shuffle my feet. "The door was open. Once I looked in and saw all the feminine touches ... is this your mom's room or something?"

The truth of it is, Aiko's never mentioned her mother. With my family baggage, I have no right asking about hers, but I'm growing desperate, standing in a gorgeously adorned closet with no real substance as to the person who owns it. It's certainly not Aiko's—the tailoring is too tall, the racks of shoes too large.

Bags crunch in Aiko's hold as her chest expands with a deep breath. And like a dark wave, pain washes across her face. "It's not my mom's. She died in a car accident when I was a baby."

"Oh. I'm so sorry." I move toward her, feeling terrible over forcing Aiko to bring up the tragedy from her past, but I'm stopped in my tracks when she follows up with, "It's Savannah's room."

CHAPTER 24
EMBER

D id I hear her correctly?

"This is Savannah's?" I open my arms wide, encompassing the closet and all that hangs here, neglected for over a year.

Aiko nods, then half-turns from the door. "I'll explain, but come with me. I don't like being in here too long."

Fair enough. I fall behind Aiko, giving one last lingering look at the delicate wisps of fabric.

"Shit," I murmur, whirling back into the closet.

The necklace is where I left it on the floor, its thin gold chain tangled and the gold heart pendant flashing with beckoning ripples. I pick it up, not wanting to leave a mess in a place that's so close to a memorial. As I rise, my hand hovers over the jewelry shelf with the heart pendant dangling like a metronome in my grip.

I stare at it.

Forever is engraved on one side. *You*, on the other.

Throwing a look over my shoulder, I check to see if Aiko's nearby and watching. She's not.

I don't know what makes me do it. Perhaps it's the constant comparison to a girl I never met. Maybe it's her connection to Thorne, continuing on despite her disappearance. Either way, I pocket a piece of her, wanting to keep her close.

"Ember?" Aiko calls.

"Coming!" I slip out of the closet, shutting the door softly behind me, and pad out of Savannah's bedroom, the necklace safely tucked away.

Aiko lingers in the hallway, waiting for me, but the suspicion's left her expression. "In here."

She leads me to the neighboring room, and when she turns on her ceiling light, I get more insight into Aiko.

Pale blue paint covers the walls, offset by a cream waffle-weave comforter on a twin-sized bed. She has a white vanity similar to Savannah's, but hers is devoid of cosmetics in favor of stacks of novels. On closer inspection, most of them are romance, with women intertwined with bare-chested men on the covers.

My brows hike up at this side of Aiko.

A vase of pink roses adorns her nightstand—real, by the way the fleshy softness slides between my fingers. Bright, framed posters hang above her headboard in a row of four—a Lisa-Frank-style collection of under-the-ocean views, like dolphins leaping above bright coral and mermaids holding hands. A few family pictures adorn her walls, the one near the door showcasing her standing stoically in front of her dad in full uniform with his hand on her shoulder. But it's the one on the opposite nightstand that draws my attention—a family of four, including Aiko and her father. A woman with soft amber-hued hair tucks her arm in his, and Aiko and Savannah kneel in front with their arms around one another.

The sight of her always steals my breath. She's me, but tanned, amber-eyed, and with honey hair. She's like ... the me I'd be if I hadn't holed myself up in my childhood bedroom, constantly studying, rarely steeping in the sun, and spending every weekend helping Dad design landscapes on his computer.

Savannah, she's what I'd be if sunshine hit my face every day. If I dyed my hair, put in contacts, and absorbed her pigment where I'm colorless and pale.

"It gets me every time, too," Aiko says behind me. I hadn't realized she was standing so close and jolt in surprise. "I'd swear you guys were sisters at the very least."

I hum with a noncommittal noise. Malcolm insists he only had one child with a woman he met once, on a night he was vulnerable. His words. In a way, I believe him. Savannah and I are the same age, and her birth has the official, genuine documents mine lack. I looked into it. I was a black market child, but even those are given a clandestine paper trail, and there was no mention of being separated from a twin, either.

I suppose, for now, I have to take Malcolm's story as the truth, unless something comes up to make me question it. Like...

"So how is it Savannah was living with you?"

Aiko perches on her bed, weaving her fingers back and forth. "She was my stepsister for five years. Dad and her mom met at a parent conference in Winthorpe, and the rest is history, as they say."

I come to sit beside her but give her enough space to be comfortable. "Are they still married?"

Aiko shakes her head. "The divorce was finalized a few months ago. After Savannah went missing ... it killed them. Her mom, Molly, couldn't accept the loss. She dedicated all her waking hours to finding Savannah. Dad helped, too, but he has to answer to the military. Every time they called, he had to go. Molly started to resent it. They fought a lot." Aiko casts her gaze to the ceiling, a faraway look in her eyes. "I did everything I could to help, too. Went to all the search parties, kept up with the flyers at school, updated the website, scoured the volunteer hotline for tips. It was exhausting. Molly, somehow, kept at it, but you could tell it was taking its toll. She lost weight, never slept, became sharp and impatient with me ... it got to the point where all she wanted was her daughter. She couldn't live as anything else but Savannah's mother. It was awful."

"I'm so sorry you had to endure that." I lay my hand between us, offering comfort.

Aiko lowers her chin and closes her eyes. "I got along with my stepfamily. Loved Molly. I'd never had a mother, and when she moved in, she included me in everything. She asked my opinion on redecorating the house, took me with her and Savannah every time they went shopping in town, warmed the kitchen with the smell of coffee and pancakes and bacon ... God, I didn't realize how lonely I was until they moved in. Dad's gone so much. I had a full-time nanny for a long time, but she was paid to take care of me. That's not the same as family. Molly and Savannah showed me the meaning of that word." Aiko's breath shudders out. "I loved Savannah, too. She wasn't the evil step-sister I was afraid she'd become after it was obvious our parents were dating. We never hung out in the same circles—I was quiet, prefer reading to people, movie nights to parties, that sort of thing—and she was all smiles and brightness *all* the time. But her friends, I don't know *why* she hung out with them. They were really mean to me. I started only drinking from lidded thermoses because every time they tripped and shoved me, I'd ruin my uniform. They flung a lot of cruel names at me, too. Before I found my backbone, I'd sit in the bathroom stalls every lunch, eating my food and crying. Savannah would tell her friends to stop if she witnessed it, but she wasn't always there, and they wouldn't always listen. If anything, I thought *I'd* be the stepsister who fucking hated the Winthorpe princess."

I let out a quiet laugh. "All that sweetness can be sickening, I agree."

"Yeah, but when she moved in, I got to know all sides of her. She wasn't always unicorn poop and rainbows. There were times she was sad, or her friends annoyed her and she just wanted to stay in. Those were my favorite nights. Curling up on her bed with a movie playing on her laptop and tossing popcorn at her for *constantly* thinking out loud during the movie." Aiko sighs again. "And she listened. She was good at hearing me out. We talked a lot. I loved having her as a sister. We often fell asleep together instead of in our own beds. She was gentle and kind. Until sophomore year."

I stiffen, withdrawing my hand.

"She changed. She started dating Thorne, and became quiet and withdrawn around the same time. Like, when you get a new boyfriend, you want to always look good, right? I mean, that's what I assume. I've never had one. But she did the opposite. Stopped blowing out her hair, lessened the makeup, didn't care about a pressed uniform or what she wore on weekends. It was weird and not like her."

"Do you think he was..." I can't even finish the thought. All I can see in my mind's eye is Thorne demanding I bend to his will. Pushing me to the brink of death and telling me to orgasm or drown.

A lot of girls, especially ones filled with delight, wouldn't handle it well. They wouldn't thrive or crave more dances with demons. That darkness would swallow their light.

"Abusing her?" Aiko predicts the rest of my question. "No. She confided in me sometimes. She told me he was different from other guys but not in a bad way. He made her question the status quo, like why she always felt the need to follow the rules, or bend to authority figures, or be a good girl. He had her try new rebellions."

Yep. That sounds like him.

"Stuff like breaking curfew, skipping class, hiking the forests at night, and hang gliding off cliffs, for god's sake. All without Molly's permission or knowledge."

I set my jaw, unable to confirm or deny that such adrenaline would fuel me as well. So far, Thorne's offered me dangerous, sexual adventure. At the heat of jealousy behind my eyes as I listen to Aiko, I'm discovering I do *not* want to know if Thorne pushed Savannah toward danger in bed, too.

Aiko's calm tone contains no judgment against Savannah for enjoying Thorne's type of self-awakenings, and for that, I'm thankful.

"I got the sense something *else* happened at the same time she got together with him," she continues. "Savannah wasn't herself because her friends were doing something to her."

My ears perk. "You mean, Aurora and all them?"

She nods. "I think they were up to no good with her. Like they got wind of Thorne's interest and wanted her to be bad with them, too, but those tasks were different. Worse. They were like … dares."

I flash back to being drugged and on my knees in front of a half-circle of cloaks, their chanting and taunting. Aurora was for sure one of them. And where Aurora goes, Belle and Delaney follow. If Savannah were a part of that group, it's not a far reach to consider that she was brutally initiated into the Virtues, too.

However, Aiko wasn't there. Not to my knowledge. I didn't see her or sense her that night in the caves, and I'd like to think she would've shrieked in outrage at the sight of me tied up and groggy from a spiked drink. Especially as a girl who loves neon, cartoon sea life, and wakes up to photos of her family every day.

And Savannah was sweet to her. Probably protective. If I were Savannah, I'd be sparse with the details, too, unwilling to drag Aiko down with me. I already am.

Aiko says, "At the same time she was falling apart, she was a good person who lured me out of my lunchtime appointment with the bathroom stall to sit with her, promising that her so-called friends would stop bullying me. And that time, it worked."

"Is this why Aurora and her crew still don't bother you?" I ask. "Even with Savannah gone?"

Aiko shrugs. She lifts her thumbnail to her mouth, chewing on it. "I've wondered that myself. I've had over a year to think about it, too. Are they doing it to honor their friend? Probably not, considering their propensity for evil. I'm pretty sure it's because they're afraid."

I straighten in surprise. "Afraid of what?"

"Of what she might've told me. About them."

The Societies? I breathe out. "What did she tell you?"

Aiko blinks sharply as if jolted from a dream. She stands just as quickly, collecting the junk food she'd tossed on the bed. "If you're warm enough, I say we have a bonfire outside on the beach. You up for it? I can find some marshmallows somewhere."

"Uh ... sure. But Aiko—"

"Awesome! Let's go."

Aiko shoots out her door before I have time to close my mouth and rise. The sharp point of the pendant's heart pokes into my thigh as I move, and I press a hand to my pocket.

It acts as a potent reminder.

Aiko and I both have secrets and sins we're not quite ready to reveal.

CHAPTER 25
THORNE

A lazy haze thickens the air in my room as I sprawl face-up on the bed and inhale the last of the roach.

Flicking it onto the ashtray beside me, I lift to my bare forearms for a peek out the window at my elusive, illustrious neighbor across the street.

She eluded me last night, my midnight visit to her room almost turning into a futile approach.

How I *loathe* failures.

I knew something was up when I pressed an ear to the hidden panel behind her wall and didn't hear anything. Ember mewls in her sleep, the whimpers and protests like a lightning rod going straight to my cock. Not one night has gone by when I'm prowling behind the wall that she's so deep in slumber, she's silent.

Another unavoidable clue occurred when I moved to the peephole, the tiniest pinprick blending into the paint on her walls, and I was blind. The unlit fireplace blackened the bedroom. There were no flames to guide me, no undulating plays of light and shadow across her exposed skin to tell me she was in bed, writing within a dream.

Where *was* she? A fire brews deep in my gut at the follow-up thought, *who* was she with?

I'd clicked open the door anyway, a glutton for punishment. Even enjoyed wandering around her vacant room, touching her things and perusing her collectibles from home, taking advantage of time I'm not usually able to take. She'd brought a well-worn children's book with her, something about lost unicorns, and a faded, beaten-up teddy bear with sewn-in buttons for eyes and a raggedy red vest. He sits lopsided on a tall-backed sofa chair in the corner. I sneer at him as I pass, not into the whole plastic-eyed watchfulness of stuffed animals. So judgy.

A teal silk scarf hangs over her desk chair. I lift it to my nose, wrinkling it when I realize it's not her scent. Must be her mother's. It drops from my fingers.

Her computer rests on the desk with its lid closed, and on a whim, I sag into the chair and open it. Ember must not believe too much in security because her laptop flashes on as soon as the computer loads. I skim the file names saved on her screen, but she's largely boring in this respect. School assignments divided by subject. If I opened each one, I'm sure I'd find documents corresponding to each title—no hidden porn or stash of dark web finds. Not my Ember.

She may be into the kinky stuff, but it's only because I'm coaxing her into it. I doubt she's diving into her own independent research.

The fact inspires me, though, and I open her web browser and click on her recent history. Maybe she *is* curious.

I read the newest searches and scowl. Curious about the wrong things, it seems.

Ember's looked into Savannah's disappearance, reading the

news articles and mining her social media accounts. I push my shoulders back at the search of my name, the perusal of *my* social media, but relax when I don't find searches like *did Thorne Briar kill Savannah Merricourt.*

My accounts are a total front, not the real me at all, but Ember spent time going through the group photos of pretend happiness and go-lucky drunkfests we held in the caves below Winthorpe. Probably so she could get a better look at Sav and compare their faces. It's exactly what I would do if I were told I took the fucking spot of a missing girl. A glance at the date confirms my suspicions—literally her first day at Winthorpe and she's getting the goods on everyone who crossed her path, including Aurora and Aiko.

The skin under my eyes tightens as I take in the wealth of information she acquired and the amount of digging she managed to do in a few hours. She's showing a level of skill I didn't think she had, accessing confidential databases and pulling up Savannah's hospital records, including her birth certificate. She also tried a few hacks on finding her birth mother, but I'm aware of the futility without even needing to check. That woman is buried deep.

Interesting. Had Ember's true heritage been different, she would've been a perfect fit for the Marks company.

Ember predominantly focused on Savannah's social life, sticking with Instagram and TikTok. For that, I'm thankful but not trustful, and a few keystrokes later, I pull up her deleted history. She'd done a good job burying it, but I'm my father's son and am confident I know my way around binary codes more than she does.

Ah. There it is. All the searches about *me.* She pulled up precious little, as I maintain a clean slate on the internet, and luckily, she wasn't savvy enough—or willing enough—to pry into the police investigations and my one and only suspect inter-view. Father is the same, relentless in scrubbing all photos of himself from the internet, unwilling to put a face to the deeds he commits.

I sit back, though, staring at the exposed files I'd had to complete a few tricks for in order to access. Why did she delete all her information gathering on me, but not anyone else? Or fail to put a passcode on her computer? It's as if she knew I'd be snooping in her room or swiping her laptop at school...

A few taps of the keystrokes, and I find the hidden tracking code in her software.

I smile.

Devious little pretty...

She set me up. Gave her nightly visitor full access to her files so she could prove there was a stranger in her room. I look up sharply from the computer and to the hidden door I'd left wide open. *Does she know it's there?*

"Not yet, sweetheart," I murmur, deleting my digital tracks in seconds.

It gives me pause, however. Perhaps I'm not being as incog-nito as I thought, and I'm very, *very* careful.

I file that possibility away for later investigation. Bored now, I push back from the desk and retreat into the old tunnels connecting my house to hers, mulling over the disappointment that she may be gone all weekend. Could she have returned to her adoptive parents? A possibility, but Malcolm's not the type to put his precious objects on loan, even for a weekend.

My concerns end up allayed when the next evening, I hear the crunch of tires and watch Ember exit the navy BMW 5-series that Malcolm has his butler drive around. It's no i8, but it'll do. Jaxon ditched me an hour ago, muttering something about going fishing while nursing an epic hangover from the bottle of bourbon we split at lunch.

Ember's hair lost even more pigment in the sun as she steps into her driveway, white as a halo and blowing in the spirited New England wind before she disappears into the manor.

"Where did you go last night, little pretty?" I mutter, staring out at the pink-and-gold-streaked sky as the sun gives into the moon. The idea of Ember meeting anyone forces my skin to contain a volcano of boiling blood. Whatever poor soul dared to ask her out will have a terrible time walking around campus with their balls bursting in my hands come Monday.

I send Jaxon a text, demanding he find out where she was and who she was with. I'd do it myself, but tonight, I'll be … busy.

Ember's home now.

I slip out of bed, bare-chested and rock-hard, going in search of everything I might need.

THERE'S no passion in the recent Noble initiations. Father, as the leader of the chapter, has declared fear-based rites to be the most preferable. Mandatory, in fact. He's also put me in charge of all the fledglings and, if necessary, the Virtues', too. You would think I'd enjoy making the freshmen cower, the girls cry, and the boys moan. Or vice versa. I've tried to take pleasure in it, standing above them and ordering them to keep slicing the knife into their skin, holding their forearm in the fire, lying chained in a coffin, or else I'll make them.

If I'm anything like my father, it should bring me joy to use my talons and scrape terror across their faces. I've often pondered whether my father would oversee the initiations with savage pleasure glittering behind his permanent pissed-off stare, then jerk off to the fond memories later. The fucked-up bastard probably did.

I'm going through the motions like he asked, being vicious when necessary, but it's just not hitting me in that pleasure spot. I'm dull as a butter knife issuing these commands. The effect of self-torture and the desperation of these idiots numbs my senses, slows my heartbeat, and frankly, bores me.

Until tonight.

At the thought of yanking Ember from her bed and dragging her to a location under my control, my blood simply fizzes. My pulse beats so emphatically, I can feel it at the tips of my fingers and toes. I'm more alive than I've been in years, and it takes an incredible amount of constraint to lessen my adrenaline with weed, bide my time, and wait.

Wait.

Wait.

Nightfall assists in my silent journey through my house, but I'm eager for the permanent darkness of the underground tunnels connecting Ember and myself.

It's after ten, meaning Father's encased in his study, likely to stay there until dawn, and my stepmother will be comatose in bed, likely hoping to continue her unconsciousness if Father decides he needs more than bourbon for his nightcap.

The staff will also be isolated in their quarters, few daring to wander the cold stone halls of the Briar estate unless summoned. I use the desertion to my advantage, padding down the Persian runners in the halls and avoiding the priceless bronze heads poking out of their displays like a seasoned cat burglar.

It's impossible to count the number of times I've snuck out and through this mansion, in hiding and in escape. It's imprinted in my muscles at this point, the dips and dives and graceful maneuvers through the dark interior until I reach the tunnel I want.

A single underground corridor attaches the Weatherby

Manor to the Briars', so neglected and cobwebbed it was most likely created in the 1800s when the manors were first built and the families bonded through the flagship secret societies. The footsteps breaking through the dust have only ever been mine, confirming my assumption that my father no longer uses this connection, if he did at all. He prefers open-faced defiance when it comes to Malcolm, not breaking and entering his home late at night with nobody knowing.

The entrance of one such tunnel is hidden on the first floor, behind one of the dual winding staircases. It's incredibly old-fashioned, requiring me to pull at a sconce before the seams appear and the wall sinks in. Then I have to push at it to open, sending out a plume of dust mites each time.

I've learned to hold my breath, lest I sneeze and perk up my father's ever-present ears.

Doing just that, I close and lock it behind me.

Ember and I won't be using it for our return journey.

Using my phone's flashlight, I navigate the pebbled walkway, forgoing the lighting of candle sconces on the walls. Blowing them all out at the end is a bitch, and I'm a man who prefers using modern technology to assist in my depravities.

When I'm at the point where I'm under the public road separating our houses, a decaying staircase takes shape to the west, and I head in that direction, carefully toeing the steps so I don't crash on my face and jab a rock into my groin. Again.

At the top, I'm faced with two options, north or south, but having done this too many times, I head north, winding behind the Weatherby walls now, and using muscle memory to feel my way across the narrow openings and take an even narrower set of hidden stairs.

There are a few interesting spots along the way, discreet sections of Weatherby Manor that I wonder if Malcolm even knows about or cares, but none of those draw my interest right now.

All I can think about is Ember. All I want is her.

At last, I reach her bedroom and run my palm along the cracked, old stone separating me from her.

Then let myself in.

CHAPTER 26
EMBER

e's coming...

He's COMING, Ember!

He's here.

My eyes pop open, the dark scarlet of my eyelids ceding to the semi-gold of my bedroom. The low-burning fire crackles, assisting in waking me up fully, but the dream maintains its grip on my skull, forcing the recall of Malcolm wandering the halls toward me, warning in a deathly voice, *I warned you. Don't do it, Ember. He'll come for you if you bow to him. Becoming one of him means forever. Forever you. You forever. Don't fall into the hole of my mistakes.*

HE'S COMING.

Scooting up on my pillows, I scrub my eyes. My time with Aiko hasn't helped these soul-stirring connections my subconscious makes between Malcolm, the Societies, Savannah, and Winthorpe High. If I had proof, that'd be one thing, but all I possess are Malcolm's warnings, Aiko's memories of her stepsister, and my rush of emotion when it comes to Thorne.

So intangible. So not right, but not enough to cause me fear.

Rolling onto my side, I stare into the lowering flames in my fireplace, my thoughts torn between being overly cautious or barging forward and—

A hand clamps over my mouth.

My scream ricochets off the dry palm and into the back of my throat, my body recoiling on instinct, back arching, legs kicking —but my lower half is caught under the sheets. The contact against the hard muscle behind me is fought by nothing but my foot, covered in soft linen.

Writhing, my arms shoot out as I try rolling onto my back to use my nails and scratch at the person holding me silent with one hand and down with the other, his forearm crushing my chest. Pain spears from my breasts at being so forcefully squished. I cry out.

"*Stop.*" My voice comes out muffled, nonsensical. "*No.*"

"I love to hear you beg, little pretty."

My whole body goes still. All except for my eyes, which search frantically until I can make out the silhouette hovering above me.

Thorne's stunning features move out of the darkness and into the firelight, an angel illuminated by the devil's flames.

"Good girl. The less you move, the less reason I have to pin you down." He leans forward, the flickering shadows unable to disguise the striking blue lurking within. "Can I remove my hand, or are you going to scream for Daddy?"

The thought crossed my mind. Malcolm's bedroom is on the other side of the manor, but he strikes me as the type to be constantly attuned and will come running at the sound of my distress. But Thorne can only be here for one reason—my initiation. If I call for Malcolm, my trials will end, and I'll no longer be a prospect for a secret society that could answer all my dreams.

Being a member of the swim team, the Girls' Code computer

club, mock trial, and every other club and extracurricular is the truest way, an avenue I was determined to pursue.

But to defy these guys, to openly deny their invitation ... they could ruin me.

I've been warned of the consequences once. That was enough.

Yes, those *have* to be the reasons as I shake my head in confirmation that I won't scream. It's not the bolt of electricity shooting down my center as Thorne's hardened touch pins me to the mattress, lust storming through his moonlit eyes.

"That's my girl," he says and pulls back.

The cold air hits my lips, wicking at the moisture he left behind. Buying time, I play dumb. "W-what do you want? What are you doing here?"

"Drink this." He pulls a plastic water bottle from the back pocket of his jeans. Maybe two ounces of clear liquid glimmers in the warm, orange glow.

I sit up, pressing against the sharp carvings of the headboard. "How 'bout no."

His gaze narrows. "Last time, I didn't give you a choice. This time, I am."

"So you can drag me to another cave? Incapacitate me while the ocean rushes in?"

"You loved it."

My shoulders tense. I purse my lips while his turn supple, and his tongue glides out, savoring the memory. He looks like he's about to devour me whole. His stare promises that he'd lick me first.

Controlling my breath under that heated gaze takes *a lot of* work. "I'm not willingly letting you drug me."

"Your choice, but you can't know where I'm taking you. Rules, little pretty. Ones I can't bend. If you don't ..." The plastic crunches its warning underneath his grip. "I'm afraid you'll no longer be a candidate. For the Society or anything else Winthorpe has to offer."

"You guys are bastards, you know that? As if being the richest kids in the country isn't enough, you have to put collars on us, too."

He inclines his head. "You're not my pet. You're a Weatherby."

I snort. "Coming from a Briar."

"Caught on to our fathers' enemy status, did you?" He holds out the bottle again. "Drink. You'll discover so much more about your lineage if you continue this process and become a Virtue."

"Coming from a Noble prince," I parry. "Who, in my limited knowledge, has no business initiating a Virtue."

"That's up for debate." Still offering the drink, he muses, "Would you rather I bring Aurora in here?"

He's got me there. Folding my arms over my knees, I say, "I don't trust you, Thorne."

"What if I promise I won't hurt you?" He smiles. "Without your permission, that is."

I shake my head. "I'll be unconscious. I won't know if you hurt me or not."

Thorne responds with the softest voice. "Hmm. My sweet little pretty."

He sits on the edge of my bed, close enough to touch. Rubs his thigh with one hand while sloshing the bottle with the other. "I'm not here to be kind and coax you into submission. I'm here to steal you from this room. Either you'll drink this willingly or I shove you back down on the mattress, pinch your nose shut, and force it down your throat." He slaps his thigh before ending on a cheery note, "So which will it be?"

"You're fucking nuts—"

He lunges.

My instant cry garbles in my throat as he slaps a palm against my forehead, and I slam into the wood behind.

"All right!" I shout, scrunching my eyes shut as I twist away from the lip of the bottle he crushes against my lips. "Fine! I'll do it."

His hold immediately releases. "Excellent choice."

The bottle hovers in my vision. Snatching it, I swill it back, locking my glare on him as I do it.

"The effects should be fairly immediate," Thorne says, his voice seeming far away. "Relax. Just like before, you'll be fully clothed when you wake. But I can't promise you won't be afraid of where you end up ..."

My blinks slow down. Blacker than normal vision. Head lolling forward, I brace for balance, but my arms are sludgy, my grip on reality even looser. "I ... I'm ... not wearing pajama pants ..."

"Bye-bye, little pretty."

The fireplace goes sideways, and my eyes close for the final time.

CHAPTER 27
THORNE

She takes her sweet time rousing.

I wile away the hour by resting my ankle over my knee on the chair across from her and catching up on next week's assignments. Ember's ahead of me—the rifling through her computer told me as much—and I'm not one to cede my top-of-the-class spot so easily. I'm not interested in the Marks Fellowship, naturally, but I can't resist giving those who want it so badly some frightening competition. I can outrun, outdo, out*rank* any one of these sycophants. Especially those who dress in a pale pink, cartoon kitty T-shirts and white cotton panties for bed.

I study Ember's bent-over form for a few minutes.

So sweet. So innocent. So mine.

A half hour later, I hear chains rattle. I dog-ear the page I'm on and look up.

White-blond hair ripples near her nose as she takes in conscious, fearful breaths. She yanks her arms again, her hair parting to reveal an uncertain expression that morphs into frustration when she lifts her head enough to notice the iron cuffs binding her wrists above her and against the wall.

Ember's knees scrape against the stone floor as she bucks and struggles. "What the hell? Thorne!"

"Right here."

Her head snaps in my direction. Enough moonlight streams in from the small, square windows to illuminate my presence. "Uncuff me. Now."

I take my time setting the text aside, uncrossing my legs, and standing. "No can do. You must be parched." I point at the full glass of water resting on the side table near my chair. "Would you like some?"

Iron clanks as she presses against the stone, her legs coming up enough to reveal a preview at the apex. "Don't come near me."

"That would be problematic, considering you want me to use this key." I reach into my pocket, revealing a silver skeleton key. It flashes in the silver-blue light.

"*Fuck* you. What is this? Where are the rest of the Society members?"

"I'm afraid they're no longer required to witness your trials. It's been left up to me."

For the first time, true fear sparks in her eyes. As it should. Another revelation is the tightening of my balls as I witness her growing terror. She kneels before me, locked up in chains, and I resist adjusting my hardening cock, a response that's never occurred in any of my initiations.

"A part of the second trial is domination and making you face your worst fear." I step closer, noting her efforts to contain her wince. "It's one of my father's favorite tests and all the kings before him. I've never much enjoyed it, but I gotta say ..." I lower to my haunches, regarding her face-to-face. "Watching you squirm while down on your knees turns me on more than watching you drown while grinding against my pelvis."

She spits in my face.

I jerk back, outrage uncoiling in my gut, ready to grow fangs and strike. But on the outside, all I do is smile before swiping the wetness from my cheek.

Then I use my fingers—fingers that were in *her*—to carefully rim my lips.

Her eyes widen, her lips curling in disgust, but she can't disguise the growing black desire of her pupils while she watches.

My mouth curves under my finger. "While I wish this came from your other set of lips, this will have to do."

She whispers, "You promised you wouldn't hurt me."

"And have I?" I make sure she sees me scan her head-to-toe. "You're still wearing what you came in, and I haven't touched one sensitive spot on your body. Carried you, yes. Propped you up for these chains, sure. But take advantage of you while unconscious? I'm not that kind of guy, Ember."

"Don't patronize me. You love torture. Can't resist mixing pain and adrenaline."

"All which require an alert participant."

She readies for another loogie, but I palm her mouth before she can get it out. She whimpers under my solid grip, the pads of my fingers pressing into the softness of her cheeks, digging into her jaw. "If I were you, I'd get back to why you're here instead of continuing a one-sided spitting contest. Can I remove my hand, or will I have to strip you bare and leave you here overnight for your punishment to really sink in?"

After a moment of aiming pure fury at me with her eyes, she gives a single acknowledging bob of her head.

"I'd say 'good girl,' but you're being very, very bad."

I make sure my voice is velvet, my tone coated with the heat of top-shelf whiskey, a mixture intended to both soothe and enrapture, then I remove my hand from her face and sit back on my heels. A hawk assessing its prey.

She blinks, likely struggling for clarity, the drug still clinging to her mind like gossamer. "You said something about facing my greatest fear. This isn't it. Why am I chained up? Where are we?"

"The bindings are a part of the process. First rope, then iron, then ..." I scrunch my eyes deviously. "Well, I can't ruin the surprise. Just as I'm prevented from telling you where we are. This is private Noble property."

Ember takes the opportunity to scan our surroundings with a sharper eye. I'm not worried. All she'll see are damp, stone bricks, possibly the pooling of stagnant water in the corners, and the long, rectangular room we're in. She won't see a door, since our exit is hidden deep in the expanding shadows. If she tunes in with her ears, she'll hear the faint dripping of condensation off exposed pipes, but not much else. We're isolated here from traffic, footsteps, machinery, *life*.

I question whether she'll look hard enough to notice the faded, century-old engravings of names on the walls, housing their bodies within.

But just in case she does, I redirect her attention. "If being trapped and bound with me in a strange, decaying room isn't a fear of yours, then what is?"

She meets my stare dead-on. "Not being perfect."

That gives me pause. Though I try to control it, she must see it on my face because she elaborates. "All my life, I've strived to be good, loved, accepted. I think I learned it from my parents— that being perfect is what will make you happy. There's my mom, who always does her hair and makeup before her job and pastes a smile on her face. Like she's going somewhere important and fancy and needs to make a good impression. She's ... she cleans houses. Every day, she dressed up for an upper-class luncheon because that's what made her happy. To look good. And my dad, he was miserable for most of my childhood, working for this terrible human who paid him half the legal minimum wage to do landscaping on well-to-do homes. It wasn't until I convinced him to create his own business and surpass his boss with better software that I saw this light bulb turn on in him. Like he was *meant* for something ... but all I did was get him fired. Mom told me to stop playing with our lives like this, that we were meant to be who we were meant to be, and that just didn't sit well. I didn't want fate to decide our future. *I* wanted to do it, to take the lead."

My eyes flare at the instant kismet I feel at her statement, but I cover it quickly, reconfiguring it to a blank expression.

"The client Dad showed his virtual blueprints to ended up calling him personally," she continues, her stare drifting to the side, away from here. "And hiring him. That was the start of his new business, and he's been in demand ever since. The downside? Dad became busier and busier, and I never saw him. But this one time, I did well in an essay assignment, and he declared a dinner celebration. Even put off work to make it happen. So, I won awards and scored A's. Excelled at all subjects. Got all those dinners with Dad."

"Congratulations," I drawl in an effort to prevent the emotional thickening of my voice. Too close. This girl is hitting *too close* to home.

"I was desperate for that happiness to continue, so I kept being perfect and staying out of trouble. My parents never noticed I had no friends. In fact, most people at school couldn't stand me because I was praised by teachers too much. I told myself I didn't care because I have my parents, and I'm on the road to success and happiness. I'm ... perfect."

I unclench my jaw, staring at her for a few seconds too long. Then I rasp out, "Why are you telling me this?"

"I'm trying for honesty." She shrugs, the chains clinging to her arms clinking together. "It's the best way to get me out of this situation and into the Virtues, isn't it?"

"That's why you want to do this? Because the Virtues personify perfection?" I lick my lips. "They don't. They twist it for their means, gift honor and position to people who don't outright deserve it, and manipulate capitalism. You've worked hard, harder than most. Sure, you were mocked for it at your pathetic public school, but Winthorpe doesn't scorn such things."

"Does the Marks family? Belle's dad?"

Her mention of my father's good friend, his replacement to Malcolm, has me snapping out of it. *Why am I telling her so much?* "Is that what you ultimately want? Will it give you the prestige—the *perfection*—you're after?"

"Yes. It's all I've worked for."

I rest my hand on my chin. "It won't gift you dinners with Daddy."

She flinches. A ripple of unease forms in my chest at the sight.

Ember rests a steady gaze on mine. "But it will make everything I've done up until now, all the belittlement, the loneliness, the *implosion* of my life, worth it."

I peer at her in turn. "You think so?"

Her throat bobs, but she doesn't break our stare. "Unless, as you say, you make me face my greatest fear and take it away."

"If you're made a Virtue, all of Malcolm's threats will be made obsolete. Your parents will be free. You will escape him … can go back to them. Is that not worth it?"

She jangles her chains for emphasis. "I know. Why do you think I'm enduring this?"

I smile. "Because you like me?"

Inconceivably, a blush creeps along her cheeks. Her skin is so pale that the flush to her face is obvious in the moonlight.

The sight constricts my abs. "While we're aiming for honesty, tell me, did you enjoy what we did underwater?"

Her chest rises and falls with increasing breaths. But she looks at the ground as though she can't stomach looking me in the eye as she whispers, "Yes."

"Would you do it again?" It takes a mountain of control to keep my voice level.

A line forms between her brows. Ember's confusion, the torture of battling her need to be good with the craving to be bad, is such a delicious turn-on, my cock strains in response. "I don't know."

"But you dream of it. Twist and turn, crying out for it."

Her chin jerks up. "So it *is* you. Visiting me at night. Watching me."

At the fire in her eyes, I decide on honesty since she gave it so freely to me. "You're irresistible to me, Ember. I can't seem to shake you, and I've tried. But your innocence, tied with your curiosity ... fuck, it kills me. Every time."

Her expression falls. "It's only because I look like her."

I exhale, long and hard. "Is that what you think?"

"What else could it be? The entire school talks like you're either a suspect or a victim, but either way, you're tied to her forever. And then there's me, coming into this world at the time she's most missed, taking all the things she had. You're drawn to me because of that, Thorne. Not because of who I am."

"Baby, you are so, *so* wrong." I move closer, our knees almost touching. "Sav and I were together, yes, but what most people don't know is, we broke up the night before she disappeared. We were done. It's a part of what had the cops interested in me in the first place."

Confusion flashes across her face. "Why doesn't anyone else know that?"

"Why should they? It was our business. She and I, we had fun together, but she ... she was pure innocence. Unwilling to ..." I pause, unhappy with the delicate territory I'm treading on.

"She didn't like what you like. In bed." Ember tilts her head, studying my face for tells that she's right, I'm sure.

I take in a hard breath before I answer. "No. She didn't."

A slew of emotions ticks behind those impenetrable black eyes of hers. Until I decide to think for her. "But you do, don't you? You enjoyed the brief adventure I gave you."

"Adventures," she corrects. "Plural."

"Right. Finger-fucking you in class. I enjoyed smelling you on me all day, little pretty."

Her breath hitches. She must be lacking air, just like I am, as it shrinks between us. We stay like that, stone still, staring hard, our breaths matching in sudden, unignorable desire.

"Do you enjoy being chained in front of me?" I bend closer until our noses almost touch. "Knowing I could do anything I wanted to you?"

Her lips part. Hot exhales hit my lips, and I suck them in, desperate for a taste of her.

"What if I wanted to do something to you instead?"

My brow kicks up before I grin. "What could you possibly have to offer with your hands literally tied?"

"My mouth."

I freeze. Air hisses through my lips.

She glances down, acknowledging the obvious response to her words. And my little, innocent, wanton girl smiles. "Do you promise we're alone?"

"Yes." I ponder for a moment. "Do you promise not to bite my dick off?"

She laughs, the sound so delightful and foreign in a place like this. "I can't exactly injure the only person who can unlock me from the wall."

Ember must read something in my expression after she says that, my reluctance to have anything non-consensual between us ripping through my mind before I can stall it. I'm supposed to keep her fearful, obedient, unsure. She can't discover any uncertainties of *mine*.

Yet she says anyway, "Feel me, Thorne. Touch me there. See how much I want this."

My eyes go back to hers, riveted. Locked. Chained as much as she is.

"Do it," she says.

My desire takes over, the addiction to this girl. I trail my fingers up her bare thigh, feeling her muscles constrict at my touch until I reach her apex and stroke the white cotton. Stroke and sink into the dampness.

"Fuck," I say hoarsely.

She grinds her hips against my hand. I cup her, rubbing my thumb against her clit through the fabric and playing with her anus with the rest of my fingers. Jesus fuck, how I'd love to bury myself in either one.

Ember moans.

My attention flies back up to her face. Her scent hits the air, and a low growl exits my throat. I'm straining against my pants and can barely keep this kneeling posture before I explode with need.

"Undo your pants," she whispers with half-closed eyes, then bites her lips while continuing to circle her hips.

The iron scrapes and tangles with her movements, reminding me that she's bound, unable to stand, mine to plunder.

And she'll be forced on her knees the entire time.

The vision is almost as potent as our very near reality. It takes severe effort not to explode in my pants. On a moan, I pull out my cock, the release of pressure a fucking paradise as I hit the air, and Ember's focus devours every inch of me.

I suppose she's never seen it before. I wonder if she's even seen *one*.

From the shocked, wondrous look on her face, I'm assuming not.

"Let's see how good you are at sucking me off," I murmur before rising, tangling my fingers in her hair and pushing my dick into that plush mouth.

I'm not gentle. I push and push until I hit the back of her throat. Ember's eyes water, her cheeks bulge, and she stares up at me as if I'm strangling her.

But the silky wetness of her mouth and the panicked movements of her tongue have me groaning, grunting as I pull out, then thrust back in.

She gags, coughs, but her throat opens with my second attempt.

"There it is," I say above her, my voice tight. "You fucking take me in so well."

She responds by circling her lips around my cock and giving a tentative suck.

That curious tug nearly sends me over the edge, but I reclaim control, fisting her hair and burying myself in her mouth until she hits my shaved pubes.

"You like this?" I say as she struggles against the cuffs. Her wrists can't move—she'll have bruises by the end of this.

She garbles a response, shifting, and I realize she's not struggling at all—rather, she's finding a better angle to accommodate me.

This girl. This *goddamn* girl. I want to keep her locked in a mausoleum forever now.

Pulling out, I give her a break, allowing her a brief stint of oxygen. She gasps, saliva dribbling down her chin that she can't wipe off, my dick shining with the same kind of lube.

It bobs near her lips, and once she collects herself, she darts out her tongue to collect the pearlescent droplets at the tip.

"*Fuck*," I grunt. Instead of grabbing her by the hair again, I inch closer, curious as to what she'll do, how she'll handle me, when I'm not taking control.

Ember uses her tongue to coax me back in. And she sucks, loud and wet, moving her head until I'm all the way back in, her throat relaxed this time, then out. She plays with my tip, flicking her tongue, until I can't take any more and move my hips, grinding against her mouth.

My palms slam against the wall above her as I adjust my legs for better thrusting. Baring my teeth, I increase the pace. Ember meets my speed, moaning and whimpering just like she does when she dreams of me.

I raise my face skyward, the last thought of mine akin to *she's dangerous* before I explode into the back of her throat, forcing her to swallow my cum as my thighs burn. Pleasure rockets through me, and my forehead falls against the stone wall, my chest heaving.

"The fellowship's yours," I heave out. "Holy fuck, it's all yours."

Bracing myself, I push off the wall, stumbling back with my jeans bunched at my ankles and my balance sorely tested.

I'm gifted with a vision of Ember, cum leaking from the corners of her lips and a fresh redness to her face. Her hair's tangled, a complete lost cause, and her nipples practically spear through her shirt.

"Did you—did you mean what you said?" she asks between gulps.

"About the fellowship?" My shoulders practically hit my ears with my heaves. "Yeah. You passed the trial. It's fucking yours."

229

She doesn't brighten like I anticipated. Her shoulders sag in, and she looks away, downcast. I have the uneasy feeling I just wilted a gorgeous flower.

But what's the alternative? Admitting to her how much she fucking affects me? Confess that was the best suck-off of my life? No. Never a Weatherby. Never *her.*

I'll toy with Ember, for sure. She clearly wants to play back. Anything else is off the table, and while I didn't mean to solidify it at the time—she had me so off-balance with that orgasm, I'm still reeling—I certainly do, now.

If she's hurt by it, all the better. She'll understand I'm serious.

She says nothing as I pull up my pants and readjust myself. Doesn't comment as I walk up to her and undo her cuffs and untangle the iron rings.

Ember brings her arms down, rubbing at her wrists, but she stays curled up on the floor. I turn, pulling a sachet out of my back pocket and grabbing the glass of water. I pour the powder into it, then offer it to her.

"Drink up again, little pretty."

"Let me guess, I have to leave the same way I came in."

Her voice is rough but resolute.

"Sorry, baby," I say. I think a part of me means it.

She accepts the drink on a sigh, chugging all of it, the water no doubt needed after the way I ravaged her mouth.

Down boy, I think as my dick grows hard and her eyelids grow heavy. She leans to the side. The glass falls from her hand, shattering against the floor.

I catch her before her head hits the ground.

CHAPTER 28
EMBER

T horne deserves as much punishment as he's given to me.

I can't hand in my assignments without a hitch in my step, prep for tests without a lump in my throat, or get ahead in class without feeling nauseous.

He's contaminated every effort I made in securing the fellowship for my own. If my name *is* called in that last assembly, I'll always question whether accepting the honor will be from my hard work or his sexual pleasure.

And then there are my dreams.

It's like a lethal hush falls over my mind, my body going stiff under my sheets, but supple in my fantasy, where the bindings to Thorne tighten to the breaking point. My skin grows hot, and my legs spread for him, aching with need. But that seductive shadow of his won't approach. No, he asks me to gag myself first, tie my spread legs to the footboard, bind one wrist to the headboard. He'll do the other.

Trembling, I obey. A *snick* of sound occurs in his hand as he steps forward, his lips quirked in a promising grin as he raises a whip.

Gasping, I fly awake. It takes me a moment to understand where my hand is and what it's rubbing, but I can't stop, not through the thick haze of dream and reality, and I finish myself off while I'm still in the throes, falling onto my back, my hips arching into the air. I slam a pillow to my face to muffle my cries.

The fifth time the pleasure abates and the shame creeps in, I peel out of bed, grab under my desk, and drag it over to the part of the wall Thorne uses to break into my room.

Not anymore, asshole.

The sound drew Dash's attention, who knocked softly on my door, inquiring if everything was all right. A check of the time showed it was close to dawn, so I was forced to think up an excuse better than deciding to rearrange my room before sunrise. I just said I thought I spotted a rat and was pushing furniture to try to find it.

I heard his gasp of horror through the thick wood, but since it's not out of the realm of possibility in a home like this, he promised he'd have pest control come during business hours.

After that, I showered, discarded my damp, accusatory underwear, and headed downstairs to have breakfast with Malcolm.

It took a few days of his usual, *"How are you?"* question for me to finally stop automatically thinking, *"I'm pretty sure I'm into BDSM with Thorne at the same time he's collecting all my dreams and insecurities for his own. And you?"* and answer, "Fine. Studying hard. You?"

It went like that for a week, then two, then three, our inquiries always skimming the surface but never diving deep. Malcolm's warnings are ever-present in my head, demanding I never speak to Thorne, commanding I stop asking about the

Societies and stick my head in the sand instead. I take it to heart but don't explain to him what I'm doing. What I've done.

Trust between us is slim, made smaller by my defiance, but it is only through being on the good side of the Societies that I can survive Winthorpe unscathed. Malcolm doesn't hold as much power at the school as the Societies, regardless of my suspicions that he's a former Noble.

And if it means finding a new side of myself, a deviant, lying, purposely beguiling version of Ember Beckett, I'm not going to say no to her. She's unleashed, and holy crap, does she ever *crave*.

Tingles spread from my neck and cling to my breasts every time I dream of Thorne. But then I wake up and remember how dangerous a line I'm treading between getting what I want versus getting what I deserve.

Except ... he's not asking for anything. Not as I keep up with my studies and get ahead for semester exams. Thorne congratulating me on the fellowship after our tryst eats at me, day after day. I never had any intentions of signing up for sex with him to get what I want. I've worked for every award, trophy, and honor I've received. For him to reduce that sacrifice to a few minutes of oral with him in a basement ... it made me feel dirty, and not in the sensual way he usually cajoles out of me.

The fellowship is yours.

Yet with Aurora watching my every move and just waiting for me to screw up, I'm not about to draw a rose on all my papers and hope for the best.

Aiko's also become my shadow, meeting me after classes and escorting me to the next, acting like it's normal since we've become close, but I sense there's more of a motive than simply spending time with me.

She misses Savannah, that much is obvious. The more important concern is ... who does she see when she looks at me? Does she want me to be the new Savannah Merricourt?

Some nights, I pull out Savannah's necklace from my bedside drawer, wondering if that's what I want, too.

Thorne's screwing with my head way too much. Or maybe it's Winthorpe.

On the third week of Aiko's incessant yet kind of endearing prattling, I've had enough. Combined with the ache for *more* because of Thorne's deliberate withholding, I think I'm coming down with my first case of angry blue-balls.

"This is the third trial, isn't it?" I mutter to Thorne on the fourth Monday with barely a word from him. "Ignoring me for weeks, pretending I don't exist even though I'm sitting right beside you."

Dammit, now I'm sounding clingy, and I hate myself for it.

I clamp my lips shut, forcing my eyes forward while Lowell explains another theory I studied two weeks ago.

After ten minutes pass with no response, I decide to hell with him. I'll take the suffering Aurora has to offer over resorting to begging this guy to talk to me.

"I haven't forgotten you."

The purr in his voice sends a trail of shivers down my spine.

"I'm simply waiting for you to make the next move," he adds.

I turn to stare at him.

"You showed me a side of yourself that has me intrigued," Thorne continues, scribbling equations on his workbook. "Instead of being your consort into the dark side, I want to see what you'll do when left to your own devices. So far, you're falling short."

I whisper my response. "You're saying I was supposed to decipher, from your assholeness with a side of extra douche, that you wanted me to make the next move?"

"Yep."

He lazily turns a page, Lowell's voice a constant drone in the background.

"So this *is* a test." Of my fucking patience in not punching him in the nose right this minute.

"Not for them." Thorne lifts his chin and flicks a glance at me. "The Societies. This is all for me, which is why I can no longer approach you. I have to report to the higher-ups on your initiate status, and I'd rather not describe to them all the ways I'm making you come. Therefore, it's up to you."

His stare lingers this time, his eyes white-blue from the sunlight streaming through the window behind us. They drop down to my chest, hidden behind a blouse, but his tongue pokes out like he can see my peaked nipples just fine.

"Did you describe to them—" I can't whisper it out loud. "What we did?"

One corner of his lips rises. "I had to. It was your second trial."

My cheeks turn so hot, they scorch my teeth. The thought of the other members, of *Aurora*, and any "dukes and duchesses" I have yet to meet, opining on what I did while chained up and on my knees ... and what Thorne claimed I'd get in return—it's not me. I'm not the girl who climbs ladders made of dicks.

"I think I'm gonna be sick."

I rise from my seat, but Thorne clamps a hand on my bare thigh, keeping me down. "Membership of the elite is not without sacrifice. Remember?"

"My sex life isn't up for their perusal—"

"All they know is you obeyed me."

I go still, satisfying Thorne enough to lift his hand, but his fingers leave marks.

"I don't need to tell them how you took my dick and sucked me like your favorite lollipop. They only care about your obedience, your willingness to submit to the Societies." Thorne purses his lips. "Well. That's not entirely true. My father would probably want every detail on how I face-fucked the Weatherby heir, but I prefer to collect *his* information, not sell my own."

My teeth clank together at his words—in outrage or desire, maybe a little bit of both, as he pockets away another dirty little secret of ours.

At the same time, Aurora pivots in her seat, hissing, "Would you two *shut up*? Some of us still care about grades." She slides her glare over to me. "Unlike others who happily rely on social status and underground privilege to get ahead."

"Like you aren't doing the same thing." *Bitch*, but I keep that last part to myself. We're still in a classroom. I at least have to pretend decorum.

"You think I don't work for my high scores?" she says in a wet whisper. "I kill myself over my studies, which is why bitches like you who give up halfway in favor of the easy route piss me the hell off. Just wait until finals." She flutters her workbook. "I'm beating your ass, Cum Bucket."

My eyebrows crawl to my hairline. "Excuse me?"

"Beckett. Bucket." Her eyes slide to Thorne. "Cum. It all goes together, don't you think? Did I not mention I hate bitches who use sexual favors to get ahead?"

My stomach pitches. I sear a look at Thorne. "I thought you said—"

He shakes his head, his rigid expression foretelling the extreme fury he wants to unleash. "I didn't tell her shit."

"I thought so." Her eyes gleam with triumph. "Thanks for confirming it."

"Ladies! Am I interrupting an important meeting?" Lowell calls, and I shrink in my seat, only just resisting hiding behind my hand.

"No, sir," Thorne says. "Miss Emmerson had a question about the calculation in 12(b) of the workbook you were explaining."

"Ah. Well, Miss Emmerson, if you face the front, I can go over it in more detail. If you look at page seventy-nine of your textbook ..."

Lowell's explanation continues, and I follow along with a roiling stomach and a terrible ache in my chest. What I want most in the world is at my fingertips, but Thorne has sullied it, made it dirty and undeserving.

"I don't want you to use your connections to the fellowship," I whisper to him with my head down, using my pencil to follow Lowell's instructions. "Is that clear?"

"Do whatever the fuck you want. Sacrifice your soul, make your daddy proud, be that perfect girl you envision in that naïve brain of yours."

His use of my confession sends daggers into my heart, but I keep my expression neutral.

Thorne leans close. "I'll always be around for a good fuck. And you love it. Find me when it gets to the point you can't resist me, little pretty."

The bell rings, causing Thorne to jump into action and slam his textbook shut. I startle, but he only looks down and tilts his mouth into that killer smile—the one he used when he grabbed the back of my head and pried my mouth open with the tip of his wet, hot dick. "I'll be waiting."

I lick my lips as he leaves, my hands curling into fists at the realization that I can still taste his salt.

CHAPTER 29
EMBER

A part of giving myself a gold star and forcing proof of deserved perfection on everything I do is putting in extra time for swim practice. Malcolm's allowed my early departures for school three times a week, so I can take advantage of a deserted rec center and put in laps. I'm determined to keep my times higher than Belle's—or any girl's, really —so I can secure my *independent* qualification for the fellowship.

I spent the last weeks scoping out Thorne's early practices to prevent any chance of us running into each other. He and his buddy rule the pool most hours, refusing access to anyone else who dares to enter their purified waters. Now that my morals have settled, I'm not even attempting to screw with them. Thorne can go fuck himself.

Thorne practices in the mornings four times a week, excluding weekends, which means Monday, Fridays, and Saturdays are mine. The rest of his schedule is focused after school.

Dash drives me before sunrise, the gnarled trees and craggy rockfaces bordering the road resembling the desperate bodies of those wailing to crawl out of Hell. The comparison draws a

239

shudder from my bones, and I focus on browsing through my phone rather than pondering when I'll become one of them.

He slows at the entrance to the Winthorpe rec center. I wave my thanks before exiting the car and dragging my sports bag and school bag with me.

I enter the deserted locker room, flicking on the floodlights one by one as I press the switch. The one above my locker needs repairing. My heart rate picks up as it flickers and buzzes above my head while I get changed, remembering Aurora's recent threats in this very spot.

I peel off my clothes quickly, the atmosphere resembling too much of a horror film before the final girl screams and dies. Pulling on my swim cap and goggles, I head to the pool deck.

Unlike in the locker rooms, the electricity stays on in the pool all night. I push into the bright, chlorinated environment with relief, planning on some quick warm-up stretches, then diving in immediately.

A small splash draws my attention. In the first lane, a dark form streaks by like a silent shark spearing through the water, then a head surfaces near the lane marker.

I freeze.

As soon as he starts to push off the wall for another underwater lap, he freezes, too.

"Seeking me out so soon, little pretty?" Thorne's voice ricochets against the porcelain tiles lining the walls. His goggles reflect the same, disguising any surprise that might be in his eyes.

Then again, Thorne's rarely, if ever, taken aback.

I cross my arms. "What are you doing here?"

"Swimming." He flashes his teeth, impressed at his own smart-ass remark.

"You don't swim on Mondays."

"And you would know this ... how?" He rests a muscled

forearm on top of the pool's perimeter, glistening under the glaring light.

"Because I studied your schedule to make sure I'd never run into you while I practiced."

"Brutal honesty. I enjoy that." He pushes off, doing a lazy backstroke toward me.

I retreat from the edge automatically, despite being on dry ground where he can't reach me in enough time to prevent my escape. Or ... could he?

I recoil another step.

"Don't run from me," he says, coy and slow. "I have a conflict on Thursday. Thus, my presence now. Remind me to thank that conflict later."

A bolt of green-eyed heat runs through me. Couldn't stop it if I tried. The curiosity over what—or who—that conflict could be is too much. Will there be a girl in bed with him now that he can't visit me at night?

Thorne must read something in my expression. "Desperate to know what that conflict is?"

"I don't give a damn."

"I'm sure." He comes up to the barrier near me, folding both arms over the top, grinning as he rests his chin on them. "Come on in, little pretty. Don't be scared."

A flash of the last time I was in the water with him bursts forward, turning the jealous streak into an inferno of desire.

Thorne pushes his goggles up, and the answering desire in his eyes can't be avoided.

"I know how you feel about sharing the pool," I say. "Finish your laps. I'll wait in the locker room until you're done."

"No, you won't."

Water rushes off his body as he lifts himself out, his rock-hard, lean swimmer's body on full display as his muscles contract, and he lands on his feet.

An unfurling sensation at my core has me skittering back. His mostly naked presence *cannot* affect me like this. He could ruin everything. Take everything.

But if I piss him off ... won't he do it, anyway?

Despite the tremor in my voice, I ask, "What do you want now?"

"What I always crave," he answers without missing a beat, striding toward me. "You. Always you."

Forever you.

Blinking against the unwanted engraving on Savannah's pendant, I stumble back, nearly crashing into the wall. Did Savannah ever hear those words come out of Thorne's mouth? Did he corner her like this?

He sees my fear, his brows furrowing. "Have you become a mouse already? I thought I'd at least be able to bat you around first."

"Forever you," I whisper while glancing to the side at the rippling waters of the pool and away from him. "Does that mean anything?"

"To whom? Me?" He points at his chest, water droplets running down and collecting at the bottom of the V of his torso. My mouth waters until I swallow it down. "Nope."

My heart misses a beat at his answer. *He's lying.*

Thorne blocks me in, throwing an arm on either side of my head and angling against the wall. He bends down, running the tip of his nose along my cheek, tasting the soft skin with his tongue. I shiver. "Are you curious how I like to use the pool to get off?"

"N-no."

"Liar, liar, pussy on ... oh. The opposite. *Wet.*" His hand moves down and his fingers press into my folds through my bathing suit, the dampness pooling against his pressure.

Whimpering, I arch back until my butt hits the wall and has

nowhere else to go. "I came here to swim laps, Thorne. That's all. I have to stay on top—"

"Do you want to be on top?" He moves until his face hovers in front of mine. This close, the color of his eyes is shattered glass. Just as sharp and deadly. "Sit on my face, Ember. But do it while I'm underwater."

I hold my breath. My attention darts to the pool, then back to him.

He circles my clit, pressing harder. "Tell me you want to."

I squirm, gasping.

"I-I-" I brush against his serious hard-on, practically impaling the thin material of his suit.

Thorne doesn't wait for my answer. He yanks the swim cap off my head, causing my dry hair to cascade down my shoulders. As the strands curl around my breasts, his pupils dilate. "I've never fucked a mermaid before, but I sure as hell would like to try."

Thorne grasps my bicep, tugging me forward. It forces him to remove his hand from between my legs, and I'm horrified over wanting to mewl in protest.

Like traitors, my legs follow him to the edge of the pool. I come to his side, where he grins down at me, releases my arm, then dives in.

When he resurfaces, he turns back to me, treading water. "Strip for me, little pretty."

I bite my lip in reluctance. That only seems to fuel him.

"There's no one here. The sun's not even up yet. I thought I was the only one who enjoyed 4 a.m. swims. Show me what I've been dreaming about."

The mention of dreams cleaves my conscience in two. I've wanted this. Fantasized about him again and again, and here he is.

My hand goes to one shoulder strap, then the other.

"Fuck yes," he croons, the effort of staying afloat doing nothing to deter his focus.

I slide down the first, exposing one breast, then the other. The warm, humid, chlorinated air might as well be coming from the arctic, with how pointed my nipples are.

Thorne's eyelids grow heavy with want. "Keep going."

Trembling, I push the rest of the suit down and step out of it, but I'm slow to stand. "I've never—never been completely naked in front of anyone before."

"Then I'm honored and fucking horny to be your first."

His strained voice brings a smile to my face, the vengeful part of me glad to return the blue-ball favor and make him wait for it. It gives me the confidence to straighten and face him full-on, exposed and vulnerable.

So vulnerable.

Thorne exhales a wet breath, his arms undulating in the water as he treads. The rippling pool can't disguise his erection. While I was hiding, he reached down and pulled his dick out, the magnifying effects of the water making it seem *huge*.

"Dive in, baby," he says with a husked edge.

But the sight of his dick freezes me. "I'm not ready. To ... you know. To have sex. With you."

The last part is uttered hastily. I don't want him to know I'm a virgin. It's like the one part of me he hasn't yet accessed and manipulated, and I want to keep it that way.

"You should know by now that I don't take what isn't offered. But I still want to drown my face in your pussy, if you're game."

His dirty talk has me flushing. Stupid, because these aren't words I haven't heard before, and he'd *just* chained me to a wall while I sucked him off. Why am I embarrassed *now*?

Right. Because it's my body on display. My insecurities are at the forefront now.

I'm so immersed in my hesitancy, I don't feel his hand on my ankle until it's too late.

Thorne yanks me to the edge, and I flail until I fall into the pool.

I come up, sputtering, pushing hair out of my face. "Fucking hell, Thorne! Can't any decision be my own?"

His eyes reflect the enduring ripples in the pool when he says, "Put your back against the wall. Arms up. You'll know when I'm finished."

"What—" But I shriek as he sinks underwater, suddenly feeling like I'm being circled by a shark, and I back up into the pool's wall on pure instinct.

And his mouth cups my sex.

"Oh my—holy—" I breathe out at the same time I turn rigid, my arms stretching out like a T.

Sensing my bone-straight response, Thorne reaches around and squeezes my ass, coaxing then pulling my legs apart. He floats them over his shoulders, my body automatically angling toward him, and holy mother, I've given him full access.

He uses his tongue like I bet he uses his dick, thrusting, circling, his teeth scraping against my clit. Moaning, I push for more of him. He answers with his fingers, some sinking into my folds and another stroking my anus, circling, pushing, entering.

So much stimulation at once has my head falling back as I stare unseeing at the ceiling, whispering his name, gyrating my hips and submitting fully to Thorne's pleasure.

I'm so into his tongue curls and bites and thrusts, I don't even consider how long he's been down there or that he might be stroking himself, enjoying cutting off his airways with both water and my pussy. But when that thought *does* come ...

Oh my. It turns me on.

Heat builds at the idea of Thorne drowning while tongue-fucking me, and on an impulsive, dangerous whim ... I sink down, too, without bothering to take a deep breath.

My chest tightens almost instantly, but I keep my eyes wide open. Thorne notices and glances up, the skin under his eyes rising with a wicked smile as I'm sure he regards his mermaid, my hair floating seductively around us as the pool reflects my pale, sunless skin and dark, nocturnal eyes.

Bubbles float up at his approving growl, but I grab the back of his head and push him back between my thighs, a lot like he did with me when I was locked up for him.

The orgasm builds, but I hold it back, enjoying keeping him under and forcing my heart into a thunderous, warning beat. My pulse thrums behind my eyes. My chest grows hot, desperate for breath. But the orgasm rivals the tightening of my muscles, the instinctive stretching of my jaw to take a breath.

I want both. *Need* both.

Thorne is indeed stroking himself, his hand a rapid blur along his dick as he reaches the brink of pleasure and death, too.

My body convulses, pleading with my mind to override the need, but it only sends me closer, almost, right there—

It smashes into me as my vision grows spotty, and I ... cease to exist.

A deep-water rush invades my soul, my thighs clenching harder around Thorne's head as a silent cry escapes my throat.

As my body slumps, that same water flows into my mouth.

Eyes popping wide, I paddle to the surface, coughing, choking, weaker, and more sated than I've ever been. My hand slams against the wall as I collect my bearings and come back to earth. My coughs turn to gasps, then heavy breathing.

"Thorne?" My voice is rough and unfamiliar.

Water lapping against the pool walls is the only response.

"Thorne?" Pushing off the stone, I tread in a circle, my kicks fervent.

I notice a dark, unmoving blob at the bottom.

"Oh my god," I whisper before diving deep.

Thorne lays on his stomach, his ebony hair doing a serpentine dance with the water's flow—his only movement.

Panicked bubbles rush out of my mouth as I get to him, hook under his arms, and swim him to the surface. He doesn't fight me. He doesn't even twitch.

White-hot panic strikes my chest. I put him in a lifeguard's hold and use a one-armed stroke to get us to the nearest ladder. Still holding him, I drag myself up the rungs first, and with great effort, I pull him up, too.

His chin sags against his chest, his wet hair flat against his forehead and covering his eyes.

Oh my god, no, no, please don't be dead, please—

A litany of pleas swirl in my head. I check his vitals—pulse slow, but there—and hold a hand to his chest. Not moving.

We took it too far. He stayed under too long.

I wasn't thinking of him in the throes of pleasure. Didn't care about his need for breath, or that he'd been under a lot longer than me. All I wanted was—

"Thorne."

No response.

Scrambling to his head, I tip his chin up, press my other hand to his forehead, and initiate CPR.

"Please, please, please work ..." I take a deep breath and press my mouth to his.

And in a single thrust, his tongue parts my lips.

My cry is muffled by his mouth and kept there when his arms circle my torso and pull me against his chest. I slap at him, use my knees, and generally become a flailing fish on top of an ocean rock.

His chest shudders with chuckles. Feeling his amusement

enrages me to such an extent, I unsheathe my canines and bite into the soft tissue inside his mouth. Hard.

A metallic tang brushes against my tastebuds at the same time as he growls and pushes me aside. When I gather myself and sit up, he rises, too, with a bloody, lopsided grin.

"You *asshole*! I thought you were dead!"

He swipes the back of his hand across his mouth, still smiling. "Give me more credit. I've been training in pools since I was five. I can hold my breath for a lot longer than three minutes. And it takes a lot less than that to get you off." He winks.

I swear, I will scrape my nails across that pretty face of his.

He must read my intent because he holds up a hand to stave me off. "Truce, little pretty. I was only playing a game."

The amused spark goes out in his eyes when his attention lowers, and he watches my heaving, bare chest.

My nipples are pebbled from cold, my soaked hair painting my breasts.

I know what I must look like to him. A washed-up feast.

A low sound comes from his throat, and he slams both palms to the tile as if he's about to prowl toward me.

"You're still an asshole." I point at him for emphasis, then get to my feet to grab a rolled-up towel from the bench.

"Admit it. You loved it." His voice is scratched with desire, probably because I'm giving him a nice view of my ass.

"Never do that to me again."

"So you want another round, do you?"

I sneer at his sheer arrogance, though he can't see. "You scared the shit out of me, Thorne. That's not what I—"

I'm interrupted by the sound of a door opening and turn in time to see half the boys' swim team funnel into the pool deck.

They spot me.

Fuck. I rush for the towel, but Thorne hooks my ankle and sends me toppling onto him before I can unfurl it.

Our wet bodies smack together, a garble of curse words tearing from my throat, but that doesn't stop him from holding me at the biceps and keeping me spread-eagle on top of him.

"You're interrupting my show, boys," Thorne says, turning his head to the crowd with an evil, shameless leer.

"Fuck you!" I'm slippery enough to escape one of his hand-locks, and slap him across the face before pushing to my feet and twisting the towel around my exposed body.

Too late, though. From the looks on these guys' faces—*Jaxon's* face—they've seen everything.

"Can we join?" someone calls. Probably a freshman. "She's got enough holes for three."

"You're all disgusting." I turn to them with undisguised revulsion.

"They're not the ones standing naked at the school's pool," Thorne says, which earns him a heel to the ribs. He grunts but looks like he enjoys it, the bastard.

"You're the worst of them all." I nail him with what I hope is a deep-seated laser beam of hate for the stunt he pulled, but before I can stalk away, he hooks me by the ankle again.

"Don't you dare," I seethe.

"There's a party next Thursday evening at my father's house. Be there."

"My last trial?" I dare to ask since the show's over, and the boys have strolled to the other side of the pool, likely to wait for the coach who will be here any minute.

"That's for me to decide." Thorne rises to his full height in one lithe move. Water droplets collect at his nipples, stream down the line of his pecs and abs. I hold back a swallow.

"Like what you see?" he murmurs.

I don't deign to answer. Instead, I spin on my heel and walk as fast as I can to the exit without slipping on the wet tiles.

"One more thing, Ember."

The drawled-out, promising use of my name has me pausing.

"Your pussy tastes incredible."

Heat bursts into my cheeks, but I don't turn around. Clutching the towel tighter, I push into the locker rooms in need of an ice-cold shower.

CHAPTER 30

THORNE

Ember's taste stays on my tongue for a full seven days, akin to the seven sins invading my body, reminding me of greed, gluttony, pride—all the things she unleashes in me whenever we cross paths.

Applications for early decisions should be taking up most of my time. I've applied to Harvard and Yale, Penn as my third, but instead of focusing on perfecting my top choice, I'm wondering what Ivy *she's* aiming for. Granted, my ED status is less stressful than most with the Noble membership behind me, but it's important that I also use my brains and talent to prove I'm more than a Noble legacy. That I could get into the Ivies with or without their help.

It's a goal I've voiced to no one, most especially my father, and after checking the applications portal one more time, I slam my laptop closed and exit my room. As I cross through the upper halls and descend the wide staircase, I take note of the decorations underway for the Societal party tonight. Our ancestral chandeliers have been replaced with black chrome ones, the theme of the evening being somewhat of a midnight masquerade. "Somewhat" because the themed decorations should be my stepmother's responsibility, but she's probably in another Oxy fugue, face down on her bed, so it's left up to me what to approve or deny. Frankly, I don't give a fuck.

The event planner finds me as soon as I hit the bottom stair. She's younger, maybe late twenties, and I don't miss the appreciative glint in her eye as she takes in my shirtless form, my sweatpants riding low on my hips.

I don't bother to disguise my discontent as she scampers close. "If it isn't Briar Junior, coming out of his cave. I was wondering when I'd see you again."

"Don't call me Junior. And don't act like we're friends."

The sharp snap of my voice has her retreating one step, but her lips form a firm line. Damn. I shouldn't have slept with her. It was over a year ago, at our last event's setup, and I was certain it'd be a one-time thing. Father rarely uses the same event planner, as most can't withstand his temper or his cold, icy veneer when he's not hot with rage, but it seems this one could.

It makes me suspicious over whether Father had her, too.

"I need a Briar to approve the ballroom's setup. If not you, then is your mother available?"

"She's not my mother, and sure, it looks terrific."

"But you haven't seen—"

"I don't care."

I swing around the staircase, leaving her far behind.

My father's in his ground-floor office, as usual, and with his door propped open, I can't escape to the kitchen unnoticed as I planned.

"Thorne. Get in here."

A sigh escapes me, but it's as silent and unnoticed as I prefer to be around this man.

"I trust the mansion's outfitted appropriately for tonight?" Father sits back in his chair, his silver-tipped hair slicked back from his angular face. I've never enjoyed looking at him straight on. It's as if his skin can't contain the skull from protruding through. The deep crevices highlight the unearthly glow of his blue eyes, even in the dim, mahogany-shadowed light.

"I don't know. Why don't you ask your wife?"

"She's indisposed. I'd like you to relay with the planner—Shelly, is it?"

"How the fuck should I know?"

"Language, boy. Especially in my presence."

I don't voice an apology. I just stand there, waiting to hear the reason he summoned me into his office instead of asking whether he knows the planner as Butterfly Snatch like I do, the tattoo of a monarch butterfly needled right on her bare pussy.

Must've hurt.

"I'd like to know your plans with the Weatherby girl." Father folds his forearms on his antique desk.

Ah. There's the reason. And a pussy he will *never* see. "I assumed you left me in charge and that I'd come to you when it was finished."

"Plans change. She's passed the first and second trials despite our agreement to have her fail, which, from your limited explanation, were quite difficult. At first, I was furious, but now I'm thinking … How do you plan to surpass those difficulties and give her the ultimate test of will?"

"That depends. Do you want her as a Virtue or not?"

"Hmm." Father steeples his hands under his chin, feigning contemplation. It's such bullshit. He's had it out for Malcolm since they were kids. Apparently, destroying Malcolm's will to live by taking away and regifting everything that matters to him in a fucked-up package isn't enough. Now he has to mess with Malcolm's surprise daughter.

But if I'm to be honest … I enjoy messing with her, too. The problem is, I want to be the sole man screwing her brain and body.

Like I've said, sharing is not my strong suit.

"After much contemplation, I've decided it would benefit our interests if she became one of us, yes," Father answers as if it was always his idea.

Our interests. Hilarious. "Then consider it done."

"You'll make it simple for her?"

"No. I'm going to torture her, body, mind, and soul, to ensure her loyalty to the Nobles and Virtues. That way, no one will question it, considering your ... animosity ... toward her dad."

"A fair point. Surprising, since you're usually too self-absorbed to consider how we reflect on the others."

Rage simmers close to the surface, but I swallow it down. "She's my responsibility. I'll make her suffer, Father. Your lessons involving Malcolm Weatherby have taught me well."

"Ah." Father smiles fondly at the memories. "Yes. Good boy. I'll see you this evening. And I *expect* to see the girl on your arm."

"Ember will be there."

"As will Malcolm. It should be an enjoyable evening if you don't keep me in suspense. Tell me your plans for her, boy. Or do I have to force it out of you and take over the ministrations myself?"

Quiet revulsion courses down my spine as I maintain my stare on his, pretending confidence, dominance. Ember isn't supposed to matter, but the thought of this man having her in his clutches—revulsion morphs into venom running through my veins. I can't let him near her. I'd gladly take his punishment for keeping silent, but experience has taught me it won't be enough to keep him from coming for Ember after he's done with me.

And so, I tell him.

When I finish, a slow, reptilian smile slithers along the lower half of his face. "Wonderful," he says. "Just wonderful."

CHAPTER 31
EMBER

Unsurprisingly, the news of my nakedness on school grounds reached the entire student body.

I've spent the past week dodging slurs, unsolicited groping, and sneers from freshmen to seniors, but the person who's taken the most enjoyment of my humiliation has stretched these days into eons.

Aurora corners me every chance she gets, hurling insults and spreading the rumor I smell like a swamp crotch since that's apparently where I get the most fulfillment.

She also went to the headmistress requesting the pool be drained due to unhygienic activities.

That has to be the most humiliating moment of my short time at Winthorpe High. Sitting in front of Headmistress Dupris's intimidating desk filled with student files and national accolades and accreditations, explaining that I only used the pool before hours to practice for the meets undisturbed, and that Aurora's had it in for me since I stepped on school property.

My excuse didn't hold any water—pun intended. It was only

when Thorne backed up my story that all warnings of suspension were lifted.

Thank god. The last thing I wanted was to involve Malcolm, who's been mysteriously absent for most of the week. It's strange how little time he spends with me, save for the breakfasts and dinners when he's here. It makes me question why he wanted me to live with him in the first place.

The loneliness in the manor, at school, and the ups and downs of Thorne's attention all became too much these past few days. I didn't take pride in flashing the boys' swim team. The more I thought about it, the more I felt sick about the way I submitted to Thorne and how we both wanted to drown for the sake of experiencing near-death ecstasy. I was so inquisitive, so ashamed of myself, that I looked it up one night, my desk still firmly resting up against the hidden door to my bedroom.

Erotic asphyxiation, it's called. Intentionally induced strangulation or smothering to heighten sexual arousal.

Oh my god. That's me.

My legs clench together of their own accord as I remember how good it felt, how *real*, and the way I struggled for breath while Thorne licked and sucked all my edges.

I'm turning into a different person. Having to deal with embarrassment, ridicule, and attention I've never been exposed to before. All while crushing on and then hating the boy responsible for most of it, who's also turned into the guy who's *saving* me from a lot of it.

Can you blame me for wanting my mom?

She's the one I turned to when the bullying became too tough, the soft arms that held me when I was the most upset, and the soothing voice that kept me sane during my worst moments.

And so, on the day I'm supposed to be preparing for this

party at Thorne's and my continued induction into a Society that could make or break me, I pull up her email.

And reply.

MOMMY. I miss you.

TEARS BLUR my vision as I click send, then shut the laptop as if that can hide my defiance against Malcolm's rules.

A knock sounds at my door. I scrape my palms across my eyes, hiding the evidence. It'd be so like Malcolm to be alerted literally one second after I've done it. "Yes?"

"It's me, girl! I'm here to help you get ready!"

Smiling at Aiko's cheer, I untangle myself from my bed and let her in. "You're early."

"Couldn't wait any longer. I'm so intrigued. Why is Thorne inviting you to such an exclusive event, and why did you tell me to bring this?" She holds up a navy travel bag stuffed with dresses I asked her to bring.

I ended up texting Aiko a few days ago about my invite. The party isn't even whispered about at school, it's so private, and I'll be in deep shit if it ever gets back to Thorne that I told her, but after the week I've had, it's about time I get the upper hand on these people, and Aiko's the one to help me do it. I rationalized that as long as I don't tell her about the Noble and Virtue titles, I'll be walking a dangerous line but not a lethal one.

Not to mention, I'm fucking fed up with the lot of them. My attempt to save Thorne's life and his mocking laughter afterward is enough to ignite the small amount of vindictiveness that lives in my normally dormant soul.

I answer Aiko as she steps inside, and I shut the door behind her. Malcolm's returned from his travels and I don't want him overhearing. "I'm sure it's Thorne's apology for humiliating me at the pool last week."

Aiko screws up one side of her face. "Thorne never apologizes."

Aiko's been with me since the start of the ridicule, lashing out at anyone nearby who dares to speak against me. I love her for it, and it only gives me more reason to trust her.

"It doesn't matter why." My lame attempts at excuses have run out, and I really don't want to tell her about Thorne's and my hookups. I'm afraid Aiko will look at me differently if I do. "How about we focus on the fact that I'll be inside that house and can maybe pick up some clues about Savannah."

Aiko's brows hit her hairline. "Holy shit."

I perch on the side of my bed and grin. "You told me the police suspected Thorne in her disappearance but were prevented from questioning him. They probably never got a warrant for his home. When I'm there, I could explore, look around his room, see if I find anything."

After all, it would serve him right, with the way he snuck into mine while I was sleeping.

Aiko steps closer, whispering, "Does that not freak you out? What if you get caught? We're talking about my missing step-sister here. It's a very real tragedy."

I nod sagely. Thorne and his crew have pissed me off enough to *want* to find evidence against them regarding Savannah, but I can't discount the hurt and pain Aiko's experienced or what I'd do if I *did* find something. Because that would mean I'm hooking up with a possible murderer.

One who's teaching me to strangle myself to experience pleasure ...

I blink out of it. "Maybe there will be a letter, or a photo, or some hidden room where Thorne enjoys collecting trinkets of his crimes. These manors have enough of those. Either way, if he didn't do it, he might be protecting the person who did." Aurora comes to mind. "I want to know, too, Aiko. I want an answer before I—" *go any further with him.* But I cut myself off before I finish the thought.

"Savannah loved him." Aiko comes to sit beside me. "I know the police suspected him, but there was no physical evidence. What do you think you could find?"

"Did you know they broke up a few days before she disappeared?"

Aiko jerks back. "What? How do you know that?"

Damn. It just slipped out. I'm not about to tell her about my time in a dungeon with Thorne, so I recover quickly. "I'm good with computers. I found it on some online forum where people were discussing the disappearance. Maybe someone on Thorne's side of things said something to the wrong person."

"I suppose so ..."

"You said Thorne pushed her to do things that scared her. Maybe he pushed her too far for the last time."

Aiko ponders this, and so do I. I've only had brief experiences of danger with him, but they've all been fairly brutal. Rising tides in a cliffside cave, dungeons, pool drownings ... most of me doesn't consider him to be a murderer, but an accident and then subsequent cover-up isn't far-fetched at all.

"She literally got into a black Town Car and disappeared after school one day," Aiko says, "but no one got the license plate, and the school cameras couldn't reveal it. Aurora and Thorne were the last people to see her. I've thought about this so much, Ember. Maybe they met up later and ..." She lowers her chin, staring hard at the floor, but it's clear her thoughts are elsewhere.

"Aiko?"

"I ... I have to tell you something."

"Go ahead." I lean over and squeeze her hand.

"I've been keeping this secret, one Savannah asked me never to tell anyone, but I don't think I can do it anymore. It's been too long, and the threat of getting in trouble doesn't feel as dire anymore. I just want to find her."

I squeeze again. "I know you do. So do I."

Aiko takes a deep breath, but she doesn't raise her eyes from the floor. "There's some sort of club at Winthorpe. A secret one."

Adrenaline shoots through my chest, but I force myself to remain relaxed. Curious. "Oh, yeah?"

"Savannah was a part of it. She said—she said it made Thorne's adrenaline junky habits pale in comparison. That there were brutal initiations, but it was all worth it because she could get into the college she wanted, assist in smoothing over her dad's scandal, and get a bunch of money put into her bank account. Like six figures."

My back goes up at that last part. I had no idea about stuffing bank accounts. "Did she tell you she was afraid of it?"

"Not in so many words." Aiko inclines her head in thought. "But I could tell she was made to do things she wasn't proud of. The night before she disappeared, she confessed she had one more trial to oversee, whatever that means, before she'd officially be made a marquise and all her families' problems would disappear."

Adrenaline swirls into dread. From the little I've gleaned, the Societies rank their members by the nobility standards of Medieval Europe. As an initiate, if I pass my trials, I'll make it to baroness. There are viscounts and dukes. And of course, a prince and princess. *Marquise* is a new one. I make a mental note to look up the noble hierarchy the next time I get a chance. "Why didn't you tell the police this?"

"She told me that my life was at stake if I ever whispered a word of it to anyone. These people don't fuck around." Aiko shakes her head in frustration. "'Club' isn't the right word. That makes it seem so juvenile. It's like ... like ..."

"A secret society?" I whisper.

"Yes!" Aiko bounces off the bed. "That's exactly it. Thorne's involved in it, too. I'm thinking this party you're going to has to do with it, and I want you to be prepared." Her eyes soften as they land on mine. "I can't lose another friend, Ember. You have to be careful. Maybe snooping around his home isn't the right move. If he catches you, or god forbid, his *father* catches you ..." Her shoulders tremble. "Ember, I don't think Thorne alone had something to do with Savvy's disappearance. I think it was them."

Blowing out a slow breath, I push to my feet, coming to a stop in front of her and resting my hands on her shoulders. Stilling them. "I won't let them hurt me. I'll be okay."

Aiko's eyes shine with tears as she looks up at me. "That's what Savvy said, too."

"Well, I'll be prepared. Her disappearance has taught me a lesson. I have to keep my guard up." I squeeze Aiko's shoulders once before releasing them. "She kind of looks like me, and I've inherited a lot of things that were important to her. I need to find out the truth, too."

Aiko swipes under her eyes, nodding. "Okay. But promise you'll tell me everything afterward."

My answering nod doesn't give away the lie. "Of course."

"And I'll stay here. Right across the street. Text if you're in any sort of trouble."

I flash back to the night, the first night, when Aiko made the same promise. I wasn't able to text her then, and by the expression on her face, I doubt she's confident I'll be able to do it now. Yet she still wants to try.

My heart swells. "I'll do you one better. How about I come back in two hours? If I don't, call the police. No questions."

Aiko's eyes widen. "Call the police on the *Briars*?"

"Yep."

"But what if nothing's wrong? What if I cause a raid on the most powerful man in Raven's Bluff, and he comes after me for besmirching his *name*?"

The sheer panic in her voice almost has me giggling hysterically. It's all terrifying but true. "The worst that could happen is you call the police, and you save my life, giving me the protection Savannah never received. The best scenario is, they break down the door to a party in full swing, and there I am, totally fine at the buffet table. Either one works for me. Okay?"

"The Briars would *never* have a buffet table."

The statement has us both laughing, lightening the mood as I unzip the bag Aiko brought. I pull out a strapless black floor-length gown, considering it *is* a secret society event, unbeknownst to Aiko, and black tie attire is required.

I decide to leave my hair wavy and down, stopping at my elbows, and to smoke out my eyes. I gloss my lips and put some highlighter on my cheeks and collarbone.

"Wow," Aiko breathes out when we finish. "You look ..."

"Ravishing?" I joke.

"Like her."

The acknowledgment sends a skitter of excitement in my belly. It's what I planned. I'd studied enough of her photos to notice how she preferred wearing her hair down with beachy waves. Any time she dressed up, she used dark, smoky eye shadow but never a red lip. In photos of galas with her father, she always preferred black cocktail dresses or gowns, nothing too glittery or ostentatious. Nothing in my closet came close to Savannah's fashion, Malcolm opting for country club chic for his estranged daughter instead of actual teenaged style. I risked asking Aiko to bring a few of Savannah's gowns, promising her that I had good intentions with them and would explain everything when she got here. Aiko agreed. As much as I'd like to think it was her trusting soul that convinced her, it was probably our heart-to-heart at her house that made the ultimate decision and my abject curiosity to find out what happened to her stepsister. Other than her family, I think I'm the only one left who wants to know.

Now that Aiko's caught on, I pull open a drawer in my bathroom and reveal the pièce de résistance.

"What's that?" Aiko leans against the doorframe, staring at the canister I'm holding.

"Temporary dye spray." I twist the can until she can read the label and see the color.

She pales. "Holy ..."

"I'm going golden tonight."

"You are going to *freak them the fuck out.*" But she grins, pushing off the doorframe. "I'm so glad you made me a part of this. Give me that. I'll get the back."

CHAPTER 32

EMBER

A iko stays behind in my room. When she's out of view, I unclench my fingers to reveal Savannah's golden pendant. I swish down the darkened halls, surrounded by the chemical fragrance of my newly golden hair and the strange, empty armored knights Malcolm has propped up in the alcoves I pass by and clasp the necklace at the back of my nape. I can't explain it, but I have the marked feeling that anyone who recognizes the necklace might have something to do with her disappearance. Savannah hid it for a reason.

I can file away any darting of the eyes or gasps of shock at the shining, polished heart proclaiming *You, Forever* for further thought, ruminating on it later tonight when I return to the manor.

Who gave this to you, Savannah? Was it someone who will be at the Briars tonight?

The pendant's cold at first, but quickly warms against my skin as I traverse the wide hallways.

Weatherby Manor really is an unnerving house filled with collectibles, paintings, and artifacts that Malcolm picks up during all his trips, but he never stays long enough in his home to admire them. I wonder if he ever did. Maybe when his wife was alive? Or did he leave her behind, too?

I never did look her up the way I did Savannah, or Thorne, or even Aurora. She wasn't my priority, but as my time in this manor continues, I'm thinking I should do some digging. Malcolm certainly won't tell me.

A gasp draws my attention away from my thoughts, right when I'm at the top stair. I stiffen when I look down. Malcolm stands in the foyer in a full tuxedo, appearing to have just been in the middle of fixing his cuffs before he glanced up and saw me.

"Jesus Christ, Ember." His broken whisper echoes through the cavernous entryway. "What have you done?"

I suppose from a distance, my Savannah appearance is striking. I flip my hair back in an airy sway, despite my heart hammering in my chest at the way Malcolm regards me. Like I'm some demon he summoned that he can't control. "I'm going out."

"Where?"

I take the stairs, forcing a smooth gait yet hanging onto the banister as though I'll topple at any minute. "I could ask the same of you."

"I have an event to attend."

"So do I."

His eyes grow small even though I'm coming closer. "You look incredibly dressed up for high school shenanigans. Where are you going?"

I clear my throat. Notch my chin. "Across the street."

The anvil I expect doesn't drop. I get a whistling inhale instead, the clenching of his jaw, and the popping of his eyes in a way that reveals his deep-seated effort to keep from going apoplectic. "You are *not* to step onto that property."

Instead of commenting on his refusal, I ask instead, "Is that where you're going?"

"Yes. Even though I don't want to, I have to."

"Why?"

For a moment, his expression softens. "It's nothing I want to concern you with. Please, Ember. Go upstairs and get out of that ... that ..."

"You've never commented on why I look like her."

He steps back. "Who? Savannah?"

I nod.

"Do you really want me to confirm, again, that you do not have a sister or a twin? Or would you rather I state the chances of a doppelgänger in this world, while slim, are still possible? I don't particularly *know* why you resemble her so much, but I find the more important question is, why are you deliberately dressed up as her tonight? Are you planning on hurting the people closest to her? Her parents? Because yes, Ember, her father will be at the Briars tonight. And if he sees you ..."

I still at his revelation, never considering that her parents might be there. I was solely focused on rocking Thorne, shaking him enough to show *some* emotion, and maybe sticking it to Aurora, too. "I ... I didn't think ..."

"No. You didn't. Go change. We'll discuss your punishment when I return."

My hands clench into fists at my sides. "I'm going with you."

He reels. "You are *not*."

I will not show fear. I will not show fear. "The only way you're stopping me is if you physically restrain me, so if you really want to go that far ... If you try to touch me, I'll fight and scream and bite—"

"*You defied my direct order not to contact the Becketts!*"

His roar rattles the chandelier above our heads. I gasp, rocking back on my heels.

Malcolm doesn't relent. "You contacted your mother. Replied

to her email. You broke our deal, which gives me the right to contact the authorities and have them dragged out of their home in handcuffs."

"Don't!" I cry. "What kind of emotionless robot *are* you? It was just a few words! I just told her I missed her!"

"And her reply was filled to the brim on her manipulations, lies, anything to twist your arm and get you back to her."

My face turns numb. "She ... she wrote back?"

"She did. And you will never read it."

I launch at him. I should've known he controlled my email and taken proper precautions, but my emotions and my broken heart got the best of me.

A lot like it's getting to me now.

I beat my fists against his chest, screaming that he's horrible and that all I want is my family. He catches my swipes like he would a mosquito and silences me just as easily.

Clutching my forearms and pressing them against my chest, he growls, "If you don't turn around and go to your room this instant, I will call the police and have your parents charged *tonight*."

"You're a monster."

"And you're a liar. Go, before I truly lose my patience."

I rip out of his hold, my heels scraping across the marble as I back up. He stares at me without blinking, his cheeks splotchy with color, before whirling to the door and slamming it so hard behind him, the walls reverberate.

I stare at the door until it blurs into a watery brown splotch. My skin is so hot, it burns, my fingertips turning red and pulsing with rage. How dare he? How *dare* he use his power on me with no explanation? With no rules on his side? Why does he get to draft my future when he's only been in my life for three fucking months?

If you're made a Virtue, all Malcolm's threats will be made obso-

lete. Your parents will be free. You *will be free of him* ...

Thorne's past words stroke against my skull with the purr of a kitten.

My upper lip peels back from my teeth. A few blinks and the front door comes back into perfect clarity. My breaths become audible, but I don't care if Dash is nearby to hear. I whirl around, lift my skirts, and sprint up the stairs, storming into my room and slamming the door behind me as hard as Malcolm slammed his.

Aiko spears up from my bed. "What the—"

"I am so *tired* of bastards running my life." I stalk to the desk, fury giving me more adrenaline than normal, and easily move it aside.

"Uh. What's happening right now?"

My bedroom is so far in the west wing of the manor and the walls so thick, I doubt she heard any part of the argument. "I'm revealing a hidden door."

"Oh. Cool." Aiko hops up from the bed and attempts to help, but I've moved it enough that I'll be able to slide through.

She says, "Can I ask why you won't be using the front one?"

"Malcolm's forbidden me to."

"I see." Aiko crosses her arms. "Wait. I don't see."

"He's been invited to the same party and has taken it upon himself to forbid me from going to it. I'm about to show him he has no authority over me."

"But what about your parents?"

I bend down, searching for some sort of trigger or hatch to open this damn wall up. "They'll be fine. If I go to this party and finish what Thorne wants, Malcolm can go screw himself."

Aiko's gasp has my hand stilling on the wall. "I knew it. You're becoming one of them. I was hoping you'd failed the first initiation at the lighthouse, but this is why you've been acting so strange and not telling me everything."

My shoulders slouch in answer.

"Ember, this is so dangerous. What were you thinking? And why didn't you *tell* me?"

I turn to her. "I didn't want to make any more sacrifices than I had to, and that includes losing my only friend."

"But this is how they lure you in. They make promises you're desperate to make happen. Savvy was *just* as frantic. Ember, you can't. You can't do what they want. It's not worth it."

"If I don't, Malcolm will lock me in here. He's terrified of something he refuses to explain, wants to keep me as one of his dusty, cobwebbed trophies, and doesn't care one bit about how I feel. He doesn't see me as a human. If I—if I don't do this and get out of here, I'll disappear, Aiko."

The reference to a disappearance makes her wince.

"I didn't mean ..." I sigh. "All I've wanted in life was to be successful in my own right, get my family out of a rut, and never have to worry about money ever again. Malcolm exploited that. It's why I'm here. But being at Winthorpe gives me an opportunity to escape of my *own* volition. If I play nice with the Briars and get this fellowship, I'll be free and finally able to help my family. If I turn into a Virtue, I'll escape Malcolm."

"A ... Virtue?"

I blow out a breath. "That's what they're called. The girls. The boys are called the Nobles."

"Wow." Her cheeks billow with surprise, but then she sucks them in. "But haven't you thought—I mean, your parents committed a crime. They stole you. I'm sorry, I know that's harsh."

"They're not innocent in this," I agree, "but I've had a lot of time to think about it, and they spoke to me about it as much as they could this summer before I ... before I left. They were desperate. Traditional adoption methods weren't working. And they're older, not an ideal pair for a birth mother searching for the perfect set of parents, and adopting internationally can take years, too. They saw an opportunity with a man who contacted them, said he worked for a doctor's office and there was a mother, homeless, who died while giving birth after hours. If they wanted the baby—me—they had to act now." I shake my head, folding my arms across my chest. "That was all a lie, of course. But at the time, they believed it. They drove six hours, met this man at the back of the doctor's office, and he handed them a baby. Six hours. That's all the time it took. I just ... I can't forgive them for a lot of that, but they loved me for eighteen years. I wish they'd told me. I wish a lot of things ..." I trail off, the emotion too thick in my throat. I don't want to talk about this anymore. "I need to text Thorne."

Aiko jolts at my sharp change in topic but doesn't comment as I pull my phone out of my clutch and type furiously.

ME: Where's the button to my wall. You know what I'm talking about.

HE RESPONDS A FEW SECONDS LATER.

THORNE: Are you trapped in your castle, Rapunzel?

A GROWL SIFTS through my teeth. Aiko mutters, "Yikes," then crawls back into my bed.

ME: Tell me, or I won't be attending your party.

• • •

THORNE: **Baseboards. Find the two seams. Push it with your foot.**

STEPPING BACK, I inspect the white molding around the bottom of the walls. There. A few feet away, I spot a small vertical seam, and an identical one about ten inches away. Positioning my foot between them, I press down.

A door-sized part of the wall sinks in, then slides open on silent hinges. *Somebody* is keeping it well oiled.

"These old mansions are so *fucking* cool," Aiko says from behind.

I gift her with one last tight smile before I step into the dark.

"Be careful, okay?" Aiko's voice fades the farther in I walk.

"Two hours," I remind her. "That's all."

She agrees but doesn't sound convinced.

I can't think about her worries right now, what with all the Malcolm-induced turmoil taking up my headspace, so I face forward, using my phone as a flashlight and texting Thorne one last instruction.

ME: **I'm in. Now tell me how the rats scurry along these tunnels from my house to yours.**

I CAN PRACTICALLY HEAR his chuckle in his response.

Thorne: The Rat King has your back, little pretty. Hang a left ...

AND I DO.

CHAPTER 33
EMBER

I t takes me a few tries to find the one brick that acts like a button to get myself out of the suffocating, stale tunnels. Eventually, I push the correct one, and what initially appeared as a dead end swings open in front of me, revealing Thorne's satisfied, cocky smirk.

"You got here in record time." He holds out a hand to help me through. Which I don't take.

I hike up my gown, revealing my calves so I can step over and through. He cups my elbow anyway, but I shake him off as soon as I'm steady.

"You running hot and cold only turns me on," he warns before closing the door behind me. It blends in seamlessly with the walls.

"Where are we?" I ask, moving from under a vast set of stairs and into the light.

I swear I hear him stop breathing behind me. It's then I remember my outfit, my *hair*.

Turning to him, I gift him with the same satisfied, cocky smirk.

What I don't expect is the deformed twist of horror in his face before he rushes at me, clutching my biceps and spitting, "What the *fuck* is this?"

His eyes dart to the pendant. At the sight, Thorne's pupils almost blow out.

I'm choking on fear—his rage is *so close* and hot against my mouth—but I say mildly, "Don't you like my outfit?"

"What are you trying to do?" He shakes me. "You have no fucking idea, do you? I thought you naïve but never dumb until this moment."

On a shaking breath, I say, "I want to know what happened to her."

"Halloween was last month. This is macabre. You can't show up in the ballroom looking like this."

"Why not? Will Savannah's abductor be insulted that another person who looks just like her has taken her place?"

"What makes you think her abductor, if there is one," he adds, "is in this house?"

"The Nobles and Virtues are lethal. You've all but said it. Your trials against me all but *prove* it. Why shouldn't I believe they're involved?"

"If you want to keep your life, you'll keep that thought to yourself."

"So you admit her disappearance has something to do with the Societies."

He releases me, raking a hand through his hair. "You were supposed to be easy prey. Instead, you're just annoying the hell out of me."

"If you're so innocent, let me take a look around your room. Access your computer files. Do all the things you didn't let the police do, then maybe I'll be less of an annoyance."

He arches a brow. "That sounds like more of one."

"Look." I grow serious. "A girl is missing. *Your* ex-girlfriend.

You should want to fish out the person responsible as much as I do. *More* than I do."

"Of course I do. I just don't want to be an idiot about it."

"It's called shock value, of which you have none. Let me enter the party looking like this. See who reacts."

"*Everybody* will react."

"Do you have a better idea? Because an entire year has gone by, and she hasn't been found."

"Yes, then you come into the picture, resume her activities, excelling like she did, thriving the way she *should*, and going after the Marks Fellowship the way she wanted to, as well."

I freeze. My chest stops moving. "What did you just say?"

Thorne lets loose a hollow laugh. "You're becoming her without even realizing it, Ember! Does that not freak you out? Do you not think you're a puppet in somebody else's play? Come on, you have to have figured it out by now."

"What are you ...?" I back away. "No. I'm my own person. All my decisions at Winthorpe are mine."

"Right," he drawls. "Just like your choice to come here was."

"How dare you," I whisper. "I told you about Malcolm and my fears in confidence, and now you're throwing them back in my face?"

He turns on me. So quickly and absolutely, my back slams against the opposite wall. "I'm your tormenter. Your tempter. Your beast. I have never given you reason to think me your savior."

I try to swallow, but there's nothing there for my throat to use. "You will not take my dreams away. I won't let you."

"You don't know what you're starting," he snarls. "My advice is to leave the same way you came in. I won't breathe a word. But if you enter that ballroom dressed like that, I can't promise I can protect you."

"Funny, I never heard 'your protector' in that speech of

yours." I swish my gown and slip away. "I didn't come here thinking you'd have my back, either."

"True. I'm only known to have your pussy on lock."

The slap rings out in the deserted hallway.

I pull my hand to my chest, my mouth falling open at what I've done.

A reddening mark is already forming on Thorne's cheek, the muscles underneath pulsing as he clenches and unclenches his jaw, reaching for control.

He won't look my way, but his arms go rigid at his sides. He says through barely parted lips, "You deserve whatever comes your way tonight."

After a few heaving breaths, I respond, "Gladly."

I don't check if he's behind me as I turn down the hallway and follow the drifting sounds of music. The last thing I'm about to do is ask him where to go, so I rely on my senses, my ears picking up the sounds of his heavy footsteps nearby. I refuse to give Thorne the satisfaction of peering over my shoulder, so I keep my chin up and my pace steady, appearing to all the world like I know what I'm doing.

The skirts of my gown flow around my shoes as I walk, and I take a sharp right, down another ornate hallway until I reach an open set of doors revealing a soiree draped in black and white silks, cascading crystals, and a myriad of ivory and ebony masks.

One such mask is offered to me at the door by a staffer dressed in a white suit jacket and black pants. "White for the ladies, miss. Is this to your liking?"

A feather-decorated eye mask rests on a small black satin pillow in his hands. It's beautiful, soft like the feathers of a dove, and my fingers hover over the diamanté detailing around the eye holes.

Thorne snatches it from the pillow and mashes it into my

chest. "She loves it," he says to the guy, then clamps a hand around my elbow and drags me inside.

"Enjoy being the center of attention," he mutters before pushing me into the center of the ballroom.

The entire crowd hushes. Champagne flutes lower from dropped jaws, heads turn as they mutter to their neighbors, and a few gasps and cries ring out.

All are masked, gorgeously attired, and belonging at this lavish affair like fishes to water. I'm the odd one out, my crushed mask clutched to my chest as I hobble on my heels and regain my balance.

This isn't how I planned my entrance. Shock value, yes, but not one instigated by *Thorne*.

I glare in the direction he disappeared, hating that I fell into his trap. Again.

"Isn't she ...?"

"New initiate ..."

"But she looks like ..."

"Oh my god, the resemblance ..."

A flush creeps across my cheeks, but I stand proud, letting them see. Forcing them to remember. Making the pendant shine.

I scan faces, searching for one appearing more vindictive or shocked than the others, but I didn't expect the masks. It's almost impossible to recognize who's who, never mind catch a kidnapper.

God, I wish Aiko were here to shout at everybody.

Movement in my periphery catches my attention. Two people, a couple, are taking off their masks, edging closer. The woman has tears streaking down her cheeks.

Oh, no. Savannah's father and stepmother.

Senator Merricourt's expression turns to stone at the sight of me, the age lines around his eyes and mouth smoothing with cold threat. An auburn head rushes toward them, body encased in a gold, sparkling dress, distracting Senator Merricourt at the same time she turns and glares at me through a white eye mask similar to mine. Aurora.

"Snake," I hear her say before she ushers them away.

I set my shoulders, prepared for this, hoping that one day they'll forgive me.

"I see our guest of honor has arrived." A bold, silken voice rises above the others.

The crowd parts to reveal a tall, slim man in a perfectly tailored tux, with a pointed chin, carved cheekbones, and thick, silver hair flowing back from his forehead.

What gets me are the eyes. They're exactly like Thorne's.

He holds out his hand. "Damion Briar. What a pleasure to finally—"

"*Get away from her.*"

The beastly growl causes my hand to pause halfway to Damion's. Turning my head toward the sound, I spot Malcolm pushing through the crowd.

And Thorne following him, his expression similar to Senator Merricourt's.

Malcolm comes to my side, a protective arm covering my shoulders. I quell the instinct to struggle since I'm not yet sure which predator I should be more wary of and which I should seek asylum with.

"Find some calm, Malcolm." Damion takes back his hand. "I was merely introducing myself to your ... daughter."

"I told you never to utter a word to her." Malcolm's arm stiffens around my shoulders, becoming so hard, it's like a boulder's been dropped.

Damion squints at his old friend. "Need I remind you, she came to me."

"I told her not to come." Malcolm's voice is rough as he looks down at me. "I *warned* you."

"Too late, my dear, departed friend." Damion gestures behind us. "Come, boy."

I twist to watch Thorne stalk to his father's side, looking none too pleased about it. When he meets my gaze, his eyes burn blue fire.

Damion says to his son, "Why don't you tell Mr. Weatherby here what's been going on with Ember at Winthorpe."

Thorne sets his jaw. His stare seems to say, *I told you so.* "She's accepted initiation into the Virtues."

Malcolm's hand falls from my shoulder, and he stumbles. I don't think I've ever seen him so viscerally affected. As I watch him, it's clear he's appalled I've hurt him like this.

Once he collects himself, he stares at me like he's never seen me before. "No," he whispers hoarsely. "Baby girl, *no.*"

"She's passed her first two trials," Thorne continues. To my relief, he doesn't elaborate, but by the way Malcolm reacts, Thorne might as well have.

"Malcolm ..." I pause. Collect my thoughts. "You brought me here under threat. Gave me opportunity under a guise. Promised me a true father with faithless intention. You barely speak to me. Can hardly *look* at me. I've lost my family, and ... and the Virtues promised to give it back to me. I'm only—I'm doing what I need to, to survive."

"This is the opposite of survival," he rasps. "If you're in their hands—no. I won't think it. Refuse the third trial. *Walk away.* I'll take you. We can leave."

"You and I both know you can't," Damion interjects. There's a musical, amused lilt in his tone. "Or do you need a reminder, Malcolm?"

Malcolm straightens. He shoots an arm in front of me at the same time he says, "Don't. She can't know—"

"Darling!" Damion calls. A pointless yell since the entire ballroom is silent and watching the exchange. "Come introduce yourself to our newest initiate."

A woman steps into the center of our ring, clad in an almost sheer sky blue gown. Her face is obscured by a masquerade mask, but the beauty of her bone structure can't be disguised. And her hair, shining chestnut under the chandeliers, falls in carefully styled waves to her pale, freckled shoulders.

I frown, her familiarity becoming more obvious the nearer she draws.

"Take off your mask, darling. Let Ember get a good look at you." Damion beckons her like a pet and nestles her against his side like a possession.

With a trembling hand, she does as he asks and won't look at anything but the ground beneath our feet.

My hand flies to my mouth when she pulls off the mask. "It's you," I whisper.

The woman in the portrait. Julie. *Malcolm's wife.* But ... there's a difference. A long, angry scar on the right side of her face, starting from her temple and cutting all the way to her jaw.

Malcolm stares at her, his very being shuddering with every breath as he wills her to look at him.

"Meet Julia Briar," Damion says, an arrogant grin pulling at his lips. "Does she ring a bell?"

"She's ... she's ..." My eyes bounce back and forth between her and Malcolm. "But how?"

"She's mine now," Damion says. Malcolm is stiff-backed at my side, unmoving. Destroyed.

I turn to Thorne. "What is this?"

"A sacrifice," he answers flatly. "A consequence. However you like to see it. The Societies take as much as they give."

"I don't want your riddles," I say, my words growing fire. "You promised me—"

"Everything you wanted," Thorne confirms. "I never said it would gain you a safe haven."

Greed. Second-guessing. Fear. It all has me tipping backward, threatening to take over my body and propel me out of these doors and away from them.

They promised all those things to Savannah, too, Aiko had said.

And look where Savannah ended up. I've ignored so many signals, and why? Passion? Lust? Exploration of a new side of myself?

"What have I done?" I whisper to myself, but Malcolm hears. He finds my hand and holds on.

"Well, what an introduction." Damion releases his wife and claps his hands. "Back to the party, everyone. Please, dine and dance."

He winks at me before he departs. "I'll be speaking with you later, my dear."

"The atrium," Malcolm blurts hoarsely. "I've kept it alive. Tended it. For you."

Julie stares at Malcolm, unseeing. And after a cluck of Damion's tongue, she follows her husband without a single acknowledgment to Malcolm. Quivering, I turn to my father, shock warping my vision.

He notices, clutching at my hand. "Now you see the danger here. The power of the Briars. I realize—I know I'm the one that put you in Winthorpe, but Damion would've found you, regardless. I was trying to preempt him, give myself time to explain to you ... but I couldn't look at you without seeing the mistakes of my past. The shame of my decisions. Commanding, intimidating, punishing you was the only way I knew how to force you to stay away. I didn't—fuck." He swipes his free hand through his hair, the damage of his decision evident in the lines of his face. "I didn't realize you were so much like me. Rebellious and determined. I'm sorry, Ember. I'm truly ..."

"Lovely sob story."

Thorne's bored tone reaches my ears, and I turn, searing him with the most hateful look I can muster. "Get lost, asshole. Leave us."

"You heard the man." Thorne gestures to Malcolm. "The Briars hold the power, and that means you're mine. And you're to come with me."

"I'm staying right here."

Thorne lowers his head, warning me through his brows. "Don't force me to make you."

I cross my arms and jut out my chin.

"Fine." Thorne sighs as if he'd rather be anywhere else, but his arm shoots out, dragging me to his side so brutally that I yelp.

"You let go of her," Malcolm says, his voice like cracking timberwood. "I'll do whatever Damion requires if you release her."

"Too late," Thorne quips, then yanks me into the crowd.

"Thorne!" I yell, smacking at his hold, but he doesn't give an inch. "This is ridiculous! You can't drag me around a ballroom like I'm a dog on a leash! I need to talk to Malcolm." It was the most open he'd been in ... ever. "Let me go back!"

Thorne deigns to stare down at me. "I can do worse than a leash. Stay by my side because you're about to lose your heart, and there's likely no one else willing to clean up the damage."

"You're talking in riddles again." I smack at his bicep, solid iron under his suit. If I weren't so furious and confused, I'd admire the way he fills one out, his devilish handsomeness. No— I've got that wrong. The *devil* has taken the suit, not the other way around. "You're just like your father," I whisper, and that stops him short.

I nearly faceplant into his side. When I right myself, I realize my mistake.

It's written in every twist to his features, the comparison to his father leading to a morphed, demonic version of himself. He says through a low, throaty snarl, "Don't you ever liken me to that bastard again."

I staunch the urge to spar with him. "Let go of my arm."

He stares at me for seconds longer, though it feels like he's peeling apart my soul, exposing the light inside me so he can snuff it out. It's so draining, I falter, but I keep my jaw rigid and my stance steady.

Then Thorne lets go.

Cold, air-conditioned air wafts between the space he leaves behind, but I don't stay long enough for the goose bumps. I swivel—

"I'm afraid I can no longer wait for our big announcement."

A voice I don't recognize drifts over the speakers in the room, and I turn with all the other guests to the small stage set up with a mini orchestra. They rest against their seats, their instruments lowered as a heavyset man with a squared-off face takes the conductor's microphone.

My brain matches his face to a name the instant he begins his speech.

"I realize that we like to leave nominations like this for the end of the Winthorpe semester, but we have a special circumstance that I can no longer ignore." The man pulls a piece of paper from his inner breast pocket. "This is especially crucial considering most of our junior members are in the midst of applying for early decision to prestigious universities."

I almost gasp out his name. Norris Marks, CEO of the company I'm dying to be a part of, talks to this privileged crowd with humor, flair, and the ability to single me out.

I feel more than hear Thorne come up behind me, his chest pressing against my back. I move forward, but he pulls me back, locking me against him with a forearm. Shivers of unease travel up my spine as I fight the restraint at the same time I search for Malcolm. My eyes snag on his as he stands at the fringes, sorrow overtaking his expression.

Dread surges in my belly at the sight. I've never seen Malcolm look anything but stoic.

You're right, I try to say with my expression as Thorne ruthlessly holds me tight. *I should've stayed home.*

"One lucky applicant will be able to write 'Marks Edelson Technology Fellow' on their application, as we've come to an early decision on who will receive the coveted fellowship that will propel them in their early career. After leaving the capable arms of Winthorpe, that is." Marks chuckles, nodding to someone in the front of the room. Further inspection reveals Headmistress Dupris, an apparent member of the Virtues.

It's an aside thought since I stopped thinking once Marks announced there was a recipient at Damion Briar's party. Damion is terrifying, cutting, a man to break apart families with nothing but an afterthought, but this night cannot ruin my dream so easily. I wouldn't be working with Damion. He's an overseer of a secret society and nothing more. I'd be with the other normal employees, learning among peers in the most respected technology company in the nation. And it's not just Norris Marks making the decision. It's the board. Faculty members at Winthorpe. He couldn't ... He wouldn't ...

This is it. The Virtues making your dream come true.

Suddenly, I don't feel Thorne holding me down anymore.

"Call it bias," Marks continues, "but we all know that to be a Virtue or a Noble means you are already the best the world has to offer, the smartest, the fastest, the most promising individual to control the mechanics of the globe. And this wonderful girl meets all of those qualifications with flying colors. In fact, she is so promising a Virtue, I doubt she'll be a baroness for long.

Ladies and gentlemen, allow me to introduce you to our fellow-ship recipient ..."

Thorne's grip grows so tight, I'm held by a boa constrictor. It's hard to breathe, but my heart doesn't care. It hammers with hope.

"... Aurora Emmerson."

Applause spreads across the room at the same time my knees go out from under me. If it weren't for Thorne, I would've fallen to the floor.

A desolate cry escapes my mouth, unheard in the rising claps and calls of congratulations as Aurora steps up to the podium and shakes Damion's and Norris Marks's hands.

Everything I've worked for, all that has kept me together while I was cleaved from my family, the reason I stayed strong in a cavernous, lonely manor and a cutthroat, ruthless school ...

"Your third trial." Thorne has bent down enough to murmur in my ear. "Superiority. Take away your dream to see if you can withstand it." His resulting laughter tickles my ear, the shivers of his amusement traveling down my neck.

Thorne slides his arm from my front, allowing me to fold to my knees so I can wretchedly stare at the line of shoes in front of me. Hearing the joy, the claps on the back, the comments of how deserving she is.

"Don't blame me, little pretty," he whispers at my temple. "Your wonderful father aimed to sabotage you from the very beginning. He even paid a visit to my father, commanding that you never get the chance to claim the fellowship. It's the most animated I've heard him in years. He must mean it." I feel Thorne's lips move into a smile. "I guess tonight proves his success."

My stomach lurches. Thorne's hold on me burns through my skin.

"Oh my gosh, this is such a surprise." Aurora leans into the mic, her voice piercing my eardrums. "Can I just say, this is wonderful. Being a Virtue has amazing perks, and my family will be so proud to know another generation continues to work with a family, a company, like the Marks. Mr. Briar, thank you for this wonderful event that has made my dream come early. My dear best friend, one who is so sorely missed and so *poorly* represented at this event by a pathetic stranger who knows nothing about her, would be so proud of me. If she were actually here." Aurora sniffles, drawing a wave of coos and assurances from the crowd. Damion steps forward and puts a reassuring hand on her back.

I can't take anymore. I push to my feet, elbowing through the crowd and ignoring the pouts and cries of protest as I unceremoniously remove myself from the pain.

Malcolm finds me at the edges, his arms open, but I halt just before receiving any comfort.

"You bastard," I say, shaking. "You goddamned *bastard!*"

"Ember, please—"

I rush out of the ballroom, ears closed to anything further, and take the stairs two at a time, my gown billowing.

But my heart hardens.

They see a victim, a broken girl—one they shattered to pieces —exiting the ballroom in shocked tears. Patting each other's backs at shattering a young girl's dream.

Finding the spot I climbed out of under the stairs, I feel along the edges of the wall, find nothing, and slam my palms against the wallpaper in defiance. Again and again and *again.* The electric sconce near my left hand wobbles, as if not fully screwed into the wall. Desperate, I yank on it, and the wall opens. I bunch my skirts into one arm and lift one leg, then the other, until I'm through, then lean to shut the secret panel behind me.

Gasping, sputtering with the effort, a clench my jaw and

force myself to breathe through the open cracks these people have made inside my body.

I *will* withstand this and become a Virtue. I'll watch Aurora take what I deserved, and once I cry and cling to my pillow for a few days, I'll do it with a smile.

The tunnels are black, so I pull out my phone, illuminating the passageway. After two or three turns, I find the steep set of stairs Thorne initially directed me to go up, and now I must descend, precarious and emotional. I heave in a breath, determined not to break an ankle on top of everything else. I peel off my shoes and hold them in the same one clutching my phone, my purse stuffed under my arm, ensuring I don't make a sound. I don't want Thorne coming after me, not so soon. I need to reformulate my spirit.

Because I will find out how to bring about the Briars' demise, and that starts with Savannah. Whatever I discover, I'll announce it to the world. There's no way the Societies aren't involved. I'll get my family back at the same time I destroy the Briars.

It's better to focus on that than how Thorne lingers in my thoughts. Did I hear regret in his tone as he ripped the future from my hands? Or was it the rasp of success?

After a few more moments, my heart regulates its beats, and I can finally breathe normally again as I approach the secret entry into Weatherby manor.

I press open the twin stone that's laid out on the other side, into the Briar mansion, opening the wall into my room, my mouth stiff, grim, and determined as Aiko is roused from the bed and takes in the state of me.

"Uh-oh. It hasn't been two hours yet. What happened?"

I lift my head and whisper harshly, "Everything."

"Come. Sit." Aiko pats the spot next to her.

I perch on the side of the bed and lean into her, unleashing

287

the sobs I so forcefully held back in front of Winthorpe's elite. With Aiko, I can let myself go, my agony show, and the loss of my parents, my future, become the most prominent wail. Yet Thorne's betrayal festers. It *hurts*.

I picture the girl who sat on her parents' couch as Malcolm stormed into the house, her body shaking and terrified, her mind a jumble of shocked confusion.

I push her out.

I think of the girl who stepped onto Winthorpe's campus on the first day, sheepishly positive, determined to make a mark on the world, however small, and securing her future with good grades and a quiet, invisible disposition.

I slam a mental door in her face.

The girl writhing under Thorne, dancing to his fingers, begging with her mouth and tasting his cum is harder to get rid of. She has nails, the teeth of a feral, erotic creature, and she wants to stay.

I kill her.

All that remains are the remnants my enemies have left behind, but they underestimate the broken glass of my soul. Enemies don't just conquer, they can inadvertently make their victims stronger, too.

That part of me, I keep. Foster. Nourish. Sharpen.

The next time I see Thorne, we'll be facing off as true rivals. He used my vulnerabilities against me, grinned as he tore up my future with fisted Noble hands.

I'm wounded now, but I'll heal. I'll harden. And I won't make that mistake again.

Because even dying embers can turn thorns to ash.

CHAPTER 34
THORNE

Ember's last words to me were that I'm a bastard. She's not wrong.

Even though I was to ruin her as soon as we met, I couldn't resist the warmth of her and the addictive curiosity she showed as I coaxed her to explore sin. We connected, she and I, on a level I doubt my father ever predicted we would.

I took note of the vileness in her eyes as she raised her head and scorched me with hate from her spot on the ground. A place I put her. She wants my head on a platter, my dick as the appetizer, and I don't begrudge her that.

But her hatred ... that flayed my skin. Made me retreat into the crowd to let her suffer alone.

She's right, though. Tonight, I acted just like my father, a true Noble king. Maybe it's time for a queen to rise, too.

My sweet, little pretty...

Let the best underground royal win.

~

Read CRUSH, the next dark and steamy read in the Thorne of Winthorpe High Series, on Amazon!

I don't have a crush on Thorne Briar, Winthorpe High's cruel, elite master.
*I want to **crush** him.*

For exclusive bonus content featuring one of Thorne's more sexy, stalkerish moments, sign up for Ketley's VIP Crew List.

Also by Ketley Allison

all in kindle unlimited

If you want more bullies and secret societies, read:

Rival

Virtue

Fiend

Reign

If you like your bad boys and bullies as standalones (no series, one book with a happy ending), read:

Backstage with Him

Craving You

If you like the dark underground princes, read

Underground Prince

Jaded Princess

If you like a grump turned into a softie, read:

Rocked by Her

Synced to Us

If you like your playboys with big hearts and bigger secrets, read:

Trusting You

Daring You

Playing You

If you like crime with your romance, read:

To Have and to Hold

From This Day Forward

ABOUT THE AUTHOR

Ketley Allison has always been a romantic at heart. That passion ignited when she realized she could put her dreams into words and her heart into characters. Ketley was born in Canada, moved to Australia, then to California, and finally to New York City to attend law school, but most of that time was spent in coffee shops thinking about her next book.

Her other passions include wine, coffee, Big Macs, her cat, and her husband, possibly in that order.

facebook.com/ketleyallison
instagram.com/ketleyallison
bookbub.com/authors/ketleyallison
amazon.com/author/ketleyallison
goodreads.com/ketleyallison
tiktok.com/ketleyallison

Printed in Great Britain
by Amazon